pillow

pillow

ANDREW BATTERSHILL

COACH HOUSE BOOKS, TORONTO

first edition

Published with the generous assistance of the Canada Council for the Arts and the Ontario Arts Council. Coach House Books also acknowledges the support of the Government of Canada through the Canada Book Fund and the Government of Ontario through the Ontario Book Publishing Tax Credit and the Ontario Book Fund.

LIBRARY AND ARCHIVES CANADA CATALOGUING IN PUBLICATION

Battershill, Andrew, 1988-, author
    Pillow / Andrew Battershill.

ISBN 978-1-55245-316-2

    I. Title.

PS8603.A876P55 2015   C813'.6   C2015-905032-4

Pillow is available as an ebook: ISBN 978 1 77056 436 7

Purchase of the print version of this book entitles you to a free digital copy. To claim your ebook of this title, please email sales@chbooks.com with proof of purchase or visit chbooks.com/digital. (Coach House Books reserves the right to terminate the free digital download offer at any time.)

Good old head, I'd had it a long time. It was a little soft now, a little pulpy, and more than a little tender … I could still use the head. I could use it another year anyway.

– Raymond Chandler, *Farewell, My Lovely*

To restore consciousness apply restoratives, twist and pull the ears, rub the neck, chafe the hands, pat the face, pull the arms and legs, and apply ice to the spine. When consciousness is regained find out if the boy knows his own name … wrap the individual in warm blankets and give him some hot tea.

– Edwin Haislet, *Boxing*

I do not understand why, or how, I am still living, or, for all the more reason, what I am living … and yet I am living, I have even discovered that I care about life.

– André Breton,
preface to the 1924 *Manifesto of Surrealism*

1

getting a sweat on

Pillow spent the last half of his run throwing straight punches up into the air, smiling and imagining three cheetahs charging, gathering momentum across the empty plain of the sky. He saw the way their hips moved, and he pictured the way their faces looked up close: calm and still, being pushed on hard by the wind. As he cooled down and stretched on the thin, fading strip of grass between his apartment and the sidewalk, Pillow came back to himself a little and laughed. But he couldn't help it. It's normal to be excited when you're going to the zoo.

Pillow was of the mind that going to the zoo was just about the best thing a person could do with a day. He'd been as a child, but the way he figured it, when you're a kid you're sort of maxed out on amazement: tall buildings are amazing, cars are amazing, subways are terrifying and amazing, grown men's feet are terrifying and amazing, and so on. According to Pillow, you're sort of getting screwed by going to the zoo once when you're eight. What they should do is let you get used to the human world, be at full size in it for a while, let the awe fizzle a bit and then bring you to the zoo. Because snow just isn't the same after you've seen two polar bears, and you can't really understand how nice it is that orangutans hold hands with their feet until you've held hands as an adult, as someone who knows for sure how soft and warm and soothing someone else's skin can be.

While he'd been boxing (and cheating) professionally, Pillow had worked out an arrangement with one of the zookeepers to buy the leftover anabolic steroids they had for gorillas who stopped making testosterone in captivity. When he started working for Breton's syndicate he'd made the introductions, and now once a month Pillow would go to the always-abandoned picnic area behind the Giraffe Park to drop off the money and pick up the shipment.

Pillow took the stairs three at a time, hitting a short hop at the top of each landing and switching his feet briskly in the air. He swung into the open courtyard hallway and saw a cake-slice boat sinking into a turbulent sea of icing.

Every third Wednesday, a box with a small wrapped parcel in it and an envelope taped to the lid would be propped up against his front door when he got in from his workout. The envelope had his money in it, and he wasn't allowed to open the parcel.

Pillow's monthly $1,000 payment was actually more like a $975 payment, because he thought it only right to pay for the zoo (tigers don't come cheap), but he didn't believe in memberships.

As he pulled his car into the lot, Pillow craned his neck painfully to look into the cheetah enclosure. Between the thin metal diamonds of fence he saw an empty patch of brown grass. Pillow wished he had more time to spare.

At first he'd tried to pace himself at the zoo, looking at one section a month, but by now he'd seen it all, many times over, so his path depended on what kind of animals he felt like staring at for a long time. There were the animals that Pillow was pretty sure were dinosaurs, like the rhinoceros with what looked like armoured plates going along his sides with a slot for the tail, or any of the crazy lizards. Another option was the animals that reminded him of people, like monkeys or, in a weird way, turtles. There were the slow, big and sad animals, like elephants or warthogs, and he could watch them just shuffle around, listlessly making marks in the dirt and sniffing their food instead of eating it. On the other end of things there were the fast animals, the giant cats and so forth; he could watch them run and still keep track of them, even the cheetahs, who ran faster than he'd believed legs could move a thing.

Most of the things Pillow really liked to do were obviously morally wrong. He wasn't an idiot; clearly it was wrong to punch people in the face for money. But there had been an art to it, and it had been thrilling and thoughtful for him. The zoo was also evil, a jail for animals who'd committed no crimes, but he loved it. The way Pillow figured it, love wasn't about goodness, it wasn't about being right, loving the very best person, having the most ethical fun. Love was about being alone and making some decisions.

A lot of the happiest seconds of Pillow's life had happened in places like the zoo. Places where wonder coated the ceiling, and twenty different kinds of piss coated the floors. Places where you could watch a pinnacle of animal movement and dexterity from a distance, with loud, horrible people beside you shouting obnoxious things at abused animals whose hurt was their entertainment.

To Pillow, none of that meant he shouldn't be happy when a gorilla looked him in the eyes and crossed its feet at the ankles. It didn't make that something he could have imagined on his own.

That day he was a little pressed for time. He had to meet Breton and Louise Aragon about a job, so he paid and beelined to the giraffes, barely stopping to watch a wolf or two while they were sleeping. As he entered the picnic area, he peeked between the trees toward the giraffes and saw that they were all eating. Pillow would have happily spared a few minutes if they'd been playing in the fake river, or passing a ball around, but he didn't feel like watching anyone else pig out. The drugs were waiting under a park bench, and Pillow casually swapped boxes and went to climb the fence out of the zoo. Pillow always climbed the fence out, wanting to keep a low profile. He wondered if anyone noticed that he'd walk in the front door and never back out.

Pillow knew he'd missed out on good animals for the month, but he was careful to spend an extra second straddling the top of the fence on his way out, looking at the giraffe's face just above the line of trees, its huge purple tongue sprawling graphically in all directions, its head bobbing and tipping around as it took steps he couldn't see.

The crime syndicate Pillow had swiftly and easily and sadly flowed into after his neurologist had told-not-asked him to retire made a lot of noise and very little money, and was skewed heavily to the crime end of organized crime, rather than the organized side.

The head of the syndicate was a mid-sized player named André Breton. He and his boys bought and sold drugs, made book, loansharked and had started two riots for fun. Breton's syndicate were mostly recruited from his days as a Marxist firebomber in Paris. They'd done low-level hack terrorist stuff until they caught too much attention and bolted the country for a spot in the superstructure and the cash to pay for pretty paintings. Breton was supposed to be a tastemaker: rich people called him in to tell them what art to buy. He used it as a way to launder money and move bribes.

Most of the time, the Breton crew hung out and got high, talked about their dreams and played parlour games until Breton gave them something to do. And tonight what Breton had given Pillow and Louise Aragon to do was guard-dog a deal to buy some stolen coins.

As often happened, Pillow ended up having to wait around outside his apartment, kicking the toe of one shoe with the heel of the other, as he waited for his ride to some place they hadn't bothered to tell him in advance.

Most of what Pillow did was watch people exchange money. He'd make collections and stand behind Breton at deals, watching the cash and making sure nobody got out of line. It wasn't usually to muscle anybody. He was supposed to be a former boxer, violence just an impression he made. The heavy wet work was handled by Breton's two favourites, Don Costes and Louise Aragon.

Pillow was in a very minor, but reasonably comfortable, spot in the organization. He knew what he was to them and what he wasn't: he wasn't particularly useful but he had uses; he wasn't exactly trusted but he was liked; he wasn't going to make much money but he wasn't going to cost them much either. Plus, he had used to be a celebrity, which is always worth a very sad and very tiny bit.

After what felt like a long time, Louise Aragon pulled up in a car so old and so black and so heavy it might actually have been a Model T. She screeched to a stop and kicked the huge, steel passenger-side door open. Pillow swung himself into the car and settled in already slumped.

'How do you do, Pillow?'

Pillow stayed still, suggesting a shrug with just the way he breathed. 'You have really flexible legs.'

'Thank you, sir. I've never stretched a thing. Sometimes one is just a marvel.'

Pillow nodded evenly, then turned to look at the dark sky framed by black metal through plate glass. He felt the car moving under him, in the way that you can feel things that move faster than your legs carry you and it just feels like sitting down.

Louise was one of Breton's go-to people. She was thirty-something and half-sad in that way fun people without a whole lot of luck get. She was the kind of friend Pillow had, which is to say a very friendly acquaintance.

'Do you want to know where we're going, Pillow?'

'I'm more curious about those legs – you don't stretch 'em even a little?' Pillow feinted like he was going to tickle her leg, reached up and snapped her bra strap when she brought her hand down to defend the leg.

Louise laughed. 'Bark like the dog you is, Pillow, bark like the dog you is.'

'Does introducing you to your wife buy me any leeway, Louise, huh? I think it gets me a little and I take space where I find it. Space is everywhere, and we need every little, tiny inch of it.'

Louise flapped her hand like it was a talking human mouth, or possibly a very stupid and hungry bird mouth, then she put both hands back on the wheel and refocused on her incredibly erratic driving.

Pillow rolled his shoulders back and took to stretching them. His shirt lifted up, and Louise poked his bellybutton. She had her bangs pulled back tight. Her haircut looked like a wave that had been ironed.

'So, just to get it out of the way,' she said, 'we're going to Mad Love. And as always, I am deeply sorry.'

Mad Love was the bar where a good deal of the money and brain cells Pillow had held on to after fighting had gone to die. It was one of the dingiest places he'd ever seen or smelled or touched. The place, like a lot of things, gave him a headache that would make other people's headaches jealous.

'Well, that's a bummer. I guess you should maybe tell me what I'll be doing there.'

'What you always do, my man: look tall and try not to fall asleep.'

'I don't look tall, I *am* tall, and I don't make any promises about sleeping.'

Louise screeched the car to a stop in an alley that looked like every other alley. 'Can you at least promise to dream well then?'

Pillow pulled one long strand of hair loose from her head and let it flop unevenly down the middle of her face. 'For you, I'll try.'

Louise looked at Pillow for an extra second and smiled at him in the way you'd smile at a picture of a really cool building that's already been torn down.

If you're almost anyone, being talented at one thing will ruin you for all the other things. Had he, after a life of not doing much, stumbled into his work at the syndicate, it's possible that Pillow would have paid his dues, learned all the angles and taken pride in the nuances of his job. But that hadn't happened. Instead Pillow had been elite at a thing he loved, and it had been one of those things you can't do forever, or even all that long. So he knew what talent was, what it felt like as you used it, and he knew, now, how it felt to do everything else.

Since retiring, Pillow had done a lot. He'd confirmed that avoiding cocaine had (while he'd done it) been a good idea. He'd gone on a pretty good streak at the sports book, then a really terrible streak at the sports book, and then he'd stopped going to the sports book. He'd put three people in the hospital. He'd waited out ten thousand cluster headaches. He'd watched deals and checked perimeters and patted people down. And he hadn't been good enough at any of it to start to care.

Tonight, for instance, he'd absently checked the alleys, he'd absently noted the colour of the cars on the street and he'd absently been keeping half an eye on the back entrance, somewhere between sitting and lying down on a folding chair next to the bar, his legs crossed at the ankle, under the dirty-yellow glow of the half-burned-out lights of Mad Love.

Louise had explained, and Pillow had listened in the spinny and unprofessional manner that was usual for him. And Bataille was now half an hour late, which was making Louise nervous and Pillow mildly curious.

The boxer rotated his ankle in a circle until it made pretty much exactly the sound of two pool balls hitting each other from across the table. It was a technique he often used in place of clearing his throat to start a conversation.

'Yes, Pillow, what?'

Pillow jabbed a finger at Louise's suitcase. 'So how much have you got there?'

'Have you ever known me to name a number.'

'I know it's less than two hundred grand. Just me and you? Bataille showing up late. Gotta be less than that. Then again, ol' Georges is a hand-over-fist gambler, and a fist-somewheres-else sex freak, and he's got to be into Breton for at least a hundred large.' Pillow moved his head from side to side, as if weighing it against itself. 'Hundred fifty's the line, and I'll bet the under. Y'know what they're giving me? To be here, I mean.'

Louise wiped her forehead aggressively. 'I really don't care. Would you please just be helpful. This whole thing is weird. Bataille's late. Just be helpful.'

'Now four hundred bucks might sound like a lot, y'know, for a night. But how many nights do you get? And how much is the man in the suit taking for himself?' Pillow stretched his arms to their full length, splayed his fingers. 'Working with your hands, you're always just working for tips. Putting your neck out there for one, two, half of one percent off the top, when the man feels like giving it to you. When he wants to look like he feels generous. You get me?'

Louise spun all the way to face him in her chair. 'Can you go outside and look around? We're sitting here, he's late. We're just sitting here, that doesn't feel like a set-up to you? A little, maybe?'

Pillow shrugged, pulled his knees back toward himself and rested his elbows on them. 'I'm sleepy.'

'Are you okay, Pillow? We can call someone else.'

Pillow's smile was about as thin as sauna blood. He finally hoisted himself up. He walked with a relaxed gait that seemed to generate power only from the hips, as if the bottom half of his body had somewhere to be in about an hour and the top half would just as soon stay home.

Pillow ducked out to the parking lot. He looked out across the street, empty and lifeless except for the street lights and the neon spinning and fading out into the cleared-out, half-cold air of the dead night. The back entrance and alley probably needed checking, but he had a headache and was enjoying the air and the view, so Pillow stayed still and right where he was and tried to distract himself by casually trying to figure out the situation he was in right now.

Bataille worked at the rare-coin archive, he had for years. Pretty much the same years he'd been shovelling chips onto the tables and paper money straight into the hands of sex workers. Bataille had finally stolen some coins worth something. The four coins he'd stolen were misprints: they were supposed to be these old Gaulish ones that showed centaurs, but some illiterate coin-maker guy had gotten confused and done them as horse bodies with four human arms for legs, instead of the other way around.

Pillow thought about how it would feel to be a misprinted centaur. You get the big dumb head, the huge shitty lungs and heart, the colicky stomach, all toppling around on the tiny arms of the smartest animal around. He imagined being that misprint and meeting some real centaurs, seeing them and knowing – not in words because you've got the stupid horse brain but in the shallow, skittish and profound way horses know things – that you were the bad end of that coin. The centaurs jaunting around all proud, doing math equations while they galloped. It was the kind of reverie that Pillow often distracted himself with in the long hours he was supposed to be paying attention to dangerous details in the real world.

He was just beginning what would have probably been a lengthy internal debate about which kind of assholes centaurs have when one of those dangerous details skidded, as if from nowhere, into the parking lot. The car stopped a few feet away from Pillow, and he dropped instinctively into an athletic stance, but forgot to pull his gun or make any move to alert Louise, which were the things he was supposed to do.

A man fell out of the driver-side door and kicked up desperately from the ground, finally closing the door as a very skinny, sick-looking man in the back seat reached forward to scratch at the window. Pillow jogged over and helped the old man to his feet.

Georges Bataille gave off the same general impression as a scrap of paper that had been loose in someone's pocket for a very long time. He had a full head of razor-thin white hair swooping out to the side. He was holding one of his hands tightly with the other, his suit tenting at the back like the world's cheapest parachute.

'Thank you, Pillow.'

Before Pillow could respond, the man locked in the car flailed his arms ineffectually at the back windows, making a hollow scratching sound. Pillow finally recognized him as Antonin Artaud, a clinically insane morphine addict who hung out around the periphery of Breton's world. Mostly he just talked crazy, occasionally made a scene and hit people up for money. Every time Artaud moved his arms, Pillow thought about skeletons and hand puppets, and hand puppets who were also skeletons.

'Don't you thank shit, Georges. You're late, Louise is pissed and you need to tell me what this back-seat situation is. Homeboy is not an invited guest.'

'I know, and I'm sorry.' Bataille took a breath and then spoke quickly, probably eager to get the details out before his suit jacket caught too much wind and carried him all the way out to sea. 'I was late. I miscalculated badly. You see, I'd left this young girl locked in an antique bureau, and just an hour before I was to –'

Pillow reached over and palmed Bataille's face. 'Georges, Georges, Georges, no. That is not the level of detail I'm looking for here, my man. Dude in the back seat, coins, go.' He released the older man's face and patted him on the head.

'That's Artaud in the back seat. I let him stay with me for a few days, I showed him the coins and he's stolen them. He was passed out when I left, so I don't know where he took them, but he's the only one who knew where they were. So I brought him to you, and now he's reacting as a threatened and deeply wild beast.'

Pillow clicked his mouth evenly. 'That was super-concise actually, thanks. Okey-dokey, so let's get your man into the bar and, uh, see what Louise thinks.' Pillow bent over to make a visual appraisal of the inside of the car. Artaud flung a limp, loose arm at the car window. Pillow waved at him.

'Why's he wearing a priest outfit, Georges?'

'He says he has the spirit of a god and the body of a priest.'

'Fair enough, I guess. So, here's the plan. I mean, we want to get him out of the car before he remembers that cars are locked from the inside, y'know? I already got my miles in today, so I'm not in the mood to chase him. He's a little agitated, you're kind of, like, an old, weak librarian, no disrespect, so I'm just going open the door and grab him. I mean, he looks like he wants a fight, but there's no way he's got more than fifteen seconds of gas in him.' Pillow threw a short flurry of punches into the air, then bounced on the balls of his feet a few times. 'Stand back, big boy.'

As soon as Pillow opened the door, Artaud crawled halfway out, supported himself against the door frame and tried to stab him with a incredibly shiny and sharp dinner fork. Pillow swayed back, pivoted around the door and push-kicked Artaud in the chest, so he flew back into the car, his arms and legs collapsing toward his sternum like it was a tiny, sudden black hole. Pillow slammed the door and turned toward Bataille, wagging his finger loosely.

'Okay. To sum it up, you're at home, you're doing some kind of horrible sex thing and you realize that you're late for a stolen-centaur-coin sale, and your lunatic friend in a morphine coma has stolen your centaur coins, so you decide to pack him up and bring him to the buy of the coins he's stolen. I get all that, ish, y'know? But why do you give him a dinner fork? That's … that's where I'm lost on this one.'

'He must have had it in his sock.'

'How is that the first thing you say? Just right to the sock? "Hey, sorry I almost got your eye stabbed, Pillow." Nope? Just out with the sock idea.'

'The foot is the most human part of the body. Think of apes.'

'Okay, I'm about done with you. You know I love apes, you know that about me, Georges, but now is not the time. So, since this is a majillion percent your fault, you're going to help me with this situation here. I need both hands, so you open the door, I'll handle Artaud, and you stay out of the way, sound good?'

Bataille's hair flapped like a tarp being used as a tent in a very gentle wind. He moved beside the car, and Pillow positioned himself on the other side, took two deep breaths, then nodded for Bataille to open the door.

Artaud did most of the work himself, launching himself out of the car face-first, making a flailing backhand jab at Pillow with the fork as he fell to the ground. Pillow dropped onto the lunatic's frail chest with both knees, grabbed Artaud's wrist and bounced it against the pavement until he finally let go of the weapon.

Pillow got off, and Artaud didn't stand but rather rolled on his side and coughed pneumonically into the pavement. Pillow reached down and scooped the guy up, throwing him over his shoulder like a strangely proportioned bag of potatoes. Bataille followed them inside. Halfway across the parking lot Artaud got some energy back and started kicking and flailing a bit, but there wasn't much horse-power behind it, and Pillow just kept walking. It felt like carrying an animate easel.

Seeing him tell the story from a third-party vantage, Pillow thought Bataille looked and sounded a lot more like a TV-movie actor than a person explaining real things that had happened to him. His hands were moving all stiffly, jutting out when he wanted to make a point, raising awkwardly to poke at his temple to show he was upset. He occasionally glanced involuntarily over at Pillow, like he was the camera you're absolutely not supposed to look at. Pillow was kind of intrigued by it, imagining what it would be like to go through life so awkward you looked like someone inexpertly pretending to do all the things you were really doing.

There hadn't been any rope or anything at the bar, so they had just held Artaud still in his chair until he finally quieted down a little and realized that Pillow could keep subduing him pretty much indefinitely. Now Artaud was sitting quietly at a table, staring intensely at the beer taps, occasionally poking without looking at a bloody spot on his priest collar and tasting the blood. His teeth were starting to stain red.

Louise finally finished up with Bataille, and she turned around to look at Artaud. She moved over to Pillow, stood on her toes and helped herself up on his shoulder as she spoke quietly into his ear. 'We're going to talk to him a few minutes, and when he tells us where the coins are, you go get them and I bring the cash home. Yes?'

'You going to pay Artaud?'

'Not more than we have to, ten grand maybe.'

'Sure, you want me to do it?'

'Would you? He is quite creepy.'

Pillow patted her on the back, moved over behind Artaud and clamped down hard on his shoulders. 'Hey there. Here's the deal: we're going to give you ten grand, you're going to tell us where the coins are, I'm going to forget that you tried to stick me with a fork that time, and everybody's going to go home with most of the blood they have in them right now.'

Artaud nodded and didn't turn around. 'I'm reminded of the first rule of improvised comedy – it's a good rule, in that it works best when you break it: yes, and?'

Pillow spun the chair with Artaud in it, shoved it onto its back two legs and held Artaud suspended like that for a second. 'You are going to focus, you are going to pay attention and you are going to talk deal with us, or I will hurt you badly enough to change your life. Not the way you need it to change either, that other way.'

Pillow let go of the chair and Artaud lurched forward, then straightened himself. He reached his arm back and laid it on the top of the chair, where it rested like a long, deflated balloon. He looked up at Pillow, his eyes swimming like a seven-year-old dropped off a fishing boat. 'A deal. How about this, I'll make you a deal, shit lips, I'll make you a really good deal. You give me a quick five minutes to myself, as you stand there in your dreary, life's-just-one-long-graveyard-shift-and-then-you-die circus tent of a white T-shirt, you give me a couple minutes and a little bit of privacy maybe, and I work myself up a feverish, Priapus-the-protector-of-livestock hard-on, and then you bring yourself over, jump on it, lift your ankles to the sky and spin yourself in a circle a good six or seven times, and then you get up, thank me, leave the room and shoot yourself in the mouth. That's my offer. You're welcome.'

The shit-talker in Pillow found the whole thing pretty funny. He made eye contact with Louise, who was less amused. Bataille looked like a movie extra who is really just a person on the street they filmed by accident – his face almost looked blurred out for legal reasons. Louise finally spoke. 'Pillow, time is a thing here. Let's turn it up a little.'

Pillow earnestly did not enjoy hurting people who weren't fighting back. Artaud *had* tried to stab him, but it hadn't come close enough to feel like a real attempt. 'I'm kind of curious where he's going with this one.'

'Oh, for …'

Artaud sprang to his feet and pointed a bony, quaking finger at Bataille. 'You don't understand the favour I'm doing. Cruelty is sometimes ugly but it has energy, does it not? Isn't that the best we can ask?' Artaud closed his eyes and turned his face to the roof, raising his hands evenly along his sides. 'I'm a cursed man, because the only place I feel truth is in my veins. I'm cruel because I love all animals.' He opened his eyes and looked down. 'I'm saying these things to you because cruelty is the only language a squealing sow truly understands.' Artaud lunged in Bataille's general direction, and Pillow wrapped an arm around his neck and pulled the lunatic roughly behind him as he put his arm out toward Louise, looking to parry whatever reach she made for Artaud.

'Easy there, sugar bear, he's fragile. I got this.'

Louise reached up to point at Pillow. 'He's going to get his balls cut off if he doesn't tell me where those coins are.

'Whoa, whoa, whoa. Easy, man. No harm, no foul. Let's keep everyone's sex bits out of this thing.'

Louise was a few inches away from them, still mad-dogging Artaud, and before Pillow could even drop his hand, Louise fell, spouting blood from her neck and teeth, and the air smelled like smoke.

Pillow released Artaud and moved for the bar, tripping over a chair. He knew he was hearing gunshots, but it sounded like steel pipes hitting each other. He got to his knees and threw himself behind the bar. Still sprawled out, he saw the briefcase with the money in it and pulled it toward him with his foot.

Artaud moved through the room, waving his arms around like a car-lot inflatable stick person with a leak in it, screaming, 'I am tired of always butchering meat and never getting a bite!'

Pillow took a deep breath and looked over the bar. He reached for the gun tucked in the back of his pants, gripped the handle and changed his mind. Pillow had never fired a gun at someone, and this seemed like a hopeless time to try it out. A man with a ski mask was using an arm the size of a rhino's leg to pin Bataille to the bar. The other ski mask was taller and skinnier, and was moving in toward Louise's body with a gun still trained on her, looking a bit like a cop on a realistic television show. There was blood on the floor. Artaud was still loose, running toward the skinny ski mask now.

Almost casually the ski mask threw out an arm and caught Artaud with the butt of the gun. Artaud fell oddly slowly, like a tree blown out of its roots. Pillow rubbed his eyes, took a breath, fumbled with the briefcase's latches and finally got them open. He gripped the open briefcase and threw it as hard and as high in the air as he could. It hit the ceiling hard, and the bills spread out and drifted down slowly, the way leaves fall off a tree that's just been hit by a car. Pillow vaulted the bar and hit the fire escape at a run, losing his legs as he met the pavement in the alley. He scrambled to his feet and took off sprinting. He reached the street, crossing it diagonally and without looking.

He was a beautiful runner.

Eventually Pillow stopped in a diner he'd never seen before. He ordered a coffee and stared into it for a long time. He watched the ripples move slowly inward from all around, showing the shaking of his hands. A pigeon flew into the window and Pillow started, almost knocking his coffee over. He hadn't realized how hot the cup was making his hands until he took them away.

The street outside was empty except for a flock of pigeons pecking away at a spilled pile of rice. Pillow made a habit of believing urban legends, so he knew he should stop them in case the rice bloated in their bellies later. The street was dark and empty, and the coffee shop was reflected in the window. Pillow saw tiles floating in the hollow road, he saw his face superimposed on pigeons who hadn't exploded yet, a dirty counter hovering dimly upside down over all of them. He watched the pigeons pick away at the pile, knowing he should move, that it was right to move.

A pigeon saved is a life saved.

The street began filling with people, and the window lights came on and the lamps thunked dark one by one. The pigeons had picked the pile loose, a couple hanging around the gutter poking their beaks around. Pillow's coffee was still full. He drank it in one gulp, took several deep breaths.

He was in big trouble. Watching the door on deals like that was usually easy money for Pillow – just sitting around looking tall, shaking some hands. But in Breton's organization, watching the door made you responsible for the door, for whatever came through the door. Pillow flattened himself across the table to look at the street signs – it was a long walk to the Bureau, but he'd need it to clear his head. It felt good to be flat on the table like that, the cold of the linoleum kissing his cheek. Pillow stayed there for a while longer, then he sat up and raised a hand over his head in one motion. He ordered one more coffee with his index finger and stayed still waiting for it. A hand with a pot came over and filled his cup and Pillow tried to thank the hand, but his mouth pulled up short and just sputtered. There was only one pigeon left now, and Pillow reached over to the window, obscuring the bird's head with his thumb.

'Haven't you heard?' Pillow asked the bird, which at that second was just his thumb with wings and legs. 'Y'know, about how big things get when you soak them.'

The bird twitched away toward another grain of rice. Pillow pulled his hand back from the window and used the hand to slap himself in the face seven times.

The centre of Breton's operation was a strange, small office in the east end of town called the Bureau. Breton didn't use the Bureau as a place to directly do business out of; it was more of a clubhouse for people to gather so he'd have them at his disposal when he needed.

Pillow entered the office, and Don Costes was the only person there, standing on a desk looking out the window. Don had been a hotshot amateur around the time Pillow was making his first title run. As Don was turning pro, his promoter got him featured in a documentary. Don had missed the weigh-in for his fight, and when the film crew went over to his apartment they'd found three transvestites playing 9–5–2 using a passed-out Don as a kitchen table. That was pretty much it for Don's boxing career, and now he was Breton's right-hand guy. He'd brought Pillow in while Gwynn Apollinaire had still been running things.

Don Costes looked like the real-life version of Captain America if you'd accidentally left Captain America under a sun lamp in a wind tunnel for sixteen years and then put him in a suit and a bow tie that didn't quite fit.

'Need to see the big man? He's expecting Louise, but you'll do.'

Pillow threw out a lazy two-finger salute and walked through the long, claustrophobic hallway that led to Breton's office.

Breton was a strange and aggressive collector. There was more stuff in his office than there was in the whole rest of the place. There was a big display behind his desk with some old jewellery boxes, preserved body parts and sculptures in it.

Paintings on the walls: an iron with seven nails in the bottom; the New York skyline with a circumcised penis in place of the Empire

State Building; a black metal staircase twisting into a solid concrete ceiling; a velvet torso with a cowboy hat in place of the head, an open file box in place of the legs, nothing in place of the arms; a ceiling fan with femurs for blades; an axe falling into a whirlpool; a giant bull eating a small amount of grass; six overlapping Persian rugs, all mostly red; something that looked exactly like a slipper and a spoon; a pressed pig's heart; a pressed dandelion; oppressed Spanish peasants waiting for a long time beside a dry stream; an avocado being blown out of glass; six glass tears; the Grand Canyon as a mostly dead leaf.

Breton was spinning around in his desk chair, wearing large mirrored lenses shaped like the silhouettes of coffee cups, his arms spread out like a propeller. Breton jumped up when he saw Pillow, stood and pulled out a chair for him, as he did every time.

Breton had one of the biggest heads Pillow was able to conceptualize belonging to a human. He moved smoothly and precisely, and Pillow was sure he had been excessively polite, excessively ruthless and impeccably dressed every day of his life. He gave the impression of a nineteenth-century gentleman scholar who'd been allowed to have too much fun in a torture dungeon for about three months too long.

'Hello, how are you today? May I offer you a biscuit?' Breton pointed with two taut fingers at the plate of cookies on his desk.

'No thanks.'

'Good, good. Do let me know if you feel peckish. It would be my pleasure.' Breton's head jolted and, remembering something, he pointed at it. 'Ah yes, did you see my new picture?'

Pillow turned around and looked. On the door: a life-sized picture of a nude woman, standing with her hip cocked to one side, dangling a strangely long-stemmed pear in front of her face.

'It's nice.'

'My mother sent it. It is a photograph of me as a child. But we have more important business. First, where is Louise?'

Pillow was slightly startled by that question. He looked down at his knees, his pants torn enough that he could see straight down the legs, blood trickling numbly down his shins. 'She's dead.'

'Most unfortunate, obviously.' Breton examined his buffed, clear-glossed nails as if they weren't perfect. 'It is one of life's finer pleasures that death's image, as it grows closer and the focus with which one chances to watch it grows sharper, only diffuses. Those lines that once seemed walls soften into mere smudges. Or, perhaps, smudges that are not so meagre.'

The exhaustion fell on Pillow like a rock cut to his exact shape. His eyes half-rolled involuntarily, then twitched back open when Breton banged the desk with a flat hand. 'I can see that time is, as always and for once, of the essence. So perhaps it is time for you to unfold the events in my direction. Talk, Pillow.'

Breton kept his hands folded over each other and on top of his desk as Pillow told the whole story in one long, tired, honest blurt. Breton would purse his lips in seemingly random places and move his hands up at the end of Pillow's important sentences, like he was the one talking. The boss was not one for social cues, and when Pillow finished, Breton sat there staring at his chest for a crazily socially inappropriate amount of time.

Eventually he nodded succinctly and began speaking, without lifting his gaze to meet Pillow's. 'I must admit to a certain respect for these fellows. I've always felt that the ideal human act consists of a slow stroll down a crowded street, firing indiscriminate shots into adorable, privately owned retail stores.' Breton raised his finger to the lips of an invisible person who had objected. 'Idiots will ask me why I have never done so, as I consider myself most of all a human, and as a close second perfect. To defend myself I will say only that there is much of the wide, patchy quilt of life to be knitted before one indulges in a thing as blunt and hopeless as purity.' He paused and used the arm of his glasses to stir his coffee. His eyes were a sort of tropical-sea blue, the kind of blue people will say isn't blue if what they're looking at is water. 'So, you are worried that you threw the money, my money, carelessly and with admirable verve into the air for the thieves to collect, and that you ran away, stumbling, into the night?' He put the arms of his sunglasses in his mouth, pulling them out and putting them back behind his ears in one motion, his eyes not blinking or looking away as the shades obscured them.

Pillow opted for brevity. It was best to just let Breton talk most of the time. 'Yup.'

'Do not worry. I understand. You did what you had to do. You saved yourself. I admire you, in touch as you are with the elemental facts of life.'

Pillow knew that Breton liked you only if you gave it back to him a little bit while doing absolutely everything he asked of you. 'I'm also in touch with the elemental facts of doing whatever it is I need to do to fix this shit. I'll find Artaud.'

Breton laughed hard enough that with a normal person you'd think they were pretending. 'As dubious a concept as merit is, Pillow, one must still reward quality. You were in charge of safety and, however unexpected the intrusion may have been, you did not handle it well. So, first we must discuss your continued role with the syndicate. In a just universe, a vacation would be in order. But I've always thought that the only true holiday would be to travel back in time to laugh at slaves. So, since real vacation is prohibited by the tepid reality to which you are resigned, I think we should find you some work. Work, as the world would tell us, is that which you do under the glare of a superior. Is that amenable to you?'

Pillow shot Breton in the chest with his index finger and thumb and made a thick clicking noise with his mouth. 'Sounds groovy.'

Breton's head twitched up in a quick double take. Pillow was maybe slightly too sleepy and loose to handle this well.

'Murders are the sorts of things that excite even the most fossilized husk of a policeman's imagination. In the not unlengthy period of time it took you to organize your limited thoughts, we can be sure that the police have been called and have begun their investigation. Artaud is, to put it as mildly as is tolerable, very unstable, a fact of which you should have been far more cognizant last night. So Don Costes will be in charge of picking him up and finding the coins. You will follow whatever instructions he gives you, and provide whatever assistance he asks for.'

Pillow nodded and noticed for the first time that Breton's cufflinks were shaped like anatomically correct human skeletons. 'Are we going to have to clip him? Artaud, I mean.'

'Only if and when I snap my fingers.' Breton took a biscuit and crumbled it in his hands, letting the remains disperse toward the floor. 'Take this seriously, sir. You are on twenty-four-hour call, you will go where you are told and you will do as you are told. This, and only this, will help you. You are responsible for Artaud and for these coins, and you are *not* in charge of searching them out. A unique situation. Now, if you will excuse me, I have other business to attend to. I hope the coming days find you well.'

Pillow decided to take a shot. 'What about Bataille?'

Breton wiped his hands together, spraying cookie dust. 'And what, precisely, makes you think that any of your business?'

Pillow paused a second, spun the biscuit plate in one spot without taking one. 'I usually make things that almost get my balls shot off some of my business. This is all about the coins, so who knew about them? There was a tip-off somewhere down the line. And it wasn't Louise, and it wasn't me. Leaves Bataille.'

Breton smiled in a thin, straight line, as cold and sharp as a razor. 'Ah, and the fractional nature of your intellect reveals itself once again. Whosoever robbed the game did indeed have a tipoff. However, you have eliminated Louise as a possible traitor for the selfsame reason that she is, was, my chief suspect. If I were tipped to rob a deal, as you say, the tipper would be the only person I would kill. And who is the only dead person? You would do well to remember it, and to cure this sepsis of the mind which has you thinking, so tragically, that some certain and small things *are*, while others, the important ones, are not. A full half of this life is a test, the other half a game. Always, Pillow, there are forces greater than your understanding at work. I will not lavish praise on a partially correct, reductionist guess. You will help find Artaud and take care of him. You will cease to bother me with such trifling things as your thoughts. Understood? *If* you will excuse me, I need to go smoke.'

Pillow honestly felt that being embarrassed was worse than most any other feeling. He imagined a rock hitting him in the head. It made him feel better.

Before Pillow could stand, Don hugged him from behind and planted a wet kiss on the side of his neck. Pillow nestled his head into the crook of Don's elbow.

'Hey there, Donny.'

'Don't let him get you down, Pillow. He'll get over it.'

Pillow set to peeling Don's hands off him. 'What is this crazy bullshit, man?'

Don was fussing with his bow tie as they stepped out the side door. 'No, no, no. I do what he tells me, I don't question it. You'll be fine; this wasn't your fault. It'll all work out. I'll put in some good words.'

Pillow squinted and shielded his eyes from the sun.

Don tipped his head back to the sky, as if parched for sunlight. 'It's that part of summer that's just about to get away from us, Pillow. You feel it? It's going to be weepy-ass fall in no time.' They reached the sidewalk and Don looked at Pillow, then reached over and touched him on the forearm. 'You'll be all right. Breton's in a bit of a twist, but I've got you covered.' Don looked over at Pillow and pushed the sides of his own mouth up, to demonstrate a smile. 'Perk up, you'll be fine. Do you want to know how good you're doing? I'll tell you your score.'

'You've been keeping track.'

'Oh yeah, I've got a ledger: 27,000.'

'That's good?'

'I can't tell you that. And I can't tell you anyone else's score. Your score is 27,000 points, and it's not relative.'

Pillow reached over and made Don's bow tie crooked. 'What now, underboss?'

'I'll start looking for Artaud today, you go home and sleep, and if I haven't found him by morning you join the hunt then. Sound good?'

'I guess it has to be.'

Don jumped up abruptly and kicked his heels together. He started walking toward Pillow's car and motioned for Pillow to follow. Pillow was too tired to even be surprised his car had appeared, let alone wonder how it got there.

Like most of his things, Pillow's car had once been nice, or at least expensive, or at very least expensive-looking. But what he'd learned in the waterfall drain of cash and the many failed pawnshop visits since was that to keep nice things perfect-looking (and value-retaining), instead of dirty or scratched or spit on by accident sometimes, you had to be one of those people who was always worrying about their things, fussing with them and putting them back in boxes, and putting oil in them, and that just wasn't in Pillow's nature. So his car was now a twelve-year-old, formerly dark-green (now green-scratch-coloured) Bentley that performed about on par with, and was as well maintained as, the average eighteen-year-old Toyota.

'I had a thought the other day.' Don did like to talk.

'Really, I had one of those a couple years back, I think.'

Don plowed forward. 'It was a thought about us, Pillow. About how we ended up … I was trying to remember the exact minute human flight became boring to me. You know? I can fly, Pillow. I'm a pilot. I'm good at flying, better than most birds …'

Pillow jumped in. 'You know something about birds? They're not all good at flying. I bet it's like people and running. You know? Like there's some birds who tore their wing ACLs when they were young and now they're just gimping along.'

'It was the same with fighting. I quit, and then I needed something else, and I thought nobody gets bored of flying. So now I'm a sky sprinter. An Olympian flyer, Pillow, I'm really good and it bores me to tears. Seems sad, doesn't it?'

Pillow nodded with deep and genuine sympathy. 'Like how fish don't realize how cool water is.'

When they got to the car, Don opened the door for him and Pillow sat down in the passenger seat with his legs sticking out onto the sidewalk, getting ready to fold himself over to the next seat.

Pillow continued: 'But it's not like that for everything. Otters do realize. They swim all day, but you can tell they still think it's fun. You can tell.'

Don leaned down, holding the door open with his bent elbow. 'Good points. I'll have Artaud here for you to pick up tomorrow. Be on time, things are going to get bad in the next little while.'

'I'll be here, Donny.'

Don looked at him and smiled, then he looked back through the car window. 'The thing of it is, I never know how to finish conversations. And then, I don't.'

Don turned his back and walked down the street, singing in full voice.

Pillow's apartment had an old doorbell that was actually a metal bell on a string. The bell pealed four times, and he woke up like he was being pulled out of a well. He tried to make out the time on his alarm clock but saw only a blur. The bell rang again. Pillow confirmed he was wearing underwear and made for the door. He used one hand to open it and pressed the other firmly to his forehead, which felt comforting.

Emily was walking away, and she turned around and laughed when she saw him. Emily was a cobbler at a shoe repair store downtown. She had been far nicer to Pillow than anyone else he'd ever consistently had sex with, and he was pretty sure the same was true for her of him. Her hair was very short and very brown, and she had a number of freckles that gave people the idea of one giant freckle over a whole body.

How it was with Emily Phipps was just one of the things Pillow was both totally sure and confused about. They'd been living in the same building for just under a year, and had been together that whole time, less a week. She'd told him a borderline-hurtful number of times that they weren't dating, just two nice people who liked each other having a good time. They slept at her apartment at least five nights a week, and Pillow was pretty sure he loved her and that, frankly, he didn't have a whole lot else going for himself that could be called good.

'Oh, hi.' She was hanging halfway between turning toward or away from him.

'What's the haps, bay-bee?'

She took a bit of a hop as she moved closer, eyeing him closely. 'I'm sorry to wake you up, but could I borrow some sugar?'

'Um, yeah, of course.' Pillow wondered if he still smelled like cordite fumes. 'What time is it?'

'Eight-thirty.' She looked him in both eyes with the corner of one of hers. 'That's p.m., by the by.'

Pillow was deeply and secretly relieved that she'd specified. 'And it's 1952? Neighbours are borrowing sugar.'

Emily let out one exact breath of laughter. 'Neighbours? You're calling me a neighbour now. Well, aren't you a peach?' She lowered her head slightly and ducked under Pillow's armpit into the apartment. Emily went over to the couch but didn't sit. Pillow peeled off into the kitchen and opened the closest cupboard and started to search through it.

The kitchen was, by a pretty good margin, the nicest part of his place. Although he was aggressively untidy, Pillow was also very conscious of germs, so the surfaces of the kitchen, while weathered, were whiter than when he'd moved in. His fridge was made of steel, and he had a gas stove with streamlined dials from back when people felt entitled to jet packs and hover cars. Beside the stove he had a three-layered metal fruit stand hanging from the ceiling. Each layer carried progressively smaller, less vividly coloured produce (starting with pomegranates at the bottom). The only plant in the whole place was a tiny potted tree he kept on the edge of the sink so that its leaves would catch the sunlight coming through the far end of the curtain's reach.

He took a look out of the corner of his eye and saw that Emily was standing still in the middle of his empty living room floor, trying not to look around. Although their apartments were the same size, shape and layout, Pillow's compared to Emily's about as well as a finger amputation compares to a manicure. All the living room had in it was a purple corduroy chair he'd found by the side of the road, a couch with a flat green sheet over it, a mismatched bed pillow and throw pillow on either arm. Between the couch and chair there was a make-shift side table, a pile of old luggage with an empty mandarin-orange crate on top. The walls were light-coloured, but with swirling greyish patterns that were either someone's idea of wallpaper or just really old stains. The only thing he had up was a patch of half a dozen postcards Don had sent him from Mexico, unevenly stuck to the wall with medical tape. The living room had doors on either end of it leading to a stark, utilitarian bathroom and a dark bedroom with a $3,000 mattress and a knee-high marble statue of a nude woman whittling a flute (both from the good old days).

Emily caught sight of the crate table, closed her right eye and rubbed it back and forth with her palm for a second. 'How about that sugar?'

Pillow spun back toward the kitchen, finally opened the right cabinet and grabbed the sugar. Emily stood up straight and looked up at him not pityingly but maybe a touch regretfully. He didn't break eye contact as he tossed the bag straight up between them. She almost dropped it but held on.

'Thanks, neighbour. I'm making a cake.'

'Gross.'

She did one of those smiles that is really just resisting smiling. Pillow felt a powerful urge to eat a tiny amount of granola out of the crevice where her neck met her chest.

Emily kept talking over her shoulder as she walked to the door. She stepped on a pair of running tights he'd laid out to dry on the way.

She noticed the tights and took another quarter step. 'Well, we can't all be ath-uh-leets, can we? Listen, Pete, I'm really sorry I've been mean this week. I'm a mean sick person. I'll work on it, but I'm not sure it'll get much better, so I might just try to be more … And we should talk. We have stuff to talk about.'

'No, don't apologize. That's …' Sometimes Pillow needed a minute to find the next word, especially when he was thinking about what brains look like when they meet air, and as he fumbled around for the rest of his sentence Emily reached up to her eye and bent over at the waist.

'Okay, okay, okay. I'm totally, totally trying to listen to you, but just now, right this second, a pimple formed on my eyelid and now I know that I have an eyelid and that I have a body and that I'm going to die someday.'

Pillow couldn't quite decide if he should laugh or give her everything he'd ever owned as a gift. 'Are you all right? Need me to pop something?'

She stood back up and breathed out evenly. She had her hand pressed flat over one side of her face. 'Popping my zits for me is probably a personal-space boundary we should stick with for the minute. I'm perfect now. Sorry. I'll have your sugar back to you in a couple hours, if that's cool.'

'Sure thing, but don't feel obligated, I've been told I'm a couple lumps too sweet anyhow.'

She shook the bag at him twice, leaned up and kissed him. The curve where the back of her head met her neck was visible as she walked away, and it seemed to Pillow he could feel the shape of it in his fingertips after she was gone.

Sometime in the several empty seconds between watching Emily leave and closing his door, two homicide detectives arrived to interview Pillow. Lieutenant Sally Avida stretched a long, bony hand across his door and stepped out from behind it. Her partner, Simon, hulked up behind her, scratching his ear.

Pillow smiled and moved out of the doorway.

'Come on in, detectives. Me casa you casa.'

Avida and Simon took two steps inside, then stopped and turned back to face him. They were trying to get him in a corner. Pillow nudged the door further open behind him.

Sally Avida was the head of the homicide division. She was tall and slight, and had one of those necks with no muscles and hardly any veins. She also had a long, curving beak of a nose, a chin the shape of a canoe, and a thin, upturned moustache tattooed on the side of her index finger.

'Pillow, Pillow, Pillow, great to see you.' Her fist bounced off Simon's shoulder like a BB hitting a tank. 'Jessica Hannah Christ, don't you just want to rest your head on him until morning. Or tuck him under your ass during sex.' She pinched Pillow's cheek. 'Get it? Because you're a pillow. Those are the things I do with pillows.'

Pillow leaned forward to kiss her hand.

Avida rolled her eyes as she took her hand back. 'That's funny. You're funny.' Although she was never less than half-joking, Avida almost never laughed.

Her sergeant, Michael Simon, was no wider than a highway and no uglier than a piece of roadkill. He had giant, bulging eyes and a few foreheads, a healthy helping of jowl hanging off a stingy slice of chin. He looked like someone who smelled like the inside of a crowded shipping container.

Simon shifted his weight, and the entire earth didn't shake. 'So I guess you know all about that shootout at the bar last night. We heard you were there.' He reached into his front shirt pocket and pulled out a loose, old cigarette and put it in his mouth.

Pillow had tried and failed many times to understand how anyone thought they were *allowed* to smoke cigarettes. He stretched to his full height, laced his hands behind his head and looked down. 'I doubt it. See, I didn't do a ton of school, but I stuck around long enough to know the difference between things I guess and things people tell me.'

Avida flicked Simon in the bottom ribs, the cigarette bobbing like an unhealthy stool.

'I told you, Sarge, the man picked up a few brain cells on layaway.' She cast a quick, careless glance back at the living room. 'Nice place, pal, I think I saw it on the cover of *Depressed and Tasteless Living* once.'

Pillow was now busy trying to get his hip to pop. Sally and Simon were known to take money. Once in a while they'd unload some stolen drugs with Breton, or tip him off for cash. They had to be playing an angle on the coins. With one last torque back, Pillow felt the hip give, and he swung his leg forward then back. 'Sorry, guys, I sort of phased out there for a second.'

'Got something on your mind? Something to share?'

Pillow grinned and clapped a hold of Avida's shoulder. 'You know what, I do! When I was a kid – I think this is important, could help you – when I was a kid I thought that *you* meant *me*, y'know, because when people said *you* they were always talking to me. I still feel that way sometimes, for like a half a second when somebody's just started talking.'

Avida waited in silence until Pillow looked her in the eyes again. 'You've eaten about twenty thousand too many punches for my taste, Pillow, but you still remind me of this very cute boy I took home once. I drank some whiskies with him – I'm celiac so I don't drink beer – and we talked, and he told me all about his little thoughts. And then I demanded that he get naked, and he did, and I left the room and came back with two raw eggs in my hands. I cracked one over each of his shoulders, then I kicked him out into the empty street, with no idea where he was.'

To say Pillow liked her style was an understatement.

'Do you know what the moral of that story is, Pillow?'

'You're really messy and kind of a cocktease?'

'The moral of the story is that when I look people in the eye and tell them what's going to happen, I tell the truth. And you're not going to touch me without my asking you to ever again. We know what you and Louise Aragon were doing there. We know about the coins, and you're going to tell us about them.'

She shrugged his hand off. Pillow kept the arm moving, rested against it on the wall.

'I don't know anything about coins. I have enough trouble counting them out to pay for an apple.'

Simon talked to Pillow's sternum. 'Think about it. Think about whether or not you're going to be protected on this. You had the door. What use is muscle that doesn't do any of the lifting? We all know how Breton treats fuckups. So if you want to get out in front of this thing, just give us a call, tell us where the coins are and we have a deal.'

'That deal you're talking about doesn't sound super-official to me. Are you off the books on this one?' Pillow looked at Simon out the side of his eye, then he got caught up with flicking a hangnail on his thumb up and down.

Simon snapped his fingers to get Pillow's attention. 'Let's just say that we have options. Where are the coins?'

Pillow nodded, riffled around in his pocket.

'I think I have like seven quarters here, y'know, from laundry day. You want 'em?'

Simon nodded and pushed Pillow's arm off the wall. 'Just think about it. Keep us in mind, and hold yourself tight, Pillow, when you go to sleep.' Simon let the air fall all the way out of the word *sleep*.

'Sure, whatever the fuck that means.'

Pillow shook a small percentage of Simon's hand.

The big man smiled as they let go. 'Like shaking hands with a lace curtain.'

Simon still had the unlit cigarette dangling out the side of his mouth – Pillow grabbed it and started examining the cigarette, turning it around in his hands to see all sides of it.

'This might be a character flaw of mine, but just so you know for later, you're going to have to fuck me up pretty good if you want to intimidate me. It's just how I am. You can talk and talk and talk, and do your cute little low-voice Lawman bit, flash your badge, but I'm not going to believe you until you put it on me. You're going to have to impress me. I've taken some *beatings*, let me tell you, and I don't remember any of 'em. Nobody's made an impression.'

Pillow put the cigarette back between Simon's lips. Avida nudged Simon further out the door.

'See you around the bend of Breton's cock.' She turned around and clapped Pillow on either shoulder. 'Nice chat.'

Avida reached in her pocket and pulled out an evidence bag, let it unroll to reveal Artaud's dinner fork. 'Just one more thing, Pillow. If I were to flip you over, would I get the cool side?' She looked both ways before she took off jogging backward after Simon.

Pillow did not usually watch television or read, so he spent most of the evening sitting on the couch listening to a five-to-one underdog win seven straight rounds and then quit on the stool before the eighth. Then Pillow watched the faucet drip and ran through the angles in his head.

Breton's syndicate was basically a bunch of crazies who liked to stir up trouble. They were always fighting with each other and getting kicked out. Pillow had avoided most of that because he was peripheral to anything important, but he was right in the middle of this one. The problem with Breton was that once you were out, you were out for good. The man was about as forgiving as a trash compactor.

The bell rang softly enough that it could have been the wind. By the time he opened the door, Emily was balancing the sugar on her head, her arms hovering a half-inch out from either side.

'I thought it might be bad form to wake you up twice in four hours, so I whisper-rang.'

Pillow took a step forward and lifted the bag off her head slowly. 'You didn't bring me any cake.'

'You would have made me feel like a fatty about it.'

He turned and made to throw the sugar onto his couch, going through the full motion before turning to her with the bag in his hand. 'That's true. I'm sorry.'

'Don't sweat it, hollow-cheeks.' She stopped and bounced her palm off her forehead a couple times. 'Okay, fuck, fuck.'

'Yeah, but we should go to your –'

She desperately shushed him with her whole hand. 'I wasn't sick last week. I was pregnant. I'm still pregnant. I was going to tell you, and then the pimple thing happened and … whateverwhatever, I'm pregnant. I'm like a month and a half pregnant right now. Screw that counting-in-weeks noise.'

The oldest trick Pillow knew was to take two very deep breaths through his nose and out his mouth. He did that.

'This is the part where you talk to me, Pete. Really. This is the part where you talk.'

She waited.

Pillow liked to think he knew a bit about women, but the bit he knew was the bit that only helps when you're both a bit drunk or sleepy and everybody has a good sense of humour and nothing terribly important is happening in anyone's life.

'Okay, fine.' Emily couldn't help it anymore. 'I am keeping it. And I know this is sort of a weird spot to do that in, but I started feeling really anxious and sad and empty when I thought about getting rid of it, and I know that's not the best reason, but I can do this and I want to and I won't ask anything ...'

Pillow put a hand on her hip. 'That's perfect. I'm in. Whatever you want to do. Whatever you want.'

After she grabbed his hand, hers stopped shaking. 'Okay. Here's the deal. I am going to have two drinks tonight, and I am going to smoke one cigarette. The last one. And you should come to my apartment and do those things with me. Or just watch me do those things. But still, come talk to me.'

Pillow whipped the sugar into the room behind his back.

As Emily talked, Pillow stared at all the different ways light shimmered off the translucent frills around her neck and sleeves. Wearing that shirt, she reminded Pillow of a lot of places and times that he had never experienced, like Western Europe or the 1920s.

The chairs and tables in Emily's apartment didn't match. They were a combination of very solid lawn furniture and very rickety restaurant furniture. It seemed like it was on purpose, though. It was the kind of place where your first guess would be that the woman who lived there had worn clear glasses without prescriptions in them when she was younger and still loved natural history museums.

They'd been talking for a long time without pausing. Pillow was fairly drunk, and Emily's third drink was just a bunch of melting ice now. Pillow had never talked to her about his health situation before.

She said, 'And how does that manifest itself, like today?'

Pillow was sort of amazed, not for the first time, by all the tiny swirls, veins and patterns moving in his drink, because the gin was a different weight than the tonic. He looked back up at Emily, and she was smiling at him, or possibly at the magical way clear mixed drinks move.

He said, 'Well, I was trembling a little bit earlier, but that's mostly gone now.'

She slid forward on the cushion. Pillow noticed and was reminded that she had a small round scar on her temple, one of those scars that is just a dent in the person's skin.

'Dude, I totally feel you on that. Last week I was shaking so hard at work, but it was only in my pinky finger, like all the tremble-juice in my whole body was gunked up in just my little finger. My littlest finger.' And she didn't nod her head in the usual way. She bobbed her head, neck and shoulders up and down. Each time she went up she'd cover the painting of a forest behind her head so only the tiny canvas sky was visible, and when she went back down Pillow could see the whole thing.

'Dude, man, we need to talk more. We need to talk about this stuff. We've been doing this for a year, and we need to get serious, and I need you to be all in or totally out. That's it.'

'I'm in. Trust me, I've watched elephants feed their babies with their trunks for a really big amount of hours. Like, a long time. I know what parenting is about. A baby elephant is big enough to be a linebacker the second it's born.'

'Dude, seriously. I need you to stop talking about exotic animals and answer my question seriously. Like a human being would. Do you know how big human babies are?'

'Yeah, I am. Yes. I can do this. It's all pretty scary, obviously, but we'll make it happen. Yeah. Let's do it.'

Pillow stopped talking after that, but he made a mental note to confirm how big human babies were later.

'We need to be … we need to let each other in. That's super-lame to say but we have to. We said we loved each other uncomfortably early and that was actually really nice, but we sort of didn't follow up on it, and we've never been on a date, and I've seen your apartment like six times, and it's a floor above me, and we need to sort this stuff out.'

Pillow rubbed his eyes. 'Yeah, we will. We're good. We're good.'

'Pete, I found out your real first name because I read that "Whatever happened to?" feature about you in *Sports Illustrated*. I'm not being pushy when I ask you to communicate with me a little bit better.'

Pillow could see the humour. 'Yes. I get it. Fire the cannons.'

Emily drained the rest of the ice cubes. 'It's. Dude. I'm not firing cannons, okay? I'm not storming your walls, all right? I'm asking you for some really basic personal information.'

'Sure. I'm sorry. Ask.'

'You've never told me about boxing, ever. I mean, I know you were good, but were you very good? Do you miss it now?'

'Those are the ones you're not supposed to ask.'

'Curiosity only ever killed cats and young children. Spill.'

Pillow rubbed the back of his neck the way he did for headaches, but he didn't have one right that second. 'Forty-seven wins, four losses and one no contest. Six knockouts. Two-belt champ at 154 pounds. Nine years ago I was about the seventh-best pound-for-pound boxer in the world. For like five months. Which sounds pathetic but is sort of amazing, all things considered. I really, really miss it. I miss it so much that I just don't think about it. I try not to. I miss it really bad. But, on the other hand, nobody fuckin' steals from me anymore, I don't have to weigh food and nobody calls me at five a.m. to do roadwork. That's running.'

'You still go running that early.'

Pillow looked at the floor and cracked a smile like a hardboiled egg rolled on the table. 'Yes, I do.'

'Why did you retire?'

'Well, I didn't exactly want to. I did it a little bit because I was getting older, breaking my right hand every fight, slowing down some, and a big bit because Julio Solis knocked me out for six and a half minutes with my eyes open. And the neurologist said I had to.'

'Jesus, I didn't realize it was that bad.'

'It's funny. I don't know this because I never watched the tape. But they told me when they were taking me out on the stretcher I wouldn't stop asking if there'd been a fight. Or if it was just practice.

I must have said it a dozen times.' He laid his right hand flat on the cushion, ran his fingers over the knuckles.

'Was there a fight?'

Pillow closed his eyes. 'I believe that it happened, you know. It must have. But I don't remember a second of that fight. If you gave me a polygraph and you asked if it happened … And sometimes right when I wake up and I know it's going to be a bad day, just for a few minutes, I let myself think maybe I'm still in the dressing room getting my hands wrapped. That I'm still getting warmed up. That it's always only just about to happen.'

He smiled at her. Pillow knew how creepy it was when someone smiles at you with their eyes closed, but he did it anyway. Then he opened them. Emily seemed upset.

'It happened. I understand that, enough people have told me, I get it. It's gone. But I was so fucking good. People don't even know. Pure boxer. If you understood, man, it was beautiful. I couldn't just sit down on a straight right, make it count, and if you can't do that you're always running, y'know. But I worked it. I fought all the brawlers and knockout artists, 'cause they get tired and they couldn't handle my footwork. I had cardio for days, and I was slick as hell. I played it smart, for years. They couldn't hit me. I move pretty good.'

Emily leaned down and kissed his hand. She sat up smiling. 'I know, I've seen you dance. I remember we went to that party and I had to go pee, and I came back and just watched you dance for a few minutes. You were bustin' it, dude, and you had your eyes closed, all blissed out, and I thought to myself, all right, self, he might be a bit sketchy, he might be a bit of a dick, he might even be a bit retarded, but nobody dances like *that* without a soul. A soul and a half.'

'I know. A lot of people have told me that actually.'

'Annnd I was right about the dick part.'

'That hurt my feelings.'

'Awww, really?'

'Yep, both of 'em. Both my feelings. I'm not retarded, though.' Pillow took a deep drink and snapped an ice cube with his teeth. 'I've been told I'm pretty far ahead of schedule, brain-wise.'

She pulled skin under her eye tight, then she let it go and stared intently at her hands as she talked. 'Okay, so the part where I'm a crass asshole, a crasshole, as someone who isn't that funny might say, is that I'm totally broke. I don't make a lot of money, and I've been frivolous, I've been very, very frivolous with money for a long time, and I have debt. Like a pretty, pretty decent amount of it. And, umm, just how much money do you have? It seems like not very much.'

Pillow tucked his chin under his shoulder and rolled with an imaginary punch. 'Depends what you mean by "not very much." Do you think nothing isn't very much?'

They both laughed.

'I have one moth in my wallet,' he said. 'I could show you, but then he'd fly away and I'd have nothing.'

Emily moaned and collapsed into her own lap. Pillow followed her down and kept talking. 'His name is Matthew. Cool guy, but he's totally cockstruck by this girl named Any Lightbulb.'

Emily sat up, pretty much over the whole laughing thing. Pillow felt slighted – the moth bit was funny, especially for on-the-spot like that.

'What are we going to do, man? Maybe I should just ditch this thing. Feel like throwing me down the stairs? Give me some of that home-cooking.'

Pillow patted his pocketless shirt. 'You know what? I forgot my coat hanger. I'll scratch you later.'

He could tell that Emily was trying really hard not to cry. Pillow wondered abstractly for a second if he really wanted a kid. If he should just let her run this thought through to the end. Pillow knew he shouldn't make another amateur-abortion joke. He knew that for sure.

Emily twisted her lip a bit too violently, then she sucked on it for a second.

'It's just the worst. Like, because I didn't make a budget. And because I didn't buy shit on sale, and because I didn't want to be counting all the time. Because of *that* ... It's not fair to the kid, I think. I wouldn't want to be as poor as me now if I was twelve.'

Pillow kept thinking it through as Emily successfully failed to cry. Eventually he came to the conclusion that his life was not going well. And one thing he'd always been good at was knowing when to mix things up. He tilted her chin up.

'Hey, I have, it's not very legal, but I could get a line on some money.'

Pillow told her the story of the coins. He slightly exaggerated their value, omitted all the violence, excluded the cops, pretended Louise had never existed and told the rest of the story faithfully. Emily listened skeptically and took a minute to think. 'So what makes you think you can get these coins before everybody else?'

'Well, first off I can take them to someone else after I find them. Fence them through Gwynn Apollinaire. She used to sponsor me while I was fighting. And she can move them. I'll get more money that way. If I can find Artaud … I'll see if he'll talk to me. I can get these coins, and that money'll sort us out for a while. Long enough to think things over, at least.'

'That's all fine, but nobody is going to get hurt? I don't get how they just took the money without –'

'I'll say what I used to say before my fights: nobody is gonna get a scratch, guaranteed.'

Emily reached over and grabbed his hand. 'This scares me, and you need to take it seriously. Nobody is going to get hurt.'

Pillow thought he could promise to try it that way, and he could be sure she wouldn't find out who he had to hurt anyway, so he didn't even feel bad saying it. 'I promise nobody is going to get hurt.'

They kept talking until the last of the summer light went out of the sky, and sometimes she would rub her palm down the whole length of her jaw and make this elegant motion with her wrist, as if flinging one drop of water off the tip of her finger.

It had started and stopped raining, and what earlier had been the whole sky was just one big pink cloud by the time they got outside. Pillow finished propping the building's side exit open, and Emily was already walking along the curb, pretending it was a tightrope. She saw him and lost balance slightly, regaining it without stopping her wave.

'I have one more serious question for you. You talk about the zoo a lot, a kind of strange amount actually, so what animal would be the best animal to be if you had to be an animal who wasn't human? Now, I'm growing fond of you and I don't want you to screw this up too badly, so I'll tell you the thing first. See, the thing is you can't be any of the ones whose whole, whose whole life, is just toil. Like penguins, or those elephants who walk for like six months just to get water and show up looking like balloons that died in your room. No, you have to pick one that plays. Those are the only right answers. Like a monkey, or a dolphin, or a kitty.'

'I think I'd be a giraffe. They clean their eyes with their tongues and they neck all day. I watch them at the zoo.'

'You're saying that giraffes just make out all day? Do giraffes know what making out even is?'

'No, they think necking is just banging their necks together a bunch of times to impress girls. Plus they're so tall and weird-looking.'

'Oh yeah, that's cool. I mean it's not as giggly and swimmy and whimsical as a dolphin but, y'know, whatever floats. Now, friend, you are going to watch me smoke my very last cigarette.' She sat down on the curb and pulled a pack of smokes out of her purse. 'The very last one.'

The air was wet and that little bit cold you have to have no imagination to resent. Pillow watched her smoke, how she'd hold it and blow it through her nose, he watched the trails rise and dissipate. Her lips would purse just a little and release, and he was trying to time it.

'Do you want to date each other?'

She reeled back laughing and covered one eye with a flat palm. 'Who is in 1952 *now*, buddy boy? So old-fashioned. Put a seed in my belly and then ask me out for a malted, huh, Bareback Buddy Holly?'

'Yup.'

Rocking back and forth, cigarette waving above her head, snowing ash. 'If you do, Peggy Sue, then you know why I feel blue … My Peheggy Suh-uh-ooo. Breaky breaky breaky Peggy Sue.' She settled down and leaned over and they kissed for a short time. She smelled like smoke and clean, human skin.

'I actually do, Pete, believe it or not.' Her eyes rolled like rocks falling down a cliff.

He pointed abruptly at her bag. 'Gimme some cigarette.'

Emily let her smile spread slowly and stretched her legs to their full length into the street. 'Okey-dokey, Smoky.' She turned at the waist and waved a cigarette in a repetitive motion in front of his face until he took it. 'Here, I'll butt-fuck you.' Emily used her cigarette to light his.

Pillow didn't cough and dropped his head to his chest; he didn't move as he exhaled. 'Holy shit, that is awful. How do you *do* that? Every day?' He took another drag.

'Oh my god, is that your first cigarette ever?'

'I used to be a professional athlete, you know.'

'You're adorable! Oh man, I haven't given anyone their first cigarette since I was like fourteen. And you hate it! You're adorable!'

Pillow flicked his cigarette into the air. 'Adorable like a fox.' Sometime since the last time he'd looked closely, a small, perfectly round flush had appeared between her collarbones. 'Like a fox you just butt-fucked.'

'Nobody said you weren't generous.'

They were much closer to the same height sitting down, with Pillow's feet splayed casually into the street, far enough that a student driver would worry about hitting them. Emily reached over and put her arm around his shoulder. She brought a hand out in front of them. With the lit cigarette still poking out from between her knuckles, she raised her hand steadily while rotating it from side to side, to give the impression of flight.

Pillow tended to do a whole lot of driving that didn't quite feel like driving. He wasn't sure how other people felt behind the wheel, but there was a strong, swirling aimlessness to his control of the vehicle that didn't read as universal. It should definitely seem like real life is happening when you're driving a car. For one thing, going far too fast and far too slow felt exactly the same to Pillow. When he looked at the speedometer, he was usually surprised by the number he saw there.

He was three hours late to meet Don at the Bureau and so he gunned it over, cars and pedestrians and buildings passing casually through the glass in a way that should have been alarming.

Pillow pulled up in front of the Bureau and saw Don leaning on the front wall, staring absently into the air, his index finger tucked securely into the deep, rounded scar that ran the length of his cheek, listening to Bobby Desnos (one of Breton's muscle-and-meth guys) telling another one of his stories. Pillow watched them through the mirrors for a second. That was another disorienting thing about cars: how much of the world behind you could be visible without you turning your head.

By the time Pillow reached them Don was laughing his ass off, and Desnos was looking a little bit offended.

'Why would you do that, Costes? I told you about this because I wanted help with my feelings.'

At a very early point in his boxing life Pillow had figured out a way to call up his fighting state of mind whenever he needed it. It had made his career, probably, and it was still helping now. Pillow wasn't one of those guys who needed to get mean to fight, he just needed to take it lightly. Making jokes, not thinking of punches as punches but as spilled drinks, party fouls. Like he was only paying attention because it was fun to get over on someone, not because that person could kill him. Pillow's recipe for success was relaxed but ready. He knew exactly how to relax, and he could fake ready no problem.

Pillow wrapped his arm all the way around Desnos's neck and kissed him behind the meth bubble behind his ear. 'Is he being mean to you, bubs?'

Don wiped a tear out of his eye and tugged on Pillow's elbow. 'You have to hear this story. Oh, my sweet lord Jesus Christ dying and shitting himself on the cross, it's good!'

Desnos rolled his eyes, the edge of his lips jerking up a little bit. 'Okay, so, I was holed up at this hotel room. And I had this new shipment that this gaping asshole over here'd hooked me up with so I figured I had to try it out, for quality control. And it was really pure. So I'm in this hotel room just tweaking my balls off. And I finish explaining this really good idea I have for how to make roulette more fun to the chest of drawers, and I hear this woman having sex or possibly masturbating herself next door. So I go up to the wall, and I listen, and she's really gettin' it, right? It seemed so private and … and I was so gakked up that I started just absolutely viciously jerking off. It was a fucking *travesty* how hard and uselessly I was slamming my meat. And she finishes a long time before I do. There's this one big thump and then she quiets down, and I'm just pulling ropes on an empty flagpole all night. Finally, hours later, I come and get a few minutes' sleep. So I wake up, and I look out my window, and I see they're wheeling a body, you know, covered in a sheet. They're wheeling it out of the room next door. Do you get it? She wasn't masturbating, she was dying! I mean … I've done some … Oof. That's a … that's a doozer.'

Pillow squeezed Desnos's shoulder. 'You're a bit of a weird guy, Bobby, has anyone ever told you that?'

'Not in a while actually.'

The best thing Pillow could say about the Bureau boys was that they weren't boring. There was always some sort of orgy or fight about to happen, someone always had a new random obsession they were talking about. Pillow realized it wasn't the sort of fun everyone was into, but he figured that as long as he was the one watching and laughing, and not the one sending love letters to female serial killers or paying prostitutes so he could cry in their laps, then he'd probably be okay.

Desnos reached out with both hands and awkwardly patted Pillow and Don on their chests, and backed into the Bureau, letting the loose-hinged door flail weightlessly open behind him.

'He's a complicated guy.'

'So, Pillow, I'll start by telling you my assumptions, then we'll move on to my plans, then we'll move on to what we're doing today.'

'Sounds good.'

'We are assuming Artaud is in town, and that he will not have the means nor the wherewithal to leave town. Yesterday I searched his apartment, and I've left a man there; we have his passport, and we don't think he has much money on him.'

'Fair enough.'

'I've put some feelers out with various narcotics suppliers, some of whom, doubtless, I will hear back from soon. Our duty, good sir, is to wait for word, and to do so in the way that is most comfortable to us. Any questions?'

'Do you have any shorts with you?'

'No.'

Pillow pursed his lips. 'That's fine, you can borrow some from me. I say we swing by my place, pick up some gear, then we can go to that creepy abandoned dock you like, run some hills, bring some Greek salads, y'know? How long are we going to wait?'

Costes nodded, then laid a hand flat out toward Pillow's car. 'Until we don't feel like it anymore.'

The creepy dock Costes liked was only actually creepy in one way, and that wasn't so much creepy as it was vaguely magical in a profound, ineffable way. The dock overlooked a nice, quiet mini-lake. On the opposite side of the lake there was a loosely spaced piteousness of cottages. What was creepy about the dock was that it seemed abandoned and unmaintained, except for three large light bulbs on top of the pillars out over the water. The lights looked like streetlamps from the rich part of a city that was also an allegory about capitalism. Smooth polished metal, the glass somehow frosted but letting the light through bright and clear, all resting on wood that was halfway rotted, rusty nails sticking out, the boards of the dock groaning and straining just from the breeze.

Having just run a pretty good set of hills, first with Don and then with Don watching while nipping at a flask of brandy, Pillow was feeling flush and calm, sitting in the driver's seat, watching the dock and waiting for the lights to flick on as the sky darkened. 'Y'know, Don, I remembered this dock differently.'

Don already looking sleepy, a little droopy and uncoordinated in the neck. 'I know, you remembered it with moral judgment in your heart. You remembered it wrongly.'

Pillow reached over and whacked Don with a hard, flush flick to the cheek. 'And what sort of a thing to say is *wrongly*?'

Don, having straightened up, smiled and drooped back down. 'A word.'

'So why are we here, Don?'

Eyes closed, Don spoke as if letting bread crumbs drop out of his mouth. 'We are waiting because we are limited, Pillow. Until Artaud pokes his head up, we might as well be looking for an echo from last year. We are *here* because one, one being me, grows tired of sitting in office space, waiting for phone calls.' Don opened his eyes again. 'You are, if nothing else, a change of pace, Pillow.'

'Then what am *I* doing here? It's one thing to need a change of pace, but the change of pace has a pace too, y'know what I'm saying? A pace that's his own.'

'I'll try to get you some money on this. I'll see if I can get you a little piece of the coins.'

Pillow looked back to the dock. The lights had come on when he hadn't been looking, and they were glowing silently and perfectly now, illuminating the rotting, mossy dock. 'See, man, you'll try. You'll try to get me just a little, tiny taste. I'm not trying to work for free.'

'You know how it is with Breton.'

'Oh yeah, I know. I know how it is. How much are these coins worth?'

Don opened his eyes again this time and tried to warn Pillow off with the way he pointed them. 'It doesn't matter.'

'Six figures?'

'Maybe on a very good day.'

Pillow laughed and gripped the steering wheel, which had, like so many other things, been really polished-looking a long time ago. 'Donny, Donny, Donny. The shit I do now, for the kind of money I do it for, it's, uh, it gets me down, a little bit. The scale gets out of whack, I think, y'know, when you've had and blown five and half, six million. It's a thing.'

'I imagine it is.'

'One time, toward the end there, I was so broke that I needed to buy food for the week, like just actual food, and I had to look for change in my couch. So that's how broke I was. D'you want to guess how much money I found, all the coins, bills, that fell out of my pocket?'

Don flexed some of his neck tendons, sucked some air past his teeth. 'I think it'll be better if you just tell me.'

'Twenty-eight hundred dollars. It was a big-ass leather couch. That's how it used to be.' Pillow clicked his tongue against the roof of his mouth. 'I owned a shark.'

'I remember. Whatever happened to that thing?'

'He was a shark, not a thing. Around the couch-change time I had him appraised by this super-sketchy Belgian dude who sold exotic animals, like, black-market overseas-type shit. And this Belgian comes in peering over his glasses, lookin' all Hercule Poirot –'

'I love Hercule Poirot.'

'I'm more of a Matlock guy.'

'Poirot and Matlock cannot be compared by any metric. They are not present on the same plane of existence.'

'Anyfuckinghoo, third-world animal-kidnap Hercule Poirot comes to look and gives me a price, not a bad price either, my man, would have paid a few markers. But right after he leaves, within five hours, Rigoberto, that was my shark's name, Rigoberto goes tits up. Stone dead. It was sad.'

'How did he die?'

'He just stopped swimming. As soon as Hercule left the scene, Rigoberto stopped moving. That's super-bad for sharks, y'know what I'm saying? And I was banging on the glass, I threw some meat in there, nothing. That was a bummer. A bummer swimming in a sea of bummers. Or not swimming, I guess. Not swimming in a tank in a living room.'

Costes let a reasonable pause fill the air. 'How would you rate your experience as a shark owner, tragic ending aside?'

'Y'know what, man? I had big dreams for being someone who owned a shark. I bought it way, way before I was making that real shark-level money too. But it was kind of a drag. I had to feed it meat all the time. I didn't even like having it in the house and I needed a whole fridge for it. And really they just look at you with these dead, black shark eyes, they don't even see you. Doing laps and waiting to taste some blood, and that's pretty much it. I loved Rigoberto because he was around every day, I mean, he was my living room wall for a few years there, but I should have bought a kangaroo or something. Maybe a koala. Something with a gentle, like, essence. Feed it some grass, have a little wrassle, give him a cuddle, that would have been nice. Yeah, man, I wasted a lot of money on that shark.'

'Why not just buy a dog? It sounds like you wanted a dog.'

Pillow drummed a quick four-beat on his lips. 'I hadn't thought of that. That would've been good. I have regrets, but hey, if wishes were fishes the whole world would be squishy. At least you don't put sharks up your nose, am I right?'

'In more ways than are countable, sweet Pillow.'

Don reached across the gearshift for an awkward upper-body car hug, then they settled back into their seats, looking out at the misty, glowing water, waiting for a phone call that would tell them where a morphine-addicted schizophrenic man was so they could speed over and grab that man and handcuff him to a chair in the Bureau and beat him with a phone book until he told them where some coins were.

Emily had gotten a whole lot of UTIS as a teenager and was now 'cautious and right and totally not unreasonably vigilant' about peeing right after sex. Pillow waited and stared at her wall, which was probably the best wall he'd ever seen or heard about. It had an old, gold-patterned square of wallpaper on it, but the rest of it was painted blue. There were three Edward Hopper prints in a line, and a black-and-white analog photo of a topless woman lying on a rock. Below the wallpaper there was a row of three other fabric swatches, different and complementary colours. Matching but not matchy.

Emily walked back into the room, sat in her chair and tried very hard not to smoke a cigarette out the window naked. She waved the unlit cigarette at him, snowing some dry flakes of tobacco onto the floor. 'Woof. You wasn't holding back there, mister. Aren't guys usually freaked out about rutting at us pregnant bitches?'

Pillow smirked. 'Oh right, I'm supposed to be weird and worried about the baby seeing my dick from the womb? I'm a grown-ass man, I know where your cervix is.'

Emily laughed. She leaned back in her chair and spun the cigarette around in her fingers. 'You're such a goon. What were you doing tonight? You were out so late.'

'Me and Don were out looking for Artaud. We're making progress.'

'Okay, okay.'

Pillow glanced over at her and shrugged, then he stared at the wall a while longer. He wondered who invented wallpaper patterns. Like who did the first one and thought it would look good on some paper and then put that paper on a wall.

'So, um, what about these coins? Is that all okay?' Emily seemed more tense than Pillow could really imagine being. Bodies are nice mostly when they're soft and easy to rub up on. Why stiffen them?

For several years now, Pillow had been trying to think about coins as little as possible. They'd been the first sign, the first time he'd known something was wrong on his own instead of some doctor telling him he'd be messed up in his fifties. He was checking out at the bulk store. He'd been bantering with the cute counter girl with the dreadlocks and the earring that was just a

58

hole. The whole place smelled like ginger and tamarind had a baby and somebody had left the afterbirth out in the sun for a few days. Pillow put his bill down, no problem, then he pulled change out of his pocket. He made a joke and the girl laughed and turned away a little bit and grabbed her elbow, and when he looked back at the change in his hand, the coins meant nothing to him. He knew what they were, he felt the weight of them, but he just couldn't make that step of really knowing, really getting that they were money, that they had numbers attached to them. He remembered the man behind him with the weirdly pouting lower lip and the yoga mat sticking out of his bag sighing, all affronted, and the girl behind the counter pulling away her elbow, reaching forward and taking three coins out of his hand and touching his arm on the way back. The ding of the till, and still just dead weight in his hand. A few chunks of metal.

He'd gone home and counted more change than he had in his whole life. Hours making change, and the change was always correct, he got pretty good at it. He'd tried to reason it out. Money had never meant much to him, until he needed it. But that wasn't the point. The point is never what you need it to be.

'They're worth enough. Six figures.'

'And what about when you find them?'

'We skip town, go live in your hometown, get jobs, free grandparent babysitting, livin' the dream, y'know.'

Emily aggressively scratched at her temple. 'I really don't like this. I don't think you should mess around with this.'

Pillow took an extra second so it wouldn't be too obvious he'd worked out the speech beforehand. 'Listen, I know that this is way outside what you're comfortable with. I feel that, but if you think about it, nothing I'm doing now is any more illegal than what I've been doing anyway. And this way we can get the money and I can quit this, and then, I dunno, get my GED and work at Burger King or something fun like that. Or I could be a dog trainer. Dogs love me, I can tell. They always lick my hand right away, I don't even have to let them smell me like you're supposed to.'

'Okay. Okay. Do your thing. But I'm not built for this, man. I just wish credit-card debt didn't make me feel like I was going to die. It's totally not supposed to do that to you, but it does. I don't know. My mother says I have an overdeveloped sense of obligation. We need money, is what I'm saying, but I still don't think any of this is a good idea.'

'Yes. Totally. First thing tomorrow I'm going over to Gwynn's house. She's really smart, and she likes me. She knows her way around stuff like this, and I'll run it all by her, and if she thinks it looks bad I'll duck out. Okay?

'Sure. Just be careful. I can't talk about this anymore, it skeeves me out.' Emily let out a deep breath. She pulled on her earlobe for a minute, then forgot about the ear, her hands hanging loosely below the chair. 'So tell me about other stuff. Personal stuff. Your childhood.'

'I don't remember that business.'

'Liar!'

'Are you kidding? I spit truth like it's sunflower seeds. Every time I see my sister she tells me some new amazing thing from when we were seven.'

Emily crossed her legs and rubbed her chin thoughtfully. She looked as much like Sigmund Freud as she could and did hope to. 'It's interesting that you referred to your youth as a business.'

Pillow made a pained face until he remembered something. 'I had an afro. I had one of those real, awesome little-kid 'fros. And one time I was out shopping with my mom and she put her hand in my hair, I was like four probably, and she called it a rat's nest. And for a long time after I thought rats were born in trees.'

Emily flicked her unlit cigarette out the window, it hit a railing and fell into the dark. 'One of these days we're going to have a personal conversation that doesn't end with you talking about animals.'

He kicked the sheets off and rolled over, giving her his back. 'Yeah, good luck with that.'

Emily reached the bed pretty quickly, and didn't stop jumping on it until Pillow tackled her and rolled them onto the floor, taking the impact on his ribs and sort of enjoying it. He felt her whole body tense up.

'I don't want to be a bitch, and I know you didn't mean to, but you can't be like that with me anymore, Pete. I have to be careful with my body. I know you were just fooling around, but you have to be careful.'

'Yeah. I'm. I'm sorry, I won't. I'm sorry.'

'Seriously. You need to promise me. And I know I was fooling around too, but you need to be careful.'

'I understand.'

She blinked as he wiped a mascara smudge out of the soft corner of her eye.

'Now and then it is good to stop sprinting after happiness and just be happy. Those of us with brain damage would do especially well to remember that, Pillow, if we could only manage it.'

There was something about having tea with elderly women that always made Pillow sit with his knees very close together and hold the cup with two fingers.

Pillow was sitting with his knees very close together on Gwynn's long, flaccid couch, the cushions denting all the way under his weight. Gwynn was sitting across from him in her lucky chair, a fancy gold-coloured thing that was oddly low to the ground; it made her knees rest higher than her waist when she sat in it.

In certain people's houses, Gwynn Apollinaire's condo would have been called the conservatory. Its main feature was a set of three floor-to-ceiling windows that faced out onto the street, their thin, paneless edges trembling once in a while when large trucks went by. The rest of the condo was lightly decorated, a small oil painting of half a gentle-seeming horse with one straight leg and one crooked one, an ornate lamp that looked like a dinosaur egg and a row of four charcoal drawings of that same lamp in the process of breaking against a kitchen counter. There was a tiny chandelier made of black glass hanging above her chair. Behind the couch there was a set of very tall doors, and Pillow could never tell if they led to another room or if they were just decorative. The doors didn't have any handles he could see, plus they were taller than any person had ever been.

The Bureau guys had been fascinated by the world's biggest man for a while. He was a nine-foot kid from the prairies. He'd wanted to be a cowboy but the weight of his bones would crush a horse's spine if he rode one, and his legs would dangle on the ground anyway. Nobody knew for sure he was the biggest man in the world until he died and they studied his skeleton at a university. At the Bureau they'd all laughed, but Pillow thought it was one of the saddest stories he'd heard. To have your bones be more famous without you.

Gwynn reached forward and grabbed him by the wrist; the veins in her hand reminded Pillow of above-ground pipes. 'I've known you for almost fifteen years and you're still such a young person. I often feel as though I was never your age. I've been here so long, looking out these windows and listening to traffic, spinning in one spot like a top.'

Pillow put his cup down. The tea had cream in it, and he'd only been sipping at it to be polite. It's not really fair to expect an eighty-three-year-old Frenchwoman to respect your veganism. He gently patted her hand, and she slumped back into her chair.

Up until eight years ago, Apollinaire had overseen most of the things Breton ran now. She'd been the one who'd brought Pillow in, paying some of his bills and betting on him while he'd still been fighting. Gwynn had run the syndicate, but she hadn't been as organized, or as firm, as Breton was now. People had done things because they liked her. She took care of you. Her big claim to fame was being held for six days under suspicion of stealing the *Mona Lisa*. She was getting a bit frail, which was how Breton forced her out in the first place, but she was still smart and connected.

'Still trying to work the old-lady bit, Gwynn?'

She had a multi-level tea stand where she kept her pipe. The top tray had a huge, loose pile of noxious black tobacco on it.

She winked, patted her stomach and picked up the pipe. 'It's the best bit, because it only gets more believable with age.'

Apollinaire had a way of making Pillow feel just as old and cool as she was.

'Do you remember when you taught me how to wink properly?'

She got her pipe lit and blew out several thick puffs, as quick and hot as a steam engine, letting the long stem of the pipe hang down, almost touching her chest as she exhaled. It really was an awful thing.

'I remember every monster I created, Pillow, and I remember some of them fondly.' She wheezed through a quick spurt of laughter. 'You winked at me in a championship fight! He had you in the corner, and you winked, ducked behind him and tousled his hair. Such style! You were a favourite, my favourite. Oh dear! I forgot the custard tarts.'

She started to get up and Pillow sat her down with his index finger. 'I'm good.'

'Still watching your figure?'

'Something like that.'

Gwynn shook her paunch proudly. 'So, before we get to your problems, I have one of my own.'

'Sure, what is it?'

'I need to apologize to you, Pillow. I should, I should have visited you, but I haven't been getting out much and ... Anyway, we should have stayed in touch, after I bought out. I apologize.'

'Don't worry about it, you lost a lot of money on me. And I wasn't exactly on the ball right around then. I wouldn't have called me either.'

She looked at him like he was the loneliest, strayest kitten she'd seen, and like she'd seen him at the end of a long career in animal rescue. 'Guilt is an indulgence of the elderly, and one I hope you'll allow me. We all owe you a lot more than apologies, Pillow.'

They looked out the window for a second. They could hear the traffic and the apartment was very still. Not even the chandelier moved.

'So, have you heard about these coins?'

Gwynn rubbed what was left of her eyebrow. 'Yes I have. And both of us would be better off if we hadn't. I wouldn't mess around with a thing like that if I were you, Pillow. Your heart is not in it. Take it from someone who has stolen the *Mona Lisa*, my boy, big scores don't feed you, they eat you up.'

'Okay. Let's say that someone has just gotten their girlfriend pregnant. And this same person needs to get the fuck out of this place and never see these people again. And say, just say, this same person finds the coins. Do you think you'd be able to move them for him?'

Gwynn took a long pause, and after she'd congratulated him and made him promise to make her the grandgodmother of his child, she took a short hobble to the kitchen for the custard tarts, because guests aren't always the only people in the room. Pillow explained his theory. Gwynn didn't seem impressed.

'So you're putting all the rocks in the Artaud basket? There's a pun available, but I'm above it.'

'I think I can flip him. I'll finesse Costes, get you the coins and if you move 'em it's a pretty decent score. We can chop it seventy-thirty.

'Okay, let's say you're right, Artaud tells you where the coins are. Why take them to me? Why not just give them to Breton and let him pay you? He would let you out if you wanted it. He let me out.'

Pillow smiled the way he used to after taking a clean punch. 'That guy wants people to kick it upstairs, so he can decide how much to give back. And I hate it. I've been kicking it upstairs my whole life. I was in a bad way when you were in charge, we both know that, but it was my own fault. You were nice, Gwynn. It hasn't been the same since you left. He's running everyone. Wants everyone committed, like we're in the army, and I'm not into that.' Pillow punched one hand with the other. 'Nobody fights for you, and you shouldn't fight for anyone else. You die alone, and you live with your friends. I've known that a long time. Since I was eight. I don't need to be on any fuckin' team. I have friends.'

Gwynn looked out the window for a long minute. Then, without turning her head, she killed the pipe and laid it back down on her tray, a thin line of smoke and smell still trickling out of the bowl.

They talked for a long while after that, about the good times, and then she gave him advice about life on the run. By the time she agreed to move the coins, they were standing in front of the window.

'Yes, I think I will, Pillow. I would have done it just for you, but I want you to know that I'll do it on my own behalf as well. This is risky enough to feel a bit like stealing. I miss stealing. I liked it. Are you sure you want to do this? It's low percentage, and I, personally, am old enough to take any risk I please. I am actually so old it would be stupid not to. For you it could be a bad idea.'

'Yeah. I'm sure. It's not nothing for you either. It could fuck with your buyout.'

She slumped forward and let her forehead press into the glass. 'I don't care. I thought it was the right thing to do, to let the younger people have their time. And maybe it was, it could well have been ...'

A giant raindrop slapped the window in front of her forehead, followed by a lot of other similar but smaller ones.

Gwynn spoke to the glass, the window fogging with every word. 'It's raining, my soul, it's raining. But it's raining rotten eyes.'

Pillow hustled over to the produce stand down the street from Gwynn's apartment to buy some groceries. It was the best fruit place in town, and for going on fifteen years now he'd been buying hundreds of dollars' worth of produce there each month. The old Korean couple who owned the place had still never recognized him. But those papayas.

Pillow was mid-squeeze on a mango when he caught sight of Julio Solis. He angled his shoulders away and tried to focus on the fruit. The man had ended his career, and here he was. Julio Solis must have been forty now, fat and happy, bouncing down the sidewalk, umbrella way above his head spraying water off it with each step, sharkskin jacket stretched tight across his chest. Solis almost ran into the apple display and stopped to look around.

'Pillow! Get over here, brother.'

Pillow put his thumb halfway through the mango, squeezed out a smile and walked over to hug Solis. Pillow reached around Julio's head and sucked the pulp and mango juice off his thumb. Julio was still hugging, and Pillow could sense that his eyes were closed.

'Howzit goin', Jules?'

Solis finally finished the hug, pushed Pillow back and looked him up and down. Pillow was under the edge of the awning and a long stream of water ran straight down the back of his shirt.

'Shit, you look good, Pillow. Me, I'm fat like the sea now, you're turning to dust! You having a comeback?'

'Naw, man, no. You were my last one. You know what the girls say, once you go Mexican you never can again.'

Solis rocked his head back and laughed, then he gestured to the street with the whole left side of his body.

'Come on, I'll show you my gym. I was thinking about you the other day, really, I own a gym now, give my father something to do so I don't kill him.'

'Oh shit, how is he? Man, he's a trip, I love Pedro.'

Solis let his chest puff down a little. 'He's himself. I'm older now, I forgive shit, I take him for who he is. He never gave me a beating like you did, like we gave each other. That was one you give each other, hey?'

Pillow rolled his eyes and neck around at the same time. 'Can't speak to it, though, Jules. You knocked me into next year.'

'Listen, bro, seriously, come let me buy you lunch. I'll … There's a kid I want to talk to you about. He's perfect for you. I know you're working out, but are you training anyone?'

'No, I'm serious, I meant actually next year. The year hasn't happened yet.'

Julio laughed, guessing and hoping it was a joke. He held the umbrella open down around his ankle. Passersby had to hug the other side of the aisle. Pillow grabbed Julio's wrist and moved the umbrella between them.

'Do me a favour – come to my gym. Look at this kid, help me out with him.'

Pillow shrugged and toed the ground. 'I've gotta go, Jules.' Looking at Julio, Pillow could tell he needed to say something else. He decided to make it a true thing. 'My girl's pregnant, I've got chores.'

'Congratulations! Great, man, that's great. Fuck, that's great. But, come on, she'll want you to make some money. I have to tell you about this kid. We could use you down at the gym. Really.'

Pillow reached across and palmed the top of Julio's head. 'What? You got some beanpole with a decent jab? You want me to teach him some tricks?'

'Pretty much, man. You should see this kid, it's like watching you out there again. Fast hands, good legs, six feet tall and he makes welterweight. Come on, man, you show him some of your old stuff, some of that cute shit. We'll give you a percentage, you teach a couple of the group classes. We pay you what we can. It's a nice set-up. He's a great kid too, you'll like him.' He spread his hands out wide. 'Come on, let's have lunch.'

'No, kid, I, uh, I can't do it. I can't be around it. It's … Yeah, I just miss it, y'know? Gets to me a little bit.'

Julio nodded and squeezed Pillow on the elbow. 'Yeah, man, okay. I felt that way too. For a long time, long time. But it feels good to get back too.' He threw his hand up in the air and then fumbled around in his breast pocket, pulling out a rumpled red business card with a picture of a speed bag on it. 'If you change your mind, you need anything, a little money, whatever, man, whatever, I'll try to help you out when I can. We have to stick together, fighters, right?'

Pillow grabbed Julio behind the neck, pulled him over and kissed his forehead. 'Right. Yup, we do. I'll, uh, I'll think about it. It was good to see you, Julio. And, really, thanks.'

Julio just nodded, smiled and walked away, not looking either way before he sprung the umbrella back up. Pillow flicked the business card twice, ripped it in half and put the pieces in his pocket. He left the stand without paying for his fruit, and on the way back to the car he stepped into an alley.

He whacked his head into the wall a couple times, knelt down and started biting the webbing of his thumb. He kept biting it harder until he drew a little blood and then he stopped, watching the blood collect and then get thinned and hustled down his wrist by the water. He laughed.

Pillow looked into the rain, enjoying the squinting, incomplete view and feeling the flow of it on his face. It's a shame how difficult it is to get a shower to that temperature. Pillow figured you probably needed the whole sky for that.

The day passed without any news on Artaud. Pillow had hung out at the Bureau playing Hollywood Gin with Don for about three hours longer than was fun. When he got home that night he put his head on Emily's lap, and she told the side of his head that if he was going to be coming home upset he needed to keep her in the loop. He told her about seeing Julio, and she seemed relieved to find out the source of the wound. This time it was Emily who waited a few beats before answering.

'Okay, I know that I'm not supposed to tell you to "just do" stuff that's a significant, like, mental-health deal for you. And if you really won't be comfortable doing it you shouldn't, and that's cool. But maybe you should just do it. You know? We need them billz, Pete. With a Z. That's how serious I am about money right now.'

Pillow thought about it; he opened his eyes and tried hard to focus them on her upside-down face. 'Maybe. I would if I could.'

'I understand, and I'm with you on whatever you want, sweet-ums. I'm using that one now, by the way, *sweetums*. But you threw me up the spat, buddy; you threw me up it pretty hard. And I don't feel bad asking that you try. You have to try to try. No more of this already-happened-already-decided stuff.'

'I get you. I will if I can.'

'And how's the, y'know, the stuff with the coins?'

Pillow used the time it took to sit up and look in her eyes right side up to mentally recheck his story. 'It's okay, Gwynn's confident. Now we just need to find Artaud.'

'Is he all right?'

'We'll see when we find him. Is that all you wanted to know?'

She tilted her head to the side, her mouth twitching neutrally. 'Boom. *Boom* means yes. That's another one I'm trying on.'

After Emily was finished eating a decent portion of a dead pig, and Pillow had eaten all of several dead plants (while avoiding looking at her plate or mouth as the food went in it), they were both still hungry. Suddenly and without warning, Emily burst into tears as Pillow was teaching her how to make kale chips (kale plus oil plus rock salt plus heat). It occurred to Pillow that they were playing a sort of sadness ping-pong. Not that whiplash high-level Asian style. They were playing basement ping-pong: a double-bouncing, swing-and-a-miss, hold-the-ball-while-you-try-to-remember-whose-serve-it-is style. He found it difficult to make out exactly what she was saying, but she seemed unable to believe how mean and strange people had been to her in romantic situations for a lot of years and situations in a row. Pillow took the time he needed to collect his thoughts, pulled her to standing, took a step back and stuck out his right hand.

'Let's agree. Let's agree to be really, really kind to each other. We can manage that for sure.'

Emily laughed a piece of mucous straight onto Pillow's cheek; he wiped it away with his left hand without changing his expression or moving his shaking hand.

'For sure.' She moved past the hand, and they hugged until the fire alarm went off, and Pillow almost tried to take the kale chips out of the oven with his bare hands when Emily gently stopped him.

Before they turned the lights off in the bedroom, they spent a long time looking at the ceiling, and Emily didn't quite agree that the white stucco looked like mountains seen from an airplane. Pillow rolled over and buried his face between her breasts in a lighthearted enough way not to be vulgar.

He spoke into her chest skin. 'Tell me a story.'

'Hmmmm. I don't know, man. Shit, I am totally cracking under the pressure.'

Pillow started moving his head around.

'Dude, that is not less pressure. Shitshitshit. Okay. Okay!' She pushed him off and sat up cross-legged. Pillow rested his chin on both his hands.

'So once upon a time there was a badger. And he was a sad badger because he'd never known another badger. He would walk around all the time looking for other badgers, but he never saw any. He was alone. So, on a hot but breezy summer day he took to the streets and –'

'Wouldn't he not know what a badger was? I mean, if he'd never seen one.'

'That's true, I suppose he'd never seen another badger. But he would go to bed at night and he'd think, "I'm a badger. I just know I'm a badger." He'd think that phrase three to five hundred times a night before he fell asleep in his one-badger apartment. And he would go out in crowds to ask about other badgers, but very few other animals would talk to him because he was very anxious around other critters, and he would rub his teeth with a small piece of quartz he carried around with him to calm down, and the quartz would make a sound like a train going really fast on tracks that aren't quite the right size for its wheels and the other animals would get scared and run away, mostly because trains are pretty scary.'

She flopped onto her back in a vaguely mummified posture.

'What happened next?'

'Oh, that was it. It just kept going on like that for a while.'

2

touching gloves

Pillow had barely been back in his apartment long enough to change and get coffee brewed before Avida and Simon walked in without knocking. Pillow wished without hope that he'd start remembering to lock his front door someday. He nodded good morning but didn't offer them coffee. They stood in silence a minute.

Simon scratched himself. 'I have to shit.'

He walked into the bathroom, closed and locked the door.

Pillow had decided he wasn't going to talk first, and he wasn't going to ask them any questions. He wanted to get the best of this one. Neither he nor Avida talked for another minute. Avida seemed less relaxed than last time, her fingers fidgeting along the hem of her blazer. Pillow turned to pour himself a coffee.

'We've got your fingerprints at the scene. How does that make you feel?'

Pillow finished pouring, then he turned around. He held the cup an inch below his lip, grinning into the steam.

'It amuses you? You sit there like a lump when I'm cracking sweet puns, and being sincerely implicated in a double murder amuses you.'

Pillow lowered his mug and placed it on the stove without drinking. He shrugged. 'I'm just in a good mood. Your news doesn't do much for me either way.'

'Ooooh, look at you. Basic reasoning like a big boy. Sure, we can't put you there that night, you're a sketchy fuck-o and you hang out in sketchy places. It's starting to paint a picture, though. Do you mind if we search the place?'

Pillow figured that was what Simon was already doing in the bathroom. 'Sure. Knock yourself out.' He winked. 'Maybe you'll find some more of my fingerprints.'

Pillow took inventory of the fridge and made a very short grocery list as the two cops searched his apartment. He felt once again annoyed by how quickly the more flavourful vegetables rot.

He had just remembered his coffee when Avida cleared her throat and prodded a shirt on the floor, using her toe to prop it against the base of the wall into the only bright circle of sunlight.

'It's amazing. Everything you own is soaked in sweat, and all your apartment smells like is one flower.' She looked over at the plant by the sink. 'A flower that isn't even a flower. The reason, in my opinion, is that there are two kinds of sweat. The first is nervous sweat, which stinks. Nervous sweat has some content, something went into it, somebody cared. And then there's exercise sweat, which is water you're done with. Just something for the wind to touch.'

Pillow blew on his coffee. It wasn't hot.

'Reminds me, that cartoon you were talking about, Sarge, what was it, the cat?'

Simon let the couch fall down with a thump. He walked over to the chair, looked at it, then he took another couple of paces and leaned against the wall, which didn't collapse or anything like that.

'It was a really good one. In this cartoon, Betty Boop sold her house. Do you know who … Oh right, I don't give a care if you understand. Anyway, Betty sells her house. It's a farm, really. She sold the farm, and as she was leaving there was a cow being milked by a cat. The cat was really tugging, and the cow was frantically drinking bottles of milk and crying and the milk was flowing. The price of the house kept dropping, and then they grouped the house with another and the price still kept dropping, and they kept selling more and more land for less and less money. Then the moon sold the earth to Saturn for twenty dollars, and Saturn took the "gravity magnet," you could tell because it had a big label on it, anyhow he took it out of the earth and everything floated away. But I didn't care about the world, all those Okie-cabin-dweller-yellow-brick-road motherfuckers can keep on floating, doesn't bother me one bit. I cared about the cow, crying and drinking milk as she's having it pulled out of her … that cat.' Simon's stomach rumbled disturbingly in three descending tones. He touched it with his palm, put his head down and walked straight out of the room.

Pillow emptied his mug into the sink. He moved close enough to Avida that they could feel each other's breath without trying. Pillow grabbed the lapel of her suit jacket precisely between his fingers. It was a very surprising fabric, maybe velvet. He checked the other side of it, it was the same colour. He looked down at her hairline.

'The fingerprints, you made that one up at home, right? Beforehand. You imagined how I'd take it, the look on my face.' He let go of the lapel and smoothed it back over. 'A lot of people have tried to guess the look on my face. They all saw me flinch, in their heads.'

Avida tipped forward, dug her face into his chest and took a loud deep sniff. She fell back onto her heels, fastened her finger-moustache to her upper lip. 'Do you want to guess which kind of sweat I smell?'

Breton seemed to want to find and revenge-kill Bataille a whole lot more than he wanted to find the coins. Since the heist he'd been working his way through the members of the Acéphale Society, a group of university weirdos who'd read a bunch of Nietzsche and were into human sacrifice. Bataille was one of the founders. The story was that they'd all sworn they'd be the one who got killed, but as of yet nobody had agreed to do the killing.

As soon as Pillow arrived at the Bureau, Breton hustled him right back out to help roust Jack Prevert, a degenerate gambler who owned a sewing-supply shop. Jack Prevert looked like a suicidally depressed guppy with hair plugs. Jack Prevert made it seem possible to smoke roll-your-owns at the bottom of the sea. Jack Prevert shovelled chips onto the table like he was bailing out a rowboat. Jack Prevert looked you in the eyes the same way most people look out their windshield on the Autobahn.

Pillow had accidentally put Prevert in the hospital a couple years back, so Breton figured he'd be useful to have along. Pillow had been trying collect on Prevert's marker from a card game, and was only supposed to slap him around a little. But Pillow'd had a bad headache that day, wasn't feeling totally himself, and somewhere between giving Prevert a light tune-up and stomping on the guy's head until his nose was a part of his cheek, Pillow had zoned out for a bit, gotten into something of a rhythm with his hands and feet and come out of it looking into Prevert's unconscious face. Pillow's foot had been pulled back a good ways off the ground, and he'd been surprised enough to lose his balance. As he righted himself, he noticed the specks of blood on his cheek, and in a voice that didn't sound entirely like his own, Pillow had said the phrase *Whoopsie poops* for the first and only time in his life.

Pillow was somewhere between ashamed and excited to see Jack Prevert again, and somewhere else between scared and excited that Breton was still on the wrong track.

The walls of Prevert's sewing shop were the kind of walls where off-white meets dirt and they get married and then after a few years invite water damage to live in the guest room and help pay off the mortgage.

There was a wire rack with five sewing machines and a fold-out plastic table with random bobs and needles on it. The cash machine was resting on a table almost its size.

Prevert was sitting on a plastic chair, staring at his hands, when they walked in. He stood as they entered. Pillow pushed him back down.

'Hey, Jack.'

'I don't owe anything. I'm paid up.'

Pillow grabbed Prevert's neck at the base of his skull, gave it a hard squeeze. 'Quit being so squirrelly, Jack. We haven't even started yet.'

Breton had walked straight over to a display of sewing machines. He poked at a needle and watched it bob up and down.

Prevert was popping beads of sweat like corn in a frying pan. 'Please. *Please*, can we do this later?'

'Georges Bataille's your pal. You guys are always hitting the tables together, and if I was a degenerate shitbird like you I'd have *already* bet good money he *already* came to you for some help.'

'Fuck, please.' Jack brought his hands to his cheeks, lifting his jowls with some effort.

Pillow wondered if Prevert trembled all the time or just when he was around. 'Listen. You have options here. My man over there –' Pillow let go of Jack's neck, turned and took a couple steps toward Breton, who had now moved on to arranging threads in a loose, colour-based tapestry '– has big, big fish to fry, as I'm sure you've heard. So tell us what we want to know, and maybe you and me don't do the same dance we did last time.' Without moving any other part of his body, Pillow threw his leg back and kicked the base of Prevert's chair sharply. Then he looked back and bobbed his eyebrows.

'That's quite sufficient, Pillow, thank you.'

Breton pulled himself away from the coloured threads momentarily and walked over to the storeroom door. He opened it and peered around the corner. 'See, you are a bit mistaken this time. Jack has no information. Jack does not even know how many fingers to put up his own asshole to have a good time. I wish, simply, to limit Georges Bataille's options, to make the fact of his capture more crystallized in its already-existent, but yet to be grossly apparent, reality. So it will be sufficient for me to simply say –' Breton cleared his throat and spoke around the corner '– that Jack lost a large amount in our gambling club the other evening. And he needs to pay us back.'

Breton looked back at them, smiled, walked to the front door, put a hand on the handle and then stopped.

A woman with string-bean-length curls in her hair and duffel bags under her eyes careened in from the storeroom. 'Jack, what did he just say? Have you been gambling again? Did I hear that?'

Prevert dropped his cheeks and started toward her, moving his hands up and down as if he wanted her to slide into third base. 'Marie, it's not what you …'

Somewhere in the back a kettle started whistling.

'No! No more, Jack.'

Prevert started trying to grab her and she slashed the air with the side of her palm, then she turned on her heel and made for the kettle. Jack's soul sagged at the shoulders. He sat back down and turned to Pillow. '*Please* go. You can't be here.'

Pillow was very confused. He looked over to Breton, who was just smiling, tapping his fingers against the door. Prevert reached up and grabbed Pillow's wrist, startling him. 'Please.'

Pillow yanked his arm away and backhanded Prevert across the face. 'Please what?'

Before he could go further, Marie came running back into the room with the kettle. Pillow only managed to make a sort of croak before she dumped the whole pot over Jack's head. Pillow lurched forward and gave her a forearm shiver to the stomach, and she hit the ground a little more softly than the kettle did. Jack's screams were a pitch Pillow hadn't heard from a person. They started low and kept rising until they were hitting somewhere above whistle-tone. His legs were twisting around sideways, and an angry purple streak was working down the whole right side of his face and neck.

'What did you do that for?'

Thick, dehydrated spit dangled from her lip. 'I told him if I ever heard about him gambling again I'd kill him. I didn't say I'd leave you, asshole, I said I'd kill you. And I heard about it.' The spit fell in a long, folding line.

Pillow looked over to the door. Breton yawned.

'A promise is a matter of honour, Pillow. Sorry to have bothered you, Marie. Any man who cannot remain in the graces of a strong woman of such rigid principles deserves worse.'

As Marie tried to stand she put her weight against the table. One of the legs gave out and bobs of thread in every colour rolled onto the ground. A long neon-green thread stuck sickeningly to the side of Prevert's face and waved around as he rolled.

She looked down at Prevert and kicked him once.

Pillow shoved past Breton and stumbled out onto the street. It was too bright for him to see for a second, and his head throbbed in three distinct places.

Breton finally came out of the shop and patted him on the shoulder. 'Promises, promises, promises. They're important to keep and stupid to make. Your usefulness has once again settled into a deep and somnolent slumber, Pillow. I will call you again whensoever it happens to rouse itself.'

Breton walked away. Pillow stood in the middle of the sidewalk, still trying to get used to the brightness of the day, his head tilted back toward the hot, cloudless sky.

Pillow wondered how many hours, if you put it all together, he had spent watching kettles boil. He wasn't like that woman in the sewing store. He couldn't leave the room and wait for the thing to start whistling on its own, come back and really believe it had boiled, that it was ready to make coffee or scald someone's face. When Pillow made coffee he would walk around, fix the rest of his breakfast, clean a dish or two maybe, but when it was crunch time, when the kettle was getting close, he couldn't help but plant himself in front of it, watch the steam start slowly flowing out the spout. Pillow didn't regret any of that time, the time he'd spent staring at steam.

Steam was the main (certainly not the only) reason Pillow hated science. The thing about science, for Pillow, was that it was really fucking hard to believe that steam was just water. And that people are just water, and that trees are just water, and that mittens are just water. They're *not*. If that kind of thinking was right, Pillow was happy to be wrong. Water was incredible on its own, in his shower, or as the ocean. Pillow didn't need to be bowled over by all the other things it could be.

Pillow could hear the street, and even though he wouldn't see it until he opened his eyes he knew that all the cars were pumping out stuff that looked like steam but was actually just gas after it had been a little bit on fire. Pillow could get on board with exhaust. It made sense as what gas would look like if you burned it carefully.

Emily was sitting cross-legged, finishing polishing a shoe as Pillow stood by the window staring at her, his leg stretched out and anchored to the side of the window frame. She looked up at him and snorted.

'Take a picture, creepo, it'll last longer.'

'That's not true.'

Emily cocked her head and looked at him out of the side of her eyes, which had small purple flecks around them from puking. She went back to the shoe, digging into scuff on the toe, her tongue sticking slightly with focus.

Pillow was remembering a whole lot of things.

Pillow had lived in the apartment complex for over six months before Emily moved in, but she still figured out the side gate before he did. The side gate was just under their apartments. It was the easiest way in and out, but Pillow had always assumed it was locked. He tried his best never to force things open, because most things he muscled just ended up breaking. People had stopped asking him to help assemble furniture, for instance. So Pillow had been making his standard orbit back to the front entrance when he saw Emily at the side gate. They'd talked a few times at the mailboxes. He called over to let her know he was there (the years had taught him that he was a very scary person to be surprised by in an alley) and she had smiled at him and transitioned from waving to putting the hand on her hip in one motion. He told her that the gate didn't work, and she listened to his whole explanation and humoured whatever half-laugh comment he'd made, and then she'd asked him if he believed in magic – not stupid magic, no wizards and capes and potions, but life magic. Caveman magic, 'behold fire!'–type stuff, like randomly looking up on the first step outside and seeing the exact second a shooting star went through the sky and being fairly sure you did it yourself in a way that isn't obvious to you but is still a whole thing.

And Pillow actually did believe, specifically, in that.

He remembered her kicking the gate at the exact right spot and how it opened wide without another touch, and how it made the longest, loudest creak he could have imagined. She'd waved him through the gate and asked if he'd like to go to a trivia night with an authentic caveman magician.

Pillow came back to the present as Emily finished with the shoe and placed it neatly to the side. She uncrossed her legs and wiggled her arms in front of her. Pillow walked over and hoisted her to her feet.

'All right, big guy. How are you doing? We good? You're okay with everything?'

Pillow dipped his knees deeply and kissed along the length of her jaw. 'Yes. I'm perfect. I called Julio. Later this week I'm looking at the kid, maybe training a little.' That information didn't get the reaction Pillow had been hoping for. He kept on, knowing he couldn't take too many coin questions. 'I even thought about names. You know, for the thing living rent-free in the apartment above your vagina.'

'Names! Cool! Yeah, let's get up in it.'

'Okay, first off, for a boy I was thinking Grampa. Grampa Wilson. Think about Grampa Wilson in kindergarten. No middle name, obviously, that's an easy out.'

Emily covered her ears and shook her head. 'Oh, and the teacher would have to say it. Oooh, you're a horrible man.'

She finished shaking her head and then she rested it in her hand.

Pillow kept remembering things, and this time he decided to say them out loud. 'I was thinking about when you invited me to that trivia night. And I got the only boxing question wrong because fuck John L. Sullivan that shit shouldn't even count, but yeah anyway, and the quiz guy had those sideburns that looked like tentacles, and you knew all the area codes, and we won the quiz because of it.'

Emily reached over and touched his hip. 'I got hos in different area codes, baby, you know that about me.'

He kept speaking through a hard, uncharacteristic catch in his throat. 'And we were talking afterward and something about the light made the spot where your nose ring used to be really clear, and I asked when you'd stopped wearing it and you seemed weirdly surprised and touched that I'd asked.'

She punched herself in the thigh. 'I wore that nose ring for five years, and nobody – my best friends, nobody – noticed when I took it out! That's crazy! I'm still mad about that. Was I just wearing a nose ring into the abyss?'

'I told you that joke about what the leper said to the prostitute and you spit your beer in this giant, perfect arc, like a fountain or a kid in the pool spits, and it went right in that guy's beer. The guy who'd asked you out and then he just wanted you to fix his boots. And nobody saw. Nobody noticed. And you told me about the crazy four-stage way you swallow. And I ... what I'm trying to say is that I still think you're a caveman magician.'

Emily hugged him hard, and he felt some happy-tears on his chest. Eventually she broke off and started fanning her face. 'The leper says keep the tip. So what's on the table for a girl's name? I need something to kill the sentiment in my system right now.'

Pillow sat down on the couch, reached forward and wagged a finger at her. 'Baby name, for a girl: Fabizness. I'd like to introduce you to my daughter, Fabizness. Excuse me, I have to discipline her: hey you're being bad, Fabizness. That's better, Fabizness. Now you're being good, Fabizness.'

Emily pursed her lips and nodded. 'Yep. You killed that sentiment. Killed it dead. That's awful. You're a very bad person.'

Pillow curled the finger back and touched his chest. 'Only at heart.'

Pillow and Don were leafing through a book of photography about honey badgers when the call came through that Artaud was at Phillipe Soupault's house, trying to buy heroin with some loosely bound play manuscripts.

When they got there, Artaud was banging on the door, occasionally shedding sheets of paper from his hand, the pages blowing up and around in the wind. They stayed sitting in the car and watching for a second. Pillow sighed, and felt somehow reminded of a three-legged cat he'd seen once. You don't see many three-legged cats, probably for a lot of reasons. He turned to Don.

'Listen, this guy took a pretty heavy shot at the deal, and he's not all there, mentally, you know what I'm saying?'

'I don't. What are you saying, Pillow?'

'I'm saying you don't need ... I'm saying it's *better* if we try not to hurt him. He's some baby-rabbit-level weak, physically, so it won't exactly be hard.'

'Didn't he try to stab you?'

'Yeah, it was just with a fork, though. You're only dangerous if you have a chance, y'know? He's fragile, so let's be careful, is all I'm saying. We don't need to fuck him up. You'd feel bad later, for sure.'

'Worried after my conscience, Pillow?'

'Yes. I really am. But hey, I'm saying sometimes I wish I'd had a heads-up before I fucked up a dude didn't need to be fucked up, and I'm giving that to you, to us, here. Anytime you can save a time you sit down in the shower after you did a thing and felt like a real piece of shit, you should. We should.'

'One should.'

'You ain't fragile, son, and I will slap the shit out of you if you get on my fucking grammar again, for real. I'm not sure, but I think that wasn't even a rule, that was a choice.'

Don smiled and pulled up short on punching Pillow in the shoulder, which was probably a good decision. 'How are you so right all the time, Pillow? How does one do it?'

'How about you just go pick him up before you piss me off too much and I have to come over there teach you a few things about life after grade school, hey, sunshine?'

Pillow was still the kind of boxing snob who would say that you're not really watching a fight unless you watch it with the sound off. Because noise is fun, and seeing is work. You listen to jokes and music, you hear people talking and it's a good time, but sound, ultimately, is lazy. It'll let you know something happened that tiny bit after it already did, and that can be fun, to realize a second after, but in a world that's full of bones getting thrown at other bones, it's not even enough to see it as it happens, let alone hear about it later. You have to spot the half-step before, sense the load-up and move before there's anything to see.

So from the car, seeing it in silence, Pillow was able to anticipate the horrible thing about three seconds before it happened, and five seconds too late. He saw Don walk up calmly, hands waving in front of him and saying something, he saw Artaud pivot around and throw the rest of his papers in Don's face. Pillow was out of the car and sprinting by the time Artaud dove for Don's legs, catching him flat-footed and tackling him awkwardly to the ground, and even though he was in the same world and air as them and was pretty close to them, Pillow still didn't hear anything as Don, his back still flat on the ground, raised his leg and brought the hard leather heel of his shoe smashing down on the hinge of Artaud's jaw. Without breaking stride or saying anything at all, Pillow scooped up Artaud's limp body, ran back to the car and gently placed him in the back seat. Don got in and sped them toward the Bureau, as Pillow stayed sitting on the floor of the back seat, holding Artaud's head stable and knowing all the time that the low, gurgling groan emanating from that head was just a weak, sad, coincidental signal of a thing that had already happened, like hearing thunder or seeing any star in the sky.

Artaud was semi-conscious by the time they got to the Bureau, but his groaning was still depressing and distracting enough that Pillow and Don laid him across some chairs in the closet and locked the door while they talked it over.

Pillow knew that this next little bit would need some finesse, and, strangely, that relaxed him. He felt a few ways, each pretty strongly: Artaud's face/jaw/brain situation was the kind of sad thing that Pillow would necessarily avoid thinking about at all costs, but the fact that Artaud couldn't talk was a really lucky break for him. The trick would be getting Artaud away from the Bureau boys, and if Pillow played his cards right he might be able to swing it.

Don was apologizing for hoofing Artaud, and talking about the things his therapist had told him to work on and how he wasn't accomplishing them, while Pillow barely paid attention, keeping a listening look on his face. When it seemed like his turn to speak, Pillow raised his fists and exploded them open, like they were fireworks reaching the best part.

'It's a thing that happened, my man. You spazzed out in a fight, happens.'

'You're an accommodating man. So many get caught up in being right. They get stuck on it, and it turns them into mean, hectoring people without realizing. Now, let's move on to how we'll extract the details from Artaud. Those coins are some money.'

'Dude, you *shattered* his jaw; he isn't ready to talk about anything. We need to get him out of here, I mean, unless you're comfortable leaving him with these Bureau motherfuckers, who will, I promise you, actually poke his jaw with a stick. That's a real thing I think will happen, like prostate cancer or cold Januarys.'

'Prostate cancer is only certain if you live long enough, if nothing else kills you before it.'

'Well, that's true, Don, but it wasn't the part of what I was saying that was important right now.'

'We need that information and we need Artaud buried and dead, tonight. That's our assignment.'

Breton, who nobody had seen enter the room, broke in on the conversation calmly and slowly, and like he was in the middle of a paragraph. 'There are ways of making him tell us where those coins are.'

Pillow was pretty good at keeping a neutral look about him when he was desperate. He turned to look Breton in the face (the eyes were a little much to ask), to look like he was giving it to the guy straight. 'Buddy, due respect and all, but sometimes things just aren't. I'm telling you. You can do whatever you want to this fucking guy, and it'll be a goddamn horror show, and maybe one of these sick fucks will get off on it, and that'll be great for him, but Artaud's not going to be able to help you. Kid has no clue where he's even at right now.'

Breton wobbled his head slightly, like a planet blowing a kiss at another planet passing just close enough to make an impression. 'Your adamancy on this issue is noted, and appreciated, Pillow. So, it seems as though the procedure must be undertaken, does it not, Don? Pillow's procedure, if you wouldn't mind.'

Costes was staring at the ground like it was a drawing of a really pretty staircase that just kept going.

Pillow laughed, keeping it casual-looking. 'Oh, don't mind me, fellas. I'm just a grown-ass man who loves it when people talk about him while he's in the room.'

Breton laughed back, ducked into his office again.

Costes took a deep breath in and threw it back out. 'The procedure is we take Artaud out somewhere that's a secret, between the two of us, and we kill him, and then we chop the important parts of his body off, and then we bury them in a few places. But because it's your procedure this time, *we* means *you*, with me helping. I'm sorry, Pillow.'

Pillow tried not to look too pleased. You can't tip it when you spot your opening, you have to wait on it. 'Why're you sorry? You're not doing anything to me.'

Don grabbed his wrist. 'Let's go get him. Are you okay?'

That was not the sort of question Pillow answered.

The closet was actually a fairly heavily trafficked area of the Bureau. It was about as big as a dentist's waiting room, and it was always full of chairs (Breton valued his hosting skills). It was also a common area for séances and sexual activity, usually at the same time.

They opened the door and flicked on the light. Artaud was sitting where they'd left him, digging his oddly long nails into the semi-padded arms of a chair, twisting his feet toward and away from each other. When the light came on, he sprung into action, like a cockroach ducking under the fridge. He was trying to scream.

'*O queseme to globa asustame.*'

Artaud jumped up, his shoes slipping against the floor, and then he climbed onto the chair and started scratching at the walls, the sleeves of his soutane sliding down his wrists.

'*O medo fai!*'

Don moved toward the lunatic, and then stepped back and waved Pillow in. It wasn't until Artaud was falling pretty much jaw-first that it occurred to Pillow that pulling the chair out from under Artaud had been, perhaps, imprudent. He caught Artaud's wrist just as he was about to hit the ground and managed to adjust him enough so that Artaud landed on his shoulder.

'*Me anseia no tooooo.*'

Artaud started sliding across the ground, kicking his legs out wildly and breaking his nails against the floorboards.

Don looked worried, not corralling-a-kidnapped-brain-injured-maniac worried, more bathroom-sink-flooding-the-kitchen worried, but he still swung around to cut off Artaud's path. 'Easy, we'll get you some of your medicine. Huh?'

Artaud stopped immediately. Then he sat propped up on his knees, his limp, emaciated wrist hanging shakily in the air between them.

'*Quesso a suavide.*'

Don hitched his pants at the knees, and Artaud grabbed his arm, the lunatic's jagged, bleeding nail digging visibly into his wrist.

'*Sempre odei, odei, odei!*'

Don firmly peeled back Artaud's fingers, then he stood up and rolled his eyes at Pillow. 'Chin up there, Arty. We'll help you, won't we, Pillow?'

Pillow did a quick shoulder check. About five Bureau boys had gathered behind him to gawk. Bobby Desnos kissed the tips of his gathered fingers. Pillow turned around; Artaud and Don were still looking at him. Pillow was still nodding blankly as he helped Artaud to his feet. He saw Don take out his pocket square and wipe off his hands.

Pillow gently cupped Artaud's swollen cheek. The Bureau boys burst into applause, some hooting.

Breton peered around the doorway. 'Ah, Pillow, adding that touch of kindness to sweeten the scene. You are a man of the living theatre. An idiot savant of pathos.'

Artaud hacked out a thick knot of blood, which landed with a slap on the floor.

Breton looped his arm under Pillow's elbow, bringing his hand up in front of them, and snapped his fingers once. Breton wasn't great at snapping his fingers. He didn't have quite enough traction and they sort of slid off each other, but that didn't really matter. Pillow felt Artaud sagging toward the ground on one side, and Breton pulling his arm back on the other.

Pillow hadn't felt so completely disconnected from what was going on around him in at least, say, ten minutes.

They drove smoothly through the abandoned lots and fields, and Pillow watched the trees float past, most of them dead and stick-like even in the summer. The fields were all scrabbled with rocks and loose soil, and the few clumps of grass that remained clung hard and stubborn and yellow. They looked to have stayed more out of spite than anything. The dusk light was leaving the sky and the liveliest things around were shadows, flickering in the headlights. To Pillow everything seemed as if it were rolling helplessly past the window of a boat or a train. As if he were seeing it all from far away.

What Pillow really wanted was to be home, but home felt about as far away to him as reincarnation does to the dead. They'd shot Artaud up with enough morphine to make an elephant constipated, and he was nodding off on Pillow's shoulder, periodically drooling blood. He'd ruined Pillow's sixteenth-best white T-shirt.

Don was on a bit of a roll.

'See –' Don looked Pillow in the eyes through the mirror '– that's the problem with casual sex. It had a really good chance to be my favourite thing in the world. Because, y'know, with how I see things, when you make a great thing casual it gets better, calmer, more relaxed. But it just didn't pan out like that. You try it and you realize there's a reason why it's called "casual sex," and not, say, "expressing your very darkest urges in a fun, caring and judgment-free environment."'

Pillow roused himself and cut in. 'Yeah, man, they could have called it "casual accidentally hurting people's feelings," or "casual not being able to ejaculate because you're a bit nervous or whatever" – those would have been fair. If they called it those things it would seem less like something you wanted to do.' Pillow flexed his foot upward, trying to get blood back into it. 'Yeah, totally, Donny, you make a decent point there. I agree with you enough that that might actually just be what I think now.'

Don reached back and patted Pillow on the thigh. 'It's really nice to have friends you like talking to at work.'

Pillow stopped the joke he was about to make somewhere in the upper half of his throat. 'Yeah. I like talking to you too, Don.'

They nodded at almost the same time and drove on in silence. Pillow looked at the moonlight reflecting in flashes off the slick, greasy skin of Artaud's widow's peak as they moved.

Don stopped the car in front of the slaughterhouse, slapped the wheel happily and turned around beaming. 'Let's get this show on the road!'

Pillow checked Artaud's pulse. It was more like half a pulse. 'It's your turn to carry him.'

The slaughterhouse had been abandoned since meat production went factory-line. It was one of those old stone buildings that makes you understand how people used to be able to stand going to work. On either side of the gates there was a metal statue of a bull. The gates themselves were tall and iron-heavy. When Pillow pushed them open, they made a long, plaintive groan, like somebody was stealing the just-okay desserts off their plates.

Pillow had, at first, been a vegan only while he was training for fights. But after seeing how his body reacted, he had decided it was best to do it year-round, to always be in fighting shape. And after he retired, Pillow still ate vegan, now looking animals in the eye and forming some opinions. Seals, for instance, definitely have souls. Pillow could tell from the way they looked at him or the cameras filming them.

There was a thought that wouldn't stop occurring to him about how people had always treated chickens. He would imagine he was a chicken and he was able – as in his chicken brain was physically big and complicated enough – to understand the whole history of chickens. Pillow was not someone to just throw a concept like this around, but if you were a chicken and somebody told you all about it … the word that shot through his mind was *holocaust*. And it had been going on for *thousands* of years. They were bred just to be killed.

Once Pillow had started thinking like that it was sort of hard to stop. What about balloons? Water balloons are made to be broken, their skin specifically cast thinner, and more easily wrecked, their destruction planned as they are built. Helium balloons seemed to want something, they seemed to have a goal. They wanted the sky more than anything, and what did they get when they were finally let free? A few minutes, a few thousand feet of climb maybe, and then that wide blue thing they couldn't help craving would kill them, make them into a few pathetic scraps and then let the scraps fall.

There is so much in the world to be sorry about, to feel sorry for, and once you start you have to draw a line somewhere. Pillow's was eating. He'd promised himself that he'd never eat a cow, or drink its milk, without permission, or eat a person, or drink its milk, without permission. And because it was an easy one to make, Pillow had also promised that he'd never eat a balloon, water or otherwise.

Don carried Artaud across his arms. Pillow opened some more slow doors for him. The killing floor was wide, and there were drains caked with blood rust in the floor. The ceiling was high, like a cathedral. Along the sides, flat metal killing tables were lined up like pews. A supervisor's office sat high at the front overlooking the floor, the windows jutting out the same distance as, and looking a little less ugly than, a carving of somebody on a cross.

Don spun around, and Artaud's head flopped like a bowling ball glued to a bungee cord. He walked over to one of the tables, kicked a leg and listened to the echo before continuing.

'These are bolted to the ground. I say we just handcuff him here. And you can take a few minutes …'

Don put Artaud down next to the table gently, as if he were a toddler who'd fallen asleep in the car. Don stood, placed a flat hand over Pillow's chest and waited for Pillow to focus on him.

'Are you ready for this?'

Pillow hooked Artaud up to the table and tested the bolts. He stood up his flashlight to light the slaughterhouse in a small vague circle, then he nodded six times too many.

Don moved into the outside orbit of light. He grabbed the side of Pillow's neck and started massaging it. Pillow pulled away. The two men looked at each other. Don ran a finger along the edge of his scar. 'You don't look like you're going to kill anyone today.'

Pillow looked back over to Artaud, the half-lit shape of the priest's body, long and thin and limp, laid out across the floor.

'Listen. Pillow. Pay attention. I brought you into this, and, fuck. I'll do it. This is on me. We'll tell Breton you did it and that'll be that.'

Pillow dug a finger into either temple and started two short, tight circles. 'Just, just give me a minute.'

'Take your time.'

Pillow felt behind him for the wall, then he leaned back and sank to the ground. He dipped his head, then squeezed it between his knees as he thought the whole thing over. The safest option was to let Don kill Artaud and be done with it, keep his head down and chill out. But the coins were still up for grabs, and Pillow had some other ideas. He just had to be sure to think it through. Adjust the game plan. Pillow knew it in the best and the only way he knew things: instantly and instinctively. He knew them for a second, to be used in a millisecond. He knew balance shifts and sagging heads. He counted blinks and forgot birthdays. Pillow looked for one thing he could use and was smart enough to keep using it. Pillow knew where everyone's toes were.

Artaud would tell him where those coins were – he just had to give him a little rope. Be a tiny bit nice to him, and let him think it was his own idea. Breton believed you had to be in control to matter, always be the one making him tell you. It was his weakness. Pillow knew he could make a play for the coins.

Pillow stood and composed himself. He walked over to Don, who was looking at the flashlight and fiddling with something heavy in his pocket. Pillow knew when people were ready to fuck other people up. Don didn't want to kill Artaud.

Don took one look over and let his head drop to his chest. 'Go ahead, Pillow. Talk me out of it.'

Pillow smiled and dipped in, tapped Don's belly with a quick, pulled one-two, then pivoted and backed up into the dark, sticking out his tongue as Don sluggishly swung back at air. Pillow didn't even fight his slur. 'I talk all day, punk, I talk when I sleep. You know what I want and you know why I want it. You talk.'

'You want to, what? Neuter the guy and keep him as a pet?'

Pillow pulled his head back, appalled. 'That's fucked-up, man. Dogs are all instinct. Eating and fucking. To take their balls … Why? So they behave? Put a collar on me, see what happens. I'd do more than bark, son, I'll start dropping –'

Don surrendered with his hands. 'Sorry, I forgot. We'll … Shit, okay, we won't kill him.' Don sighed, then looked back at Pillow, who shot him a quick, corny thumbs-up. 'You are the weirdest pacifist in the world, you know that, Pillow?'

Pillow sidled back into the light and tousled Don's hair, then he hopped up to sit on the metal table. Realizing his feet still touched the ground, he moved into more of a lean. 'I feel you on that. I'd be a really strange thing to put in a crying baby's mouth.'

Don laughed and looked over at Artaud, shaking his head. 'This is no joke, Pillow. All right? Breton is taking this shit seriously. So I need to know you have a plan.'

Pillow threw his arms loosely over his head. 'Fire away. Gimme all the questions.'

'What's the point? You going for the coins?'

'Not that one. Fire away with more if you want, though.'

Don paced away cursing. Pillow followed him, tugged on his arm to stop him.

'Listen, Don. I know the deal, I know what you're risking and I'll tell you what happened here. I asked to be left alone to snuff Artaud, you waited outside. I promised you down the line he was dead, I shot the gun, I faked the whole thing. I faked it because I'm an unreliable idiot, and I got it in my pulpy, punched-out head that it was, y'know, maybe sort of wrong to kill this poor guy for no fucking reason. Breton'll buy that.'

Pillow guessed that Don was smiling. 'No he won't. But that's fine. It's … You're a sweet boy, Pillow.' Pillow nodded in sincere agreement. Don continued. 'You best take care of this, though. Artaud is officially your problem. I'm not involved in this after tonight. You let him recover a couple days, and then …'

'I drop him at the front door of a hospital nowhere near here, and nobody hears from him again.'

'Sure, sure. And *nobody* shows up with those coins. If they sell, Breton will kill us both. But really, is dropping this lunatic off in the middle of nowhere so much better than just punching his ticket now?'

Pillow made himself look confused. 'Yup. It is. Why wouldn't it be?'

They both stayed silent for a long, comfortable stretch of time. Pillow eventually broke in. 'Now what do we do? Like tomorrow.'

'Well, Breton still wants me to help him find Bataille. We're talking to Bataille's people, trying to smoke him out. You –'

'Stick my thumb up and sit on it until he tells me to do something. I know.'

Artaud groaned thickly and rolled over, a long trickle of piss flowing slowly away from him, gathering dirt as it moved.

Pillow shuddered and turned back to Don. 'Seriously, though, what now?'

'I just told you.'

'Now I'm talking about what we do three seconds from now.'

'Of course! You're an in-the-moment kind of guy. I say we hang out in this gross and amazing building.'

'I can spare you a couple minutes. But one other thing …' Pillow paused long enough that Don leaned in, then he tagged him hard on the shoulder and took off at a sprint. 'You're it!'

The two men played tag until Don quit, because games don't stay fun when the skill level isn't properly balanced.

They walked over to the only window in the giant room, allowed themselves to be illuminated by the moon. Pillow pulled his arm over the top of his head, scratched his back and looked out the window. The arm dropped and settled around Don's shoulder like an untethered curtain. They stood for a while in silent, sweaty community.

Pillow could take only so much quiet. 'I only know one thing, buddy. Whatever really happened that night, it's not going to make any kind of sense.'

Don turned into him and slapped Pillow in the middle of the chest.

'We're talking about the world, Pillow. Trying to have the world make sense is like trying to balance a battleship on a wineglass.'

Don tucked his head into Pillow's armpit, and the two men settled into the familiar companionship of uncertainty as they watched some stars die.

Somewhere far away a whole packet of party balloons was being forgotten in a junk drawer, never to be animated with breath, and some other tragedies besides that.

Pillow's only non-athletic shoes were a pair of black boots, and three months prior, the zipper pull on the back of the left one had broken off in his hand. Since then he'd been carrying the small piece of metal around in his pocket, gingerly using it as a hook to get the zipper down, like a sardine key.

Pillow and Emily had gone out for a drink, or more accurately two soda waters.

It wasn't as if Pillow usually gave a particularly detailed or lengthy description of his day, so he and Emily had talked about more interesting things. They'd talked a little bit about how tall people die younger, and also a little bit about how left-handed people die more often in accidents because handrails and things like handrails are made for people to fall in a certain right-handed sort of way.

Pillow knew he was a good liar because so far none of his bigger lies had been found out. Emily didn't seem to realize how dangerous and illegal the coin thing was, Don wouldn't tell Breton about Artaud, and the cops didn't have anything solid on him.

Pillow's record was holding true. Nobody had ever suspected him of cheating while he was fighting. He'd never failed a dope test, or been suspended, and he'd juiced for pretty much every fight, sometimes to get an advantage and other times just to get by. EPO, shooting lidocaine in his hands, diuretics to cut weight, anabolics for recovery, he'd done it all. It was about cycles. If you cycle off early enough you can always fade the test. That was how he'd have to play it now: one big cycle and then jump before he was pushed.

The key words were: *very, very careful.*

Emily came out of the bathroom seeming puzzled. Pillow walked over and touched her stomach, which still felt the exact same.

'Are you okay?'

'I have a doctor's appointment tomorrow. I didn't tell you about it and I don't know why, but you can come if you want. Sorry for the short notice.'

'No problem. I'll be there.

'That's not really what was bothering me, though. I was just thinking about this nightmare I had last night that I was addicted to biting the caps off beer bottles. The really solid ones you have to pop off with the – ' she made a levering motion to represent a bottle opener, '– and I knew it was super-bad for me, that my enamel was dying, but I just kept doing it. What do you think it means?'

Pillow didn't say anything, just nodded several thousand times.

When they got outside the air was sudden and cool, and Emily skipped over a sidewalk crack on her last step out of the building and bounced on the balls of her feet. Pillow complimented her hair, and she told him that he was wrong, that, in fact, her hair was a colour most commonly referred to as 'mousy brown.' Pillow told her that it seemed to him more of a Disney mousy brown. A wearing-impossibly-puffy-glovesand-hanging-out-with-a-dog-and-stealing-steamboats-and-whistling-when-you-talk-and-building-a-life-for-yourself-in-a-magical-kingdom sort of brown.

Emily stopped bouncing and tucked her head between her shoulders, and the very top of her cheek was reluctantly turning a bit red, from the air being so sudden and so cool.

Pillow was aware that Mickey Mouse is actually black, but he figured that there were more important things than being totally right all the time.

On the way home he couldn't help thinking about coins, Artaud's mouth and the thread on Jack Prevert's face, and he worried the zipper pull so much against his leg that it drew blood through his pocket.

The next morning Pillow, partly because he had paced Emily's living room instead of sleeping and partly because he was nervous about the afternoon training session at Julio's gym, ran all the way downtown without thinking too carefully about how he'd get back to his apartment, and decided to just hang out in the architecture garden for a while.

The architecture garden was this strange two-level park with a structure that looked like a castle wall in it. On the top level there was a large, flat gravel courtyard with very tall sculptures in a circle around the outside. The sculptures were all elevated on steel or concrete pillars. One had a miniature two-floor house with walls on three sides. Another had a small biplane made of metal at the top. The sculpture furthest from Pillow was a big block of concrete extending out toward the highway with a metal chair attached to the end. On the ground, there was a stool with a very old-looking bike wheel welded to the top.

Pillow leaned against one of the castle walls and looked over the courtyard, sometimes focusing on individual sculptures and sometimes letting the whole thing loosely into his focus. From where he was standing he could see the sculptures and the highway behind them at the same time.

Lieutenant Avida and Sergeant Simon emerged from the berry-bush-lined stairs under the chair, Avida skipping up the last step and using the railing to swing heavily around. Simon followed her not quite as slowly as an elderly hippo would have and slightly more enthusiastically.

'How goes, Pillow?'

'Pretty good. How are you?'

'Oh, you know, we're all right. Catching a lot of cases lately, though, like that one from yesterday … What happened there again, Sergeant?'

'Jack Prevert popped an aneurysm not unrelated to the full kettle of boiling water poured on his face.'

'Oh yes. Of course. And remind me, why would we bother, Mr. Thing I Used To Practice Kissing and Cuddling When I Was a Lonely Twelve-Year-Old? Get it?'

'Because I'm a pillow.'

Avida snapped her fingers and pointed at him.

Simon answered her question. 'Because we think he was there strong-arm debt-collecting, and that set the wife off to kill the husband.'

Pillow yawned. He looked over Avida's head, admiring the lines of the chair against the cloudless sky. When he looked back down they were both waiting in silence. 'Oh, were you two done? Hey, I'm a straightforward guy …'

Simon snorted as loud as a lot of people would shout at a rescue helicopter.

'And the way I think, with a thing like that, a guy getting a kettle thrown on him, right? With a thing like that, either you've got the goods right away, and I'm arrested, and you'd have brought eight guys and I'd have already called my lawyer. Or you two love my company. And I'm a lot more charming than I am guilty.'

Avida leaned over and spun the bike wheel; it kept rotating as she talked. 'We aren't talking about lawyers here, Pillow. We're talking about trying to find some lost money. If you won't talk to us, should we talk to Breton? Does he know about these little chats? We talked to Don Costes yesterday, and it seemed like he wasn't aware. Why wouldn't you tell them? One wonders.'

Avida seemed edgy – she knew he was after the coins, but they couldn't do anything about it. The less official they kept it, the better.

'I don't know what you're talking about,' said Pillow. 'And if you want to tip your hand to Breton, you can be my guest.'

Simon stepped up and pushed his face close to Pillow's. Simon had about a hundred pounds on Pillow but the cop still only came up to his collarbones. Pillow grinned and stuck his chin up.

'There's nothing more dangerous than being smart for a second, Punchy. Don't walk home alone or anything reckless like that. You're bleeding an awful lot.'

Pillow looked down and noticed a thick line of dark red blood rolling down his leg, smeared into the cracks of his dry skin. He flipped Simon's tie up into his face, sidestepped him and did a quick Ali-shuffle. 'That's it for me, kids, unless you have any other advice.'

Avida smiled vaudeville-wide. 'You look a little worse for wear there, Pillow. You stressed out? The body is a candle, Pillow.' She patted the top of her head. 'This end is for burning.' She dropped her hand and nodded at her feet. 'And this end is so you don't tip over.'

The cops turned and crunched back toward the stairs. Pillow stuck around another few minutes wiping absently at his leg until the bike wheel stopped spinning and the huge, oblong shadows of the park were still again.

Julio's gym was cramped and tight, and now that Pillow was really looking around, he liked it. The walls were the usual collage of posed photos and old fight posters, glued up in wide, crooked blocks at random intervals. You could tell it was a one-man shop – most of the pictures and posters and the only belt up were Julio artifacts – but Pillow looked around and thought that some of the kids looked decent. The gym was in sort of a strip-mall area. The windows stretched all around, each covered by a different flag, the gym bright with sunlight through fabric.

Pillow had agreed to go look at the kid at Julio's gym that day. He was ready to skip it, but Emily wanted him to, so he figured he may as well come to the gym. It also helped that sitting alone in his apartment and thinking about Artaud and the coins had mostly been a random, aggressive back-and-forth between nausea and whatever the feeling is when you want to cry but you're a grown man and that's actually physically sort of hard to do.

Pillow slung his leg over the top rope and moved into the ring. He tested the canvas and started moving around, shaking his arms out, up on his toes circling to his right and throwing the odd jab. He picked up the pace, eventually closing his eyes and feeling Julio. Moving away from that right hand. He started throwing more punches, really sitting down on the right. He saw a glancing shot cut Julio's brow. Julio moved in and Pillow clinched him, dragged the laces of his glove over the cut, then broke the clinch, rolled Julio's straight right and hit him with a counter-uppercut to the solar plex. He felt the ropes behind him and bounced off, switching his feet quickly and taking the angle. It was all right there. Julio was beatable; Pillow saw him folding.

'Damn, my man still has legs.'

Pillow opened his eyes. Fat Julio was there in his old-man sweatsuit, arm draped lazily around the kid's waist. The kid was tall as hell, a bit skinny in the legs, but he looked athletic. His face wasn't that marked up. Good skin.

'This is Kevin.'

'Nice to meet you, sir.'

Pillow started skipping in the air, jumping over an invisible rope, moving it with his arms. 'How do you do, boo-boo?'

Kevin looked a little puzzled, a little like it might be a permanent state.

'I'm going for a Yogi Bear–type vibe. See what I'm doing here, with my legs and hands and shit. You should do this, but with a real rope.'

Kevin seemed to realize that now was a time to smile. He turned around and fished a rope out of his bag, moved over to an open spot by the mirrors.

Pillow did a couple double skips and shouted over to him, 'And stay outta dem pic-a-nic baskets.'

Kevin looked over his shoulder to acknowledge that a joke had been made.

Julio smirked up at Pillow. 'I don't think he's seen that cartoon.'

Pillow stopped air-skipping and looked over at the kid untangling his rope as he stretched his neck out. 'Well, Jules, first impression: if he did see it, he'd think it was a documentary.'

Pillow watched the kid hit the bag for a while, then he worked the mitts with him. It took about six seconds for Pillow to size the kid up. This wasn't some hotshot prospect Julio was giving him. The kid was card-filler. Julio was hoping to squeeze enough wins out of him that he could put him in a squash match with a real prospect. Of course they wouldn't give him a real one. Still, it felt good to be back in the ring, and the kid had an okay jab, he was just raw as shit, and slow on the trigger. The kid had fast feet and bad footwork, the classic trick case. To anyone who didn't know shit about boxing, he'd look like a champ. Almost ten years out of the ring, and if they gave him two weeks to train, Pillow knew he could still take the kid apart. It wouldn't even be fair.

Pillow showed Kevin a few good exits, worked on his balance a little, and the kid listened. After the mitts were over, Pillow was a bit dizzy so he let the kid get some water and sat down on the edge of the canvas. The kid came back smiling and started taking off his wraps.

'Hey, thanks a lot. It's, it's, it's a real honour to train with some-one like you. I watched you when … um.'

Pillow smiled and slapped the back of Kevin's head. 'When you were a kid. A child. An infant. A fuckin' newborn fawn. I know I'm old, motherfucker, all right, you won't hurt my feelings.'

Kevin laughed and nodded. 'Good to know, gramps.'

They both sat there smiling and nodding until Kevin got his wraps off and stood. Pillow hopped up, stuck out his hand and pulled Kevin standing.

'Have you got your miles in today?'

Kevin looked down. 'Nah, I slept in. I was planning to just run home.'

Planning nothing. The kid was lazy, but Pillow let it slide. 'Hey, no sweat, I'll run with you.'

Kevin looked back up at him sidelong. 'That's okay, man. You look tired. I'll just do it.'

'I ate a big lunch, gotta work it off. Flush the poisons and so forth.' Pillow turned abruptly and started to leave the gym.

Kevin hesitated then followed. 'Really, man, it's okay, none of my other trainers have run with me. You can drive behind me or something. Lots of them do it.'

When they got outside, Pillow got distracted by a trash-can lid that had somehow ended up stuck in the top branches of a tree. He stopped and looked at it a second. Pillow imagined the hum it would make in a heavy wind, imagined the lid floating and hover-ing a while, deciding to settle there. Sitting, thinking it could be a mistake, the way anything different can be a mistake.

Kevin had started bouncing around to keep his legs awake. Pillow felt sorry for Kevin, for Kevin's nose and eyebrows and mom. The nicest thing would be to break the kid's knee, make sure his brain couldn't get anywhere near a good fighter in a bad mood.

'Fuck that noise. I always hated that shit, some fat asshole driv-ing a golf cart while you're sweating your balls off. I'll run with you. Who can't run? Lemmings can run, and they'll jump off a cliff 'cause it's *there*.'

About eight kilometres in, Pillow's headache got so bad that the world of his vision shrunk into a black pinhole from the corners. He keeled over a bit and after a second Kevin grabbed him around the waist and guided him off the sidewalk to the grass. Pillow breathed deeply for a while. It was a very hot day. It had been a very hot day and a half since he'd slept.

'Well, Kevvy baby, I might should've winked a few times before I came here.'

Kevin looked at Pillow like he was deer whose head was already mounted on the wall. 'Hey, it's all good. Don't worry. Just take your time. You sure you're good?'

Pillow wiped his forehead, then he snapped his fingers at Kevin. 'Shit, son. Just because I'm a broke-down wreck doesn't mean you're done training. Gimme some Superman–Banana action.'

'What?'

Pillow waved vaguely. 'Tummy down, arms and legs up, engage your core, then, y'know, flip over. You feel me?'

'Oh yeah, sure.' The kid got down on his stomach. 'I've never heard anyone call it that.'

'What does everyone else call it?'

'They just say it like that, then they say *switch* when you're supposed to.' Kevin laughed. 'Most them don't say *tummy* either.'

Pillow looked up at the sky; it was so empty he could have forgotten about clouds if he tried a little. He counted off in his head. *Banana*. Kevin switched over onto his back. Pillow watched for a few seconds and nodded. 'Just say *switch*, huh? I'm a bit more whimsical than those old sacks of shit. Oh, that reminds me, lesson time, here we go, *Superman*.' Kevin rolled over again. 'If you ever have to do an interview, a longer one, just learn like six words they don't expect you to use. In this business, that passes for a personality.' Pillow leaned forward and pinched Kevin's earlobe, folding it over and then letting go. Kevin looked up startled. Pillow winked. 'That's sign language for *banana*.'

After he'd put Kevin through a quick plyometrics circuit, Pillow told the kid to sit down on the curb and drink some water. Kevin took a mouthful, spit it back out into the street, then had a deep drink.

'So what's your record?'

'Julio didn't tell you?' Kevin laughed and wiped his mouth. 'He doesn't have the best memory.'

Pillow let out a loud snort. 'Who does? That stuff's for pussies.'

'I'm eight and two. Six kayos.'

'Good, man, good.' Pillow hooked Kevin's nose with two fingers. 'You broke this – ever do your jaw?'

'Nah. You?'

Pillow stood and took a few steps, making sure they were solid. 'Oh yeah. Twice. First time, I broke it laughing.'

Kevin dribbled some water down his chin, then wiped it. 'In a real fight?'

'Yup.'

The kid shook his head, grinning. 'So you were winning?'

Pillow rocked his head back a little. 'Shit no. I was getting the *piss* beat out of me. Yeah, man, he was banging – this was Angulo – he was banging me to the body, clinching the shit out of me, roughing me up. Real dirty fight. The ref wasn't doing anything, eighteen-foot ring, the whole set-up, so I tried to fight him on the inside. And this is a lesson, this is a lesson: I was landing shots, landing all my shots, but they were just bouncing off him. He looked like he was getting his nails done, meanwhile I'm getting my ribs caved in about five times a round. So round eight or nine, I don't remember, he's got me in the corner, throwing a million punches, I'm too tired to get out. And I look down and he's so excited he's got his elbows, like, 100 percent flailed out to the side. Like he wanted to float in the ocean, y'know? So I look at it and I lean in his ear and I say: "D'you leave your water wings at home?" Pillow could tell he was slurring a bit, but Kevin seemed to be following. 'And I laughed, I mean, I know that's not an amazing crack, but in the ring, context and all, on the fly like that, it seemed pretty good to me. So I'm just hanging out, laughing at my own joke, and he pushes me into the turnbuckle and snaps my jaw in half with a left hook.' Pillow rubbed his jaw, remembering screws.

Kevin was shaking his head. 'You're crazy, man. Why would you laugh when you're getting beat up like that?'

Pillow was back to looking at the sky. 'It was funny.' The kid looked up at Pillow the way Pillow looked at shits he was really, really surprised had come out of his body. All of a sudden he didn't feel like talking to Kevin anymore. 'I have to get a move on, pal. This was fun, I'll be …' Pillow lost the last of the sentence and let it trail off. Kevin grabbed his hand and shook it, said a bunch of thankful things Pillow didn't bother following. Pillow looked at the kid again, imagined cuts over his eyebrows, imagined telling him he could still win, imagined pouring water down his throat, imagined lying. Pillow hugged Kevin hard, and when they broke he put his hand around the kid's jaw, cradling it a little.

'What do you call a sheep with no legs?' Kevin was too confused to say anything. Pillow finished the joke anyway. 'A cloud.'

Pillow was too keyed-up to nap, so he just lay down in the back of his car, rubbing his hands against the vague fuzziness of the ceiling for about an hour. It made him feel better, refreshed enough to give Gwynn the kind of attentive visit she really deserved at this point in her life.

Pillow figured Artaud might need a little energy (which in Artaud's case was to say cocaine and opiates) to revitalize himself. Gwynn had been allowed to keep a small dealing operation out of her place after she bought out. Mostly she just sold pills and coke to her art friends.

Pillow got out of his car and then immediately leaned against it, doing a quick supported back bend over the roof and taking a couple of cleansing breaths. He twisted the skin on his chin around for a bit, then he stood up straight and looked up at Gwynn's window. She saw him, smiled and waved. Gwynn had a strange way of waving. She'd start with her hand down on her hip and move it slowly up, still half-cupped, and then at the top she'd open it. Opening it was the wave.

'So, four people went hiking and they stood by the edge of a cliff. It was a beautiful cliff, and when they looked out they could see the clouds wisping off into nothing, they could see more dirt and more trees than they could imagine on their own. At first they stood far back, and they looked, and they looped arms around each other's backs.' Gwynn turned around and pinched Pillow's forearm gently. She kept talking, her loose, dry hands resting on the inside of his knees. 'And then one of them walked right up to the edge of the cliff, and she looked out, and she breathed so deeply that the others could see her chest move in and out, and they could feel their own chests move in sympathy. And she turned to them, she told them it was beautiful, so much more beautiful, to look straight down at the little bit of dirt under them than at the wide, stupid panorama. She said, "Come to the edge." And they said, "We can't." And she kept insisting. And they said, "We can't, we will fall." And she asked them one more time. And they came. And she pushed them. And they floated into the vacuum of infinite space, never to return.'

Gwynn lifted her hands and brushed them against each other. 'That, dear boy, is a thing I never said. It's a thing I should have said. You'll find that, when you've got the time, and the world has forgotten you, and you're doing your tallies alone. You'll find the best things you said were the things you didn't, or they were the things you only said to the cold night air in front of you as you walked home so light-footed and so drunk and so sure that life was just starting. That it would keep on starting. When time was just a thing you checked on sometimes so you wouldn't be late to the next party.'

Pillow ran a hand over his face and enjoyed the hard scrape of his stubble. 'We weren't all sitting around reading sad books and diddling ourselves and falling in love with boy painters, Gwynn. I *know* time, all right? I spent my whole life watching clocks count down. Listening for bells to ring. But it doesn't help a bit when it actually runs out. When it keeps running.'

Gwynn slapped him on the leg and turned back around, looking out the window. 'Diddling myself. Psssh. The boys who called themselves painters fell in love with me, buster.' She jabbed her upper chest with her thumb. 'And, when I was feeling generous, I let them do the diddling for me as I closed my eyes and imagined old men with rotten teeth and tweed jackets and thick yellow nails. As I came and came and came. I'm an eighty-three-year-old woman who was an amazing thirteen-year-old girl. I had a *youth*. It was only everything else that was sad.' Gwynn pushed a thin, almost translucent, piece of hair out of her eyes. 'I'm going to assume you want something.'

'You're good at that.'

'What?'

Pillow laid his hand out flat, as if expecting an answer to be placed on it. 'Assuming.'

'I've been told I'm also passably talented at being told what the fuck you're doing.'

'I've got Artaud all to myself. I've got, maybe, a couple days to get him talking, during which time I need him to give me the coins, and hopefully not die of withdrawal.'

'You've never seen my office, have you, Pillow? Almost nobody has. I'll show you.'

Pillow offered her a hand up.

Gwynn kept looking at him for a second and then hoisted herself up with his hand, sliding up his forearm and settling into an old-school arm-in-arm, directing him with small, certain pushes toward the doors that were way taller than they needed to be. All Gwynn did to open them was put her hand flat against them and keep walking.

The room was huge and almost empty. The ceiling was all glass; the walls were covered with different tricks of light from the sun catching angles in the pane. In the middle of the floor there was a small tree in a pot, and a chair a couple feet in front of it. Gwynn took Pillow to the chair and told him to sit.

'Watch this tree while I get your stuff.'

Gwynn shuffled over to the corner and opened a wall safe. Pillow looked at the tree; it looked like a fully grown tree but tiny. Its leaves formed a clean circle at the top, like leaves do in drawings.

Gwynn kept talking over her shoulder.

'Some would say I'm too old for a diary, Pillow. But I thought myself too refined for a diary when I was the right age, seven-some-odd decades ago. I regress years each day. I was born a hundred-and-nine-year-old woman and I'm the perfect age now. You're always young enough to do something the first time. That's something I'm only just learning. My diary is about this tree.' Pillow turned around and looked at Gwynn flipping through a wide assortment of sealed bags like they were records in a store. 'I bought that tree when it was a seed, and for the last seven years I've recorded every change. I note each leaf that falls, and how it falls, I record the exact day they start turning. What the colours turn into. I have a whole section about how the shadows differ by season and by hour of the day.'

Pillow was back to looking at the tree. No leaves fell. He was sweating under the focused light of the ceiling. Gwynn dropped two baggies and a pill bottle into his lap and then rested a hand on his shoulder.

'What's going on, Pillow? Is anyone on to you?'

'We're good, Gwynn.' He closed his eyes for the next lie. 'Nothing to worry about. I'm closing in on these coins. Artaud will give them up soon. Are you ready?'

She used her free hand to flick at an imaginary bug. 'Some people, people more worried about being right than being original, would say that I was born ready. I'll just say that I was born one time, and I'm ready this time.'

Pillow pocketed the baggies and stood. Gwynn was looking at the tree.

'I know it's silly.'

He grabbed the back of her head and pulled it in to his chest. He spoke with his jaw moving against the top of her head. 'It's a great tree, Gwynn.'

Pillow couldn't help but wonder if that was how any tree wanted to live, in a box being watched. Everything written down.

Paper is made of trees. So was the box.

Gwynn pushed back and spread an arm toward the doors. Pillow noticed that the top of the door brushed against the glass ceiling every time it opened. He could see the little scuffs along the whole arc. A long spear of light hit him in the eye.

At the door Gwynn stopped and dug into the closet. 'Here, you should take this.' She pulled a long knotted walking stick out of the closet. It was bluntly ugly, but solid-looking, like something a very old and stereotypical shepherd would use to support himself as he walked up a heath.

'Why?'

Gwynn shoved the stick into the crook of Pillow's arm, spun him and pushed him toward the door. 'Artaud. He'll like it. He found it at a market in Paris, and he carried it around with him all the time for a while. He traded it to me for heroin. I don't even think he remembers I have it. But he'll like it, give it to him.'

Pillow tapped the stick on the toe of his shoe. Gwynn kept looking up at the tree on the floor of the other room.

When he got back to his car, Pillow looked at the clock. Emily's appointment started in five minutes. Pillow really hoped they didn't do the thing where they show you a grainy picture of the baby and then tell you how big it is in terms of fruit, but he knew they would. Pillow sat in his car, trying to think of better places to stash Artaud, as the clock counted off minutes until the appointment started and then it counted off a few more. Pillow looked out the windshield. It felt exactly like sitting still.

Driving sleepily back to the slaughterhouse gave Pillow some mostly traffic-free time to think over his game plan. The whole thing was a foot race, and he was the only one on track. Bataille was in the wind without the coins, and now it was between himself, whoever knocked off the original buy, and the cops. Avida and Simon were in it for themselves. They'd keep the whole thing unofficial in case they found the coins and managed to work a deal. Breton had written off the coins, and Don would be in just as much trouble as him if he told about Artaud. The only real wild card was the robbers. Everyone else was predictable, but he didn't even know who those crazies were – they just came in shooting.

As long as Don kept his mouth shut, Pillow thought he had the advantage, strategically. Only the cops realized he was looking for the coins, and they couldn't tell anyone, and even if everyone did know they wouldn't think he was a real threat. Apollinaire was the trump card. Everybody else, Breton included, thought there was only one way to move the coins. If he could just get Artaud to tell him about the coins soon, he could get away clean. He and Emily could move somewhere sunny, somewhere with beaches and sea turtles older than the telephone. The sort of place where Emily could fix shoes and learn to windsurf, and his kid could become a world-class long-distance runner.

The slaughterhouse seemed less creepy during the day, but a lot dirtier. Pillow could pretty much see staph crawling up the walls. The sun was highlighting all the dust in the air. It looked the way snow in a storm looks, falling or floating back up. Artaud was lying down exactly where Pillow had left him, one arm twisted up at a weird angle chained to the table, the other folded under his head like a double-jointed airplane cushion. Pillow figured he should probably buy Artaud a blanket, maybe a pillow. The roof was obscured by the light, making it seem absent and opaque to Pillow, like a sky that was all cloud.

Artaud woke up as Pillow reached him and started spazzing out and contorting himself away from the table. Pillow watched a long shallow gash pucker open on the priest's wrist.

'Okay, enough of that, Artaud.'

Artaud bent himself around the table leg, closing his eyes and letting out one muffled wail, sounding like a whale whose blowhole had been packed with wax.

Pillow sat down cross-legged and scooted under the table. He snapped his fingers in front of Artaud's face. 'Hey! Morphine! Food!'

Artaud kept his eyes closed tight, but his long, wracked limbs started relaxing in gradual stages. Pillow reached out and cupped Artaud's hip. He left the hand there awkwardly.

'So, you're probably pretty confused, and I want to help you out, so we should get some basics straight. The first thing you need to know is that you're safe. You have a broken jaw and a pretty bad concussion, but that's all healing. I'm not here to hurt you. Actually I'm here to help take care of you. The drugs I'm going to give you are just the drugs you like. The food I'm going to give you is just food, and the water is water. Is that all okay with you?'

Artaud opened his eyes, nodded and then turned his head to the floor. Pillow let go of his hip and took out a small notebook and a pen. 'It's important that you don't try to open your mouth too much, okay? You can write down whatever you need to say. Do you have any questions for me?'

Artaud stayed still. Pillow watched him for a while, then he put the pen and paper down on the floor, crawled out from under the table and set up the morphine shot.

Pillow held the syringe up to the blinding sun, watched the air bubble bounce back and forth, framed by illuminated dust, which, he'd recently learned, is mostly just dead skin. Pillow hadn't been surprised to learn that one. It made sense to him, that this was a life you spent breathing in skin.

The thing for Pillow was this: he didn't want to find the coins, he wanted to have found the coins. He could see it all, how far away he was from being done. The fact of doing it, pumping Artaud for information, lying to everybody, moving through the day, was tiresome to even imagine. And that wasn't how Pillow was used to wanting things.

When he'd been fighting, what he'd wanted was to fight, to train, to be a boxer. To be a boxer every day. The imaginary titles, all that imaginary glory, and the money could (and did) come and go. What he'd liked was beating people. Looking someone in the face, knowing what they wanted to do, them knowing what he wanted to do, and still getting over on them. Seeing guys fold, crack like seashells hit with a tennis racket, under the pressure. Watching all those plans and all that confidence fall out of their eyes. Watching their shoulders sag that little bit and knowing he hadn't just won a game, he'd dominated someone who was used to dominating. That wouldn't be the payoff this time. He wouldn't see it. He'd have to imagine it. Imagine those numbers in the bank, disappearing day by day, as worth it. Understand the money, the time that passed warm under a roof, as the results of effort.

Artaud wasn't going to give Pillow what he wanted until he stabilized a little, but Pillow wanted to start setting him up. He put the needle between his teeth, picked up the smoothies he'd brought and walked to the side of the room Artaud was staring at. He placed everything down in a neat line.

'All right, Antonin, that's your first name, right?'

Artaud sprayed a thin mist of blood out from between his lips in response.

'Antonin, you need to drink these smoothies I'm making for you, all right? That's important.'

Artaud reached weakly up toward Pillow's face, and Pillow caught the hand and pulled it firmly, but gently, away. He laced his fingers through Artaud's, bouncing their hands against the floor.

'Hey. Take it easy. I want to tell you one more thing first. You listen to me and you get your morphine, okay?'

Artaud looked him in the eyes. Artaud's were that light blue shade that people wear contacts to get. They were rimmed with dark red blood, the rest as white as the boring part of an egg. Pillow shook their hands, then held them still and close to his chest.

'I've seen you around, Artaud, you know that? I've seen you around, and I've seen you talk, a lot. And I've seen nobody listen. I think you've got some shit to say. So I'm not going to ask you to tell me anything you don't want to tell me. I'm not going to ask you to do anything you don't want to do. And I can't promise I'll understand, but I will pay attention to you. I'll get you drugs, I'll get you food, I'll keep you alive. And you can tell me whatever you want to tell me. And after a while, after you think I've paid enough attention, enough care, you're going to tell me one thing I want to know. Sound good?'

Artaud didn't nod or move his head or look up from the floor. The shattered extra hinge of his jaw sagged a little and then tensed back into place.

'Oh, I almost forgot, here's your walking stick. Gwynn said you might like it.'

Artaud bolted upright and snatched the stick from Pillow's hands. He lay down flat, gripped the stick in his arms and legs and squeezed as hard as he could. He kissed the top knob of the stick, and a large, bloody, chapped piece of his lip came off stuck to it.

Pillow wondered if love and adoration and being obsessed with sticks could all be the same thing.

Artaud finally sat up. He let his jaw sag in a way that must have been painful and locked his eyes on Pillow, and then those eyes started to cry.

That walking stick was either the worst or the best present Pillow had ever given someone, and with Artaud it was hard to tell.

Artaud looked down at the needle and squeezed Pillow's hand. Pillow turned the arm over. He took off his belt, handed it over and then uncuffed Artaud and watched the rest.

There was a small but significant part of Pillow that was still convinced that all the people who were squeamish about needles were actually faking it. It was the same part of his brain that couldn't help thinking he should weigh more with an erection, no matter how many times he'd woken up, stepped on his scale and been proven wrong.

Artaud, needle now stuck firmly in his arm, stopped and looked back at Pillow.

Artaud started moving his lips slowly with no sound behind them. Artaud's eyes, huge and blue and unblinking, his head tilting to the side, the deep black bags underneath creasing a little with humour, his shoulders heaving with breath. Pillow reached up and ran his hand through Artaud's hair, which fell to the sides like a field of wheat with a truck moving through. Artaud leaned forward and kissed Pillow on the lips. Pillow could smell and taste the metallic bite of blood from Artaud's mouth. When he pulled back, Artaud nodded at him and shot the morphine straight in without looking back at the needle.

Pillow considered himself an open-minded, deeply freaked out person at that exact minute. The little notebook he'd given Artaud was propped open, with a short note inside that he must have written while Pillow was preparing the needle.

A localized numbness. Local in the same way the whole of the universe is local. You have provided me with the only possible tonic. I cannot thank you enough.

Pillow sighed. Pushing Artaud was going to be a lot of work, and he needed to be sharp for it. So he just sat quietly and let Artaud enjoy himself. The guy's wrist had swollen to almost the size of a grapefruit. Pillow poked it with his finger. It was hard as a rock who'd never met another rock. Pillow pinched the abscess between his fingers and shifted it back and forth. Artaud was staring at the ceiling, mouthing something, small droplets of blood flipping off his top lip.

On the way back to the car, Pillow took a brief pause and looked out at the forest behind the slaughterhouse. They were sparse, vaguely dead woods, but still pretty in the way that trees and soil are no matter what. They were the sort of woods where seeing an alien landing or a backwoods marriage would have just made Pillow nod and shrug.

A deer walked out onto the path behind him. The deer sniffed the grass for a second and then it kept walking, in that way deer move where it seems like they're hurt but it's just how their joints are.

Pillow followed Emily down the stairs, enjoying the fluorescent lights reflecting in the polished cement of the walls and floor. Emily was holding the thick metal door open with both arms.

She was in the middle of making it very easy for him not to tell her about Artaud. It seemed like she'd pretty much tapped out of hearing about his business. She hadn't said anything to that effect, but Pillow figured it was up to him to honour the agreement. Emily didn't want to know.

'So, Peter, the reason I called you down is that I'm going to show you how I became so broke. I'm going to share this with you, even though … No, scratch that. Because it is really humiliating. You need to see.'

'I'm sure it's not that bad. Do you know how much cash has gone through my hands? It's shameful. That's not a thing I say much either. I'm actually ashamed of it.'

Emily shook her head slowly. Rapped on the sliding metal door of a passing storage locker. 'Just wait. You make a lot of strong calls on things you don't know very much about. That's something I've noticed about you.'

Possibly the only bonus feature of their apartment building was that everyone got a free storage locker in the basement. Pillow had never opened his, having lost the key shortly after moving in.

Emily hustled down the long, smooth, shiny hallway. She threw the door to her locker open unreasonably hard, and then jumped back a little, startled by the noise. 'See how strong I am? This guy, bodybuilder.'

Pillow's jaw went slack as he turned the corner and looked inside. It was packed to the ceiling with old hobby items. Hiking poles, ski poles, remote-control boats, remote-control planes, models, a sewing machine, a pottery wheel, a chemistry set, a snowboard, a diorama-making set, an easel, golf clubs, two chess boards, a boogie board and several knitting needles jammed randomly through huge, mixed balls of wool.

'Are you a …'

Emily shook her head wistfully.

'I knew you were going to say that, and I really hoped you wouldn't. And I'm just generally pissed the concept of "hoarding" has gotten so much play lately. I'm a hobbyist, okay? I have hobbies. I have almost all the hobbies, and I keep the things that I bought for them in case I want to go back and do them again.'

Pillow nodded sarcastically as he peered at a fairly accurate charcoal drawing of Charles Lindbergh.

Emily slapped him on the arm, instinctively and almost simultaneously reaching out with her other hand in apology. 'Just because you're a boring, lame monogamous hobby-haver doesn't mean the rest of us should feel bad for occasionally losing interest in stuff we once thought was by far the coolest way a person could or would ever want to spend their time. You might take a page out of my book, mister.'

Pillow cast another look around the storage locker. 'I wish I could, but trust me, I have no spare talent. I used it all. I think we might be the two bad ends of that scale, sweet bits.'

Emily pulled her shirt up to cover her face and then blew it down. 'I knoooowwww. But I loved each of these hobbies so much the first three times I did them. Dude, when I finally figured out how to blow glass … But as soon as I get, like, the tiniest bit good I just start hating the thing, whatever it is, so much. I cannot tell you how much I loved RC boat-racing for six weeks two years ago. That was a fair quit, though. It's a viciously competitive subculture.'

She did a deep memory-shudder. 'So I keep them around, like a huge weirdo, because I always think, y'know, maybe I'll love one of them again. Maybe I just needed a break from it. But no.' Emily listlessly poked a set of calligraphy pens. 'This stuff looks exactly as shitty and pointless to me as it does to you.'

She craned her head all the way to the side and sighed as she looked over a scale reproduction of the Battle of Waterloo. Pillow was watching her very carefully as a small drop of water leaked down from the ceiling, and hit her neck, and she started for a second, then remained still as the water rolled slowly down the curve of her neck.

'Hey, how about you teach me about one of them?'

'What?'

'One of the hobbies. Teach me about it. What was the last really good one?'

Emily straightened up and took a solid grip on her chin. 'None of them. I'm going to call it. It was all wasteful and sad, and all I need to do is look at this place to know it.'

Pillow pulled the hand off her chin, then he put the chin in his mouth. Emily pushed back and slapped at her face.

'I hate that! I hate it every time you do it. There's no call to slobber on a person.'

Pillow grabbed the chin again. He tilted it up a little, then he let it go wherever it wanted. An idea occurred to him. 'Hey, can I have that key? Maybe I'll take up …' He picked up a wooden ring with fabric in the middle.

'Needlepoint.'

'Yeah, maybe I'll take up needlepoint.'

She looked at him quizzically, then tossed him the key. 'Sure, I've got the spare anyway.'

'They gave us two?'

'Three. I lost one.'

'Well, fuck a duck.'

'Please don't do that. I have often wondered what you do at your "zoo."'

Pillow was genuinely offended. 'I wouldn't do that, it's wrong.'

'Yes. Bestiality is wrong. That's sort of a given. For most people.'

Pillow waved the key at her. 'But it shouldn't be. People think it's wrong just because it's gross. And that's not the reason. A dog can't tell you they're not into it. No matter how much you think you know what a dog wants, you don't. People should keep that in mind.'

Emily wrapped a hand around his waist and cast a quick, sighing gaze over the locker. 'You're a moral man.'

Pillow nodded. 'I'm sorry about the appointment, I –'

She pinched him hard on the hip to stop him. 'I gave you the option. And you won't have it next time. But I gave it to you this time.'

They stood in silence for a little bit, then Pillow turned her and walked them out the door. She broke his grip, turned and squinted at him.

'I don't think needlepoint is for you, though. You're more of a Fimo clay man. Scratch that: Sculpey. Back in the day, when Sculpey came around everybody was like, "Fimo can suck a dick!"'

Pillow closed and locked the door, then they linked arms.

'So, I'm a Sculpey guy. You can tell, can you?'

She patted him on the shoulder. 'Oh yeah, I can spot 'em a mile away.'

That night it took less than the length of time it takes to eat a very small amount of brown rice and eggplant for Pillow to remember how much he hated spending time alone in his apartment. He went for a long walk and ended up at Mad Love.

After the storage-locker reveal, Emily had become 'sleepy and grumpy and gross' and refused to let Pillow sleep over. He took it in stride. It gave him a planning evening.

He had a few drinks at Mad Love, trying not to think about exploding heads, and kettles, and money he didn't have anymore, and money he didn't have yet. Then Pillow hung around in the parking lot, looking up at the bright, flickering sign and feeling the heft of the rock in his hand. He'd gathered a bunch of them in a line behind him and was making plans for where he was going to throw them. Pillow wasn't doing as much productive thinking about the coin business as he'd planned to. He had the rock thing pretty much sorted out, though.

'Pillow?'

He spun around, ready to make a huge mistake with a medium-sized rock.

Don covered his face with his forearms. 'Watch out, Pillow, Jesus, it's fucking me. Don't go caveman on me, fella.'

Pillow came back to himself quickly. 'Donny! Sorry, shit, I'm sorry.'

Don grabbed him around the waist in a sort of side-hug. 'What are you doing here?'

'I was going to pelt this bar with a bunch of rocks.'

'Is that a good idea?'

Pillow felt dizzy. Don sat Pillow down on the curb, rubbing his back and talking him down. 'Pillow, we should leave. This is a place you go to hurt yourself. Let's not be seen around here, with the cops and all. Let's go over to my house and we'll have some drinks there. Okay?'

Pillow nodded. 'Yeah, yeah, let's go. I really do want to bust up that sign, though.'

Don stood and offered his hand. He hoisted Pillow up. 'All I'm saying is throw peace a lay every now and again.'

Pillow laughed and started to walk away. He turned around and Don was looking at him like he was crazy.

'I said every now and again, not every time. I meant that we should each throw one rock, and then run away.'

Don caught the very bottom corner of the *E*, Pillow hit the join where *O* and *V* met square. They saw the sparks start to rain down onto the entrance, and they could hear the shouts and curses as they turned the corner.

Don owned more cushions than anyone could really need. Pillow was stretched out across a number of them on the floor as Don paced across the room, occasionally swigging an obscure green liqueur as he listened.

It felt good to talk about the pregnancy with someone who wasn't the pregnant person.

'Okay, do you want to hear my one and only parenting idea? I think it could help. No disrespect, but you don't seem to have given much thought to child rearing.'

Pillow waved him on. He liked to think of himself as a person who knew what to do with advice.

'This is only for a boy. When you give him the sex talk, right, when he's like eleven or twelve. The birdsies and beezies. My talk is just one word: *cunnilingus.*'

Pillow snorted.

'I'm serious. Almost every man has a dick, and a few of those are going to be bigger, harder, veinier, better-smelling, whatever. A dick, no matter the dick, is never that nice. But if you are the eleven-year-old boy who eats pussy, that's the kind of shit that makes you *special.*'

'Fair point. It's like with anything: if you want 'em to make the pros, you gotta start 'em young. But I think that's the only talk I'm ready for. I know what I'm going to say. I think I'll tell the kid, if it's a him, a her or a dealer's choice, I'll tell the kid that it's a wonderful thing, a wonderful part of life. And you have to be careful with wonderful things, because you can fuck them up, and they can fuck you up really easily. And I'd just tell them, y'know, fucking isn't wrong or bad, but there are a lot of bad reasons to fuck. The good reason is that you like the person, and they're nice to you, and you want to be nice to them back. And if you're open and really into it, that's what sex can be. It can be the best way to be nice to someone. That's what I think I'll say about birds and bees, and snails and puppy-dog whatevers.'

Don didn't give Pillow's sex talk much thought. He started up again.

'I want your take on this: yesterday I had a sexual fantasy about a girl scratching her shoulder, but I had it because I was scratching my shoulder. I pulled my shirt to the side and I reached in, and then I thought that if I saw someone doing that it would be really cool and interesting. That strange, frank physicality. You're in the middle of a crowded Portuguese restaurant and – oops, there's some collarbone. In any event, I think it's a reasonable thing to see and think is hot, but I'm not sure how standard the shoulder scratch is as an auto-erotic act.'

Pillow agreed in a fluttery and fundamental way he felt in his chest. Having gotten drunk with Don about fifty times, he knew he wasn't supposed to agree out loud. They had a rhythm. 'I'm sure you and your collarbone are going to be very happy together.'

Don nodded and grinned into the mouth of the bottle. 'Be careful, Pillow.' He sat down and, having misjudged the distance, scooted forward and looked Pillow in the eyes. 'With Breton, and with all of this. I know you're freaked out, but you're going to have to move Artaud soon. Tomorrow, at the latest the day after. Breton thinks it's important you killed him. He'll take care of all of us if we're loyal.'

Pillow motioned for the bottle, and Don gave him a doubtful look before handing it over. The stuff tasted like a fermented honeydew melon.

'I have one theory,' said Pillow. 'All you guys have tons of them, but I just have one good one. And it applies to you and Breton, especially. Shit champagne. So, champagne is good. Who doesn't like champagne? Thousand-dollar champagne is so good that you'll ignore a lot of stuff to drink it. There can be a hair in it, a bug, a squirt of piss even. It takes a whole lot to make thousand-dollar champagne not drinkable. But if there is a flake of shit in it, that champagne is now shit champagne. And nobody should drink shit champagne. Shit champagne has got to be poured out right away, so you're not tempted, because you can't reason or haggle or compromise with shit. It just is what it is. A pickle is still a cucumber, no matter how long you keep it in the jar.'

Don's head rocked back with sudden realization. 'Pickles are *cucumbers*?'

'Umm. Yup. Yeah, they are. Did you not –'

Don's face reddened. 'I hate pickles. I never eat them.'

Pillow was rolling around on floor, slapping a spare cushion.

'All right. Laugh. But I understand. It makes sense now that I've been told it once. But I honestly, I just never thought about pickles.' Don took a big swill from the bottle and laughed it back out. 'Well, I'm glad that I could cheer you up. But you know what, Pillow? I like you, I do. But your attitude about this is bullshit. You spend all your time thinking the syndicate, the whole way we do it, is dumb. You play aloof, and you make fun of it, and then you complain when you're not included. It's a fucking syndicate, Pillow. We all bought in.'

'You know the things I've done. I've been around a long time, man. What did you spend to buy in?'

'You're oblivious. I'll tell you how I bought in. Breton and Bobby Desnos pick me up from my house, random Tuesday. They drive me out to the middle of nowhere and they pull over by the river. And they tell me to walk down this really steep hill, so I walk down the hill, and they tell me to look at the hole they dug, so I look at the hole they dug. They tell me to get on my knees, so I do. Breton puts a gun to the back of my head, he stops a second and then he flicks off the safety. I remember that sound and I remember the sound of him pulling the trigger. That sound of invisible things shifting. Then I died. No taste, no smell, no touch, no hearing, no air. The whole world was just this nothing I could feel. For about half a second. And then I opened my eyes, or maybe they were open the whole time,

127

but either way I could see again and the grave was still there, and the sky was still there, and my hands were still there, and I kept waiting. I didn't turn around for a long time. From my memory I'd have to guess about two hundred thousand years. When I did turn around Breton came forward, dropped to his knees and told me he loved me.'

'That's crazy. Nobody's doing that to me. If that's in, I'm staying out. You let him get over on you like that?'

'No, Pillow, you don't understand. It's not about him and me. It's not about getting over on someone, it's not a contest. I'm not my ego. It's about pushing yourself. Agreeing to life until you die, and then a little bit past that. It's the only way. I don't mean to be shitting on you, but that's who you are working with. That's how we all feel. And I hear you, Pillow, I do, and you should be tempted and you should be frustrated, I would be if I was you. But you should hear me as well. We're telling each other to be careful. And we should both listen.'

Pillow wiped his eyes. 'I'm supposed to listen to a forty-year-old man who found out what pickles are two minutes ago?'

'You're not supposed to. But it would be wise to.'

'I hear you. Thanks.'

'By the way, I'm actually thirty-*eight*-years experienced. And I know what pickles are, motherfucker: pickles are pickles.'

Don insisted on walking Pillow to the subway station. The subway stop was being renovated, so there was a large construction tarp by it. As they got to the entrance, Pillow heard Don let out a little yelp behind him. Before he could turn around, a huge hand grabbed him behind the neck and he felt the insistent press of a gun barrel in the small of his back. The hand shoved his head into the construction area and then against the wall and frisked him. Then a leg no bigger than a spruce tree kicked him prone. His face was pressed into the ground, loose pebbles nestling softly into his cheek.

Pillow shifted his hips and twisted his head a little to look. He caught a flash of a skinny ski-masked person with a gun in Don's face. Don looked almost bored, his hands stretched out above him, drooping at the wrist a little. The huge hand twisted Pillow's face back down, and he closed his eyes to keep out the dirt.

'All right, Costes. You deliver a message to Breton. You tell him those coins are in play. And when we find them we want the same deal Bataille got. Fifty grand on delivery and twenty after it goes through.' There was a long pause. They were muffling their voices but they sounded half-familiar. 'Can you give that message, or are you done with those kneecaps?'

Pillow managed to get his face turned sideways. He started moving his hand slowly down, finding some purchase between the giant kneecap and his back. The ski mask was twitching out around the shoulders, waving the gun in Don's face. Don closed his eyes and breathed.

'So the message is that some anonymous winter-sports freak knocked off his deal and wants to sell his already-bought coins back to him. Coins they don't even have yet. That's the message? Sure thing, I can deliver it. I can do a lot of things. Can I tell him for whom I'm speaking?'

Ski Mask drove a knee straight into Don's crotch and slammed the butt of the gun into his kidney. As Don started falling, Pillow gripped the knee on his back and shoved up as he bridged his hips. The big guy on top of him got off balance and started tipping over. Pillow got to his feet and caught the big one with a body shot and he let out a muffled, injured breath. Pillow hadn't even started to turn his head when something that felt a lot like a car, but probably wasn't a car, hit him and his knees gave out, and there seemed to be no directions anywhere in the world.

Pillow woke up on the subway with Don holding his head up straight. And for the whole ride he was at this rave he'd been to eight years ago. The lights of the tunnels moved past, and with each shuddering stop more people came on, and it seemed like they were dancing. There was a girl sitting across from him, and he was sure he'd seen her before. He was almost sure it was Louise Aragon. She wasn't standing up and dancing with everybody else. Her eyes were on her book and she wasn't looking at the lights but the lights were looking at her, moving across her face and slipping off and into the dark and she was scratching at a hole in her tights at the very top of her knee. Pillow felt Don pulling at his shoulder like a chicken wing and telling him that they had to go, but his whole torso felt like a bottle floating in the ocean, and his legs were buzzing in a tight band around his knees. He stayed sitting.

Pillow didn't want to leave. He wanted to dance.

As Don was calling the doctor – actually a veterinarian who'd lost her licence for dealing ketamine – Pillow fell asleep sitting at the kitchen table. When he woke up he didn't recognize his apartment until he saw his running gear drying above the sink. He took to asking Don whether they'd flown home and where Don's plane was. Don moved Pillow over to the couch and cradled his head, gently shushing him, occasionally twisting the skin over his ribs to keep him awake.

The vet took almost two hours to get there, and by the time she arrived Pillow had come back to himself enough to bluff a couple of the cognitive tests. She gave him a cold compress for his head, prescribed rest, laying off the painkillers, and really hoping he didn't have a brain bleed. Don asked what they should do if Pillow did have a bleed, and she snapped her glove off, shrugging.

'Take him out behind the stables and shoot him.'

Everyone was tired enough to laugh.

Pillow spent the whole next day somewhere in between being incapacitated by a headache and too depressed to move. After Don left, Pillow had a shower. He sat down in the tub, standing only when the water lost the last hint of heat. The cheap walls of the bathroom looked like the sides of a cardboard box full of water. In his bedroom he decided to lie down on the floor instead of the bed for a little bit. He stretched his hands out in front of his face and stared at them for a long time, then he called Emily.

Telling people not to worry over the phone is the most certain way to have them be frantic when they finally do see you.

Emily moved to touch his head instinctively, and then pulled her hand back to her mouth. Pillow sat her down. He explained a version of what had happened that he was trying very hard to believe: that he and Don had seen a homeless man getting beat up by a group of teens, and one of them had hit him with a tree branch. Emily held her hands tight to her temples as she listened. Pillow had to think for a longer minute than usual to give his thoughts.

'Listen, listen, listen, listen. This isn't a catastrophe, it's a concussion. Everyone has them all the time. Life is a concussion. Okay? I'm not going to be forgetting my last name tomorrow. I didn't go out. I just had my bell rung a little. I got hit by a kid with a stick, that's it.'

'Pete, what are you talking about? You had to stop fighting because –'

'It's not repetitive. I had to quit because I'm not supposed to take repetitive blows to the head anymore, okay? That's what the doctor told me. My head has been healing for almost ten years. I took one shot. One shot. I'll be fine.'

'Do you think I haven't looked this up? Do you think I haven't looked this up for hours? I'm not an idiot, Pete. I've thought about this. And I know that your sixties aren't going to be a good time. I know that, and I'm fine with it. We have time now, and we're going to make it great. I'm sure of it. But you can't be getting in fights anymore. Ever. You need to get out of this, the coin thing, bouncing, steroids, all of this.'

'It was nothing to do with work, the coins, none of that stuff. It was random. I was walking home. We saw a homeless guy about to get his ass kicked, what were we going to do?'

'Leave, like someone who can't be in fights anymore. That's what you do now. Like everybody else, you just walk away and feel shitty about it later. You need to be scared. For me. You have to leave it behind you, Pete. I don't care about money, you have to look out for yourself.'

'I know this is bad. I understand and I accept that I was, that I am, irresponsible, and I'll make changes. But you have to give me time. I can't just walk away from the guys I work for without a word. I need a couple weeks to figure things out. But I'll do it. I'll do whatever I have to do. Okay?'

She said, 'Kiss me,' and after a bit of a pause he grabbed her wrist.

Emily was still upset and Pillow needed proper rest, so after a while she left. Pillow stayed sitting on the couch, either afraid or unwilling to move around too much. It felt like there was a very large shard of glass pressing into the middle of his forehead, and he got the idea that if he moved, the glass would go right through his skull. While Pillow sat still, waiting for his headache to go away and for his left foot to stop buzzing, the sun moved and set. The undersides of giant clouds turned a familiar pink and gently faded to black, and by the time Pillow stood to get a drink of water it was well into the night. He didn't realize how dark it had gotten until out of the corner of his eye he caught sight of a stray cat disappearing into the bushes behind the apartment complex, one loose, impossibly long strip of plastic dangling from its tail.

When Pillow walked into the slaughterhouse, Artaud was doing that thing just past sleeping and just short of being in a coma, moving his legs and arms out in front of him like a dog dreaming about running. If it's possible to spoon a knobby old walking stick, he was doing that too. Pillow said hello in a consciously loud voice. Artaud woke up, gazed around a little aimlessly and shuddered himself to a seated position. He kept his bony neck craning oddly from side to side, occasionally tipping his head and letting a weird amount of blood spill out the side of his mouth.

'How're you doing there, big guy?'

Artaud responded by flopping back down flat, turning himself away and into the fetal position. After a second or two he was snoring again, these heavy, horrifying blood-drenched heaves, each snore ending with the sound of a broken tip of bone flapping under the pressure of breath.

Pillow was ready to feel a little hurt before he realized Artaud already had a note laid out on the table.

Dear Pillow,

My mind is moderately troubled; I won't bother to go into the reasons. Your influence has helped me, and I hope when my situation improves, when I am able to exert a more sensible influence over my own brain, that I may improve yours.

I know what you want. What I ask is merely that you are sensitive to the folds in the fabric of our friendship. I wish to help you, as you do me, but I also wish not to be used.

Although I grow weary of it and thrill has long since disappeared into the wake of this rickety boat, I am badly in need of some more drugs. Whatever you have will help. I would bury a thousand ships in the sand to touch the shore once more.

My soul on your lips,
Antonin Artaud

Pillow finished reading and looked over at Artaud, still curled in a very long, very sad ball with his hands clawed over his eyes.

Pillow had one last chance to bail out. It would be easiest, and kindest, to kill Artaud. Pillow had one big dose ready, and that'd be all. Artaud would probably thank him. He'd be grateful, and for Pillow it could be over. It could all be over. Breton would let it lie, Gwynn and Don would still be his friends. And he'd be right where he was, right where he'd been. Pillow walked over and sat on the couch, he shook Artaud's shoulder. He ran his hand over the priest's cheek, the skin was tight and hot and yellow, infections blending together. Artaud's pulse pumping anemic and laboured in his neck. Pillow knew Artaud wouldn't wake up, that he wasn't about making it easy. Artaud wouldn't decide for him. It was all on Pillow.

Pillow went outside and paced. He started talking to the giant metal bull, listing reasons, mixing reasons to keep Artaud alive and go for the coins with reasons it would work.

Because you're clever.

Because you see the angles.

Because you'll fight anyone, anywhere, anytime.

Because you don't fight for free.

Because you don't fight for peanuts.

Because you know how to win.

Because cheating and trying are the exact same thing.

Because you've been fucked plenty.

Because it didn't hurt.

Because it did hurt and you didn't care.

Because kids need money.

Because women like winners.

Because you're never scared.

Because you're always ready.

Because people get scared for you.

Because she even talks to you.

Because everyone has to want something.

Because you're not exactly father material.

Because there's a prize.

Because you're a prizefighter.

The giant metal bull didn't seem to care. He kept pacing. He slapped both sides of his face hard. He dropped the death-syringe and stepped on it.

Because when your brain's that fried you'll want help too.

Because you can see the future.

Because it almost is already.

Because you go until the bell rings.

Because food is just fuel.

Because it's all just fuel.

Because you're a rocket ship.

Because fuck the moon.

Artaud was still passed out when they got to the gym. Pillow paused outside to give himself some time to think. Even though it was supposed to be new, Julio's gym already had that dirty strip-mall feel to it. The boxing gloves painted across the front door had already mostly faded away. A typical boxing gym, the place had probably looked worn out before it opened. Pillow turned off the car and sat. Finally he hustled up the steps and into the gym.

He saw Julio at the back, watching two kids spar, shouting 'Heeeeeyyyyyyy' every time someone landed a punch. Pillow charged straight toward him with his head down. He could hear the slap of hand pads, the speed bags rattling, the chains of the heavy bags creaking. He could smell the sweat and wet leather and hear some trainer counting off reps from the corner. Julio's belt (which used to be Pillow's) in a glass case above the office door. Julio had switched to a purple velour track suit, fluorescent lights reflecting at different angles off his bald head.

Pillow hugged him from behind, then swung around and leaned deep into the ropes.

'Pillow! Hey, man, hey. You came around! Here for the job? Kevin really liked the session you had.'

'Not quite, Jules. I came to ask a favour actually. Can we talk somewhere private?'

Julio eyeballed him sidelong. Pillow ran lies through his head, hoping to start believing them.

'Sure thing, sure thing. Come to my office over here.'

They walked to the back, and Pillow ducked a bit entering the room even though he didn't have to. Julio closed the office door whisper-soft.

'Listen, Pillow … I want to help you. I do, brother, I do. But …' Julio walked around behind the desk, squeaked his chair into reclining. Pillow stayed standing. 'I hear things, you know? About you. And hey, we've all, you know, we've all … Not judging, but it's my place here. My money, right? If you want to work here, I'd love it. Train fighters, that's cool. But I'm not into anything else. I'm trying to keep it all clean. I don't want no trouble.'

Pillow settled into a chair and grinned, faux-sheepish. 'None of that stuff, Jules. You, well, you remember how it was with the girls, back in the day. And that's where, that's where I've got myself in a spot.'

Julio laughed and rubbed his head, spun his chair in a full circle. 'What's going on, you need for me to take one off your hands? Because I'll do you that favour. Because we're tight like that. Brothers.'

The noise Pillow made sounded forced enough to be called a guffaw. 'Don't get too excited. I just need a place. I've got an old squeeze coming into town for a few days, and she wants to stay with me. But I'm shacked up, y'know, with my girlfriend. So I just need a little privacy, a quiet place. So I was wondering if there was a room.'

Julio came around the empty desk and sat on the edge. 'Yeah, man, it's in the basement. The door locks and all. It's got a cot. You can get in through the back door, have some privacy. I'll set you up. It's not free, though. I don't have to tell you nothing is free in a boxing gym.'

'Money's tight, man, I mean I can ...'

Julio shook his head, fake-offended. 'I don't want your money, man, what do you think I am? No, come look at the kid again. Kevin wants you to train him, full-time. You should do it, you were good with him. Get you started with him, then we get you working with some of the amateurs, building kids up. Everybody always knew you'd be a trainer, man. When you were fighting that's what everyone said.'

Pillow looked at the corner of the ceiling. 'I told you, I just –'

'No. I don't wanna hear it. I give to you, you give back. I respect you too much to give you shit for free. We're going to make a deal.'

Pillow shrugged. 'Yup. You got a deal. I feel bad for the kid, though.'

Julio laughed, then a serious look passed over his face. 'This is what it is? It's about a girl, right? Not that I don't believe you, man, really, I believe you, but I have to make sure. I can't take any chances with the gym here.'

Pillow reached across and grabbed Julio's kneecap.

'I get it, Jules, I do. Nothing to do with what you're thinking. I swear. It's … this kid thing, it's kind of kicking my ass. And I think I do just one last hurrah, then I can get my head straight. That and …'

'And you're as much of a sucker as you always were.'

Pillow let go of the knee, let his hand dangle. It touched the floor. Julio laughed and hugged him around the shoulders. Pillow closed his eyes.

Artaud slept the rest of the afternoon. He slept in the car as Pillow waited for the gym to clear for the day. He slept as Pillow carried him around the back. Pillow left him on the dirty cot, his head resting on a rolled-up shirt, his hand stretched out over his head, one arm cuffed to the bed frame and the other clutching the walking stick, as he wheezed slow, laboured breaths, tiny bubbles of blood expanding and popping at the corners of his mouth.

A few seconds before he woke up the next morning, Pillow realized he'd forgotten all the drugs for Artaud at the slaughterhouse. He took his time gathering everything, double- and then triple-checked to make sure he didn't forget anything again. He finished and looked up into the wash of light across the ceiling, breathed a bunch of dust and thought about coins.

Pillow had only lately begun to think of himself as someone who could see the wonder in things. A person who could see the way light moved through trees or the way a big dog nuzzled a small cat as important. But he just didn't get the coin thing. Like, who looked at round bits of metal and decided they should be *the* thing. Pillow could think of many, of almost any, things more amazing than metal.

A dog eating its own vomit. What does it *mean*?

These things that people seemed to hoard and love had always left Pillow a little cold. As an adult it's money, as a kid it's candy, or at least that was how he remembered it being. Kids went mental for candy. Oddly enough, considering that he would have had to think for quite a while before recalling what he'd eaten for breakfast, Pillow remembered what a chocolate bar tasted like, or at least what chocolate bars had tasted like twenty-seven years ago.

He'd eaten candy like everyone does as a kid, but he'd never been as enthusiastic as the others, and when one coach told him to eat better, he'd just stopped eating junk food altogether. Thinking back on it, he realized what he must have known at the time: candy was a phenomenon, another lovely minute you could take totally for yourself in the middle of a world full of other people in other bodies with better brains and better bodies and better coaches. But candy minutes made him uneasy because they weren't earned. Anyone could drop a piece of chocolate on their tongue and taste, anyone could scrounge a few quarters, and to Pillow that just wasn't how magic happened. Or maybe it was, but it wasn't how magic *should* happen. It should be random. He could get himself ready for magic, work hard so that he'd see it when it came, but he didn't want to plan for it. His goal was always to be prepared but also open, empty of expectation. Fuck candy and money; all birds have to do is move their arms and they fly.

On the way out, Pillow saw that he'd left the front door open. He took a running start, jumped and caught the high ledge of the door, swinging his legs out and landing softly into a jarred, disoriented headache. Pillow took a quick knee and sighed, regretting how easy it is to forget you're hurt once you've been hurt for most of your life. He finally stood, rubbed his neck and started toward the empty parking lot.

Then he saw Georges Bataille standing behind the giant bull.

'Hi, Pillow. You're not going to kill me, are you?'

Pillow dropped his arms and ambled over, dawdling so he could take it all in. He'd been wrong the whole time. Bataille had the coins. Breton had known, but Breton wasn't here, the coins were still in play. Pillow leaned heavily against the pillar of the bull statue.

'I don't think I will, Georges. But you're here and I really doubt you can outrun me, so you've taken your chances already. How did you find me?'

'I hate nothing so much as discussing driving directions. I'm going to tell you about the coins instead.'

'Do you have them?'

'I can get them. Let me explain.'

Pillow crossed his hands behind his head; holding them in one spot at the back made his head feel pleasantly stable and definitely attached to his body. 'Sure, teach me.'

'Do you know what *numismatics* means? It's the study of coins that have lost all value. I work with worthless coins, and finally, just once, I found some that were worth –'

Pillow kicked himself off the pillar and walked toward Bataille, rolling his hand around at the wrist. 'Let's wrap this up and get to the part where you tell me where they are.'

Bataille was anything but stupid; he moved two paces back for every one Pillow took forward just to keep the distance.

'So the Artaud line was bullshit, you've had 'em the whole time.'

Bataille smiled. 'I have always had everything in this world. André Breton differs on that point. I needed the money, and at the last moment, I felt defiant. So I brought Artaud, knowing him to be an effective straw man, knowing that he would wave his arms in time with the breath of the wind and scare any winged creature. And a few mammals of limited perspective as well. A scentless figure is a terror to animals of instinct.'

'That's some cold shit. Isn't Artaud your friend?'

Bataille tilted his head to the ground and thought. The breeze blew through his hair like it was a cluster of dandelion seeds. 'I've always thought the words *friendship* and *guilt* to be interchangeable.

The only responsible position is to be excluded, by everyone's choice but your own.'

Pillow reached out and grabbed Bataille's shoulder. 'Man, I think you're really gumming up your own works there. Sometimes you just be nice, y'know? Eases things up.'

Bataille shrugged the hand off, his nostrils flaring like somebody was eating an apple in the library. 'I did not come here to be moralized upon by –'

Pillow reached out and grabbed Bataille's nose between his thumb and forefinger, closing the nostrils. 'No, you didn't. You came here because you've packed up your house and moved to a little town called Fucksville. You came here to give me all the detail I want, and let me decide what I want to do with them. Clear?'

Pillow released the nose, and Georges rubbed it for a minute, calmed himself and started in again, in a consciously slow, easy tone.

'Clarity is one trap door in the community-theatre stage of truth, but I understand you. What would you like to hear?'

'Why you ruined your own deal, where you've been, why you're coming to me now, where those coins are and how much you want for 'em. In that order.'

'As soon as I tell you where the coins are my life is worthless. They're all I have. I just want to make a deal.'

'You're not wrong, Georgie-pie. I guess that's why I asked those questions in the order I did.'

'I ruined the deal out of a false belief that I had arranged a better deal. Breton would never have allowed me to cancel our deal, and if I simply did not appear, you and Louise Aragon would have tracked me down in a matter of hours, so I brought Artaud to distract you all until my, at the time, new buyer was ready to make payment.'

'So the deal gets knocked over, your buyer gets scared off, probably didn't realize you had a deal in place for the coins anyhow, and you lam it. Okay. So you're a nutjob, but that all makes some kind of nutjob sense. Why are you coming to me now?'

'I hid for several days in the house of a student with whom I have developed an intellectual relationship of practicality and trangression, and eventually I thought of Gwynn Apollinaire. She would be the only one capable of moving the coins, but in case you are not aware, I owe her several thousands of dollars and several millions of unpaid favours. But I was desperate and so I went to her, only to see you leaving. And it all fell into place. Breton, as is his way, pushed your loyalty too far, and you'd had the same realization I did. You were still under my enforced apprehension that Artaud was the ground upon which to make that play, so −'

'You're coming to me with the coins so your debt to Gwynn doesn't come out of your end.'

Bataille did a gesture that fell somewhere between nodding and bowing.

Pillow didn't need time to think. 'Gwynn'll go full price. The seventy you were going to get from Breton.'

The thinning ends of Bataille's eyebrows perked up. 'And my percentage?'

'You get seven grand. You're down to a finder's fee.'

The old man nodded and set his shoulders. 'Fair. Give me two days.

'Days? Do you even have the coins?'

'I will need to make a swift exit. And seven thousand does not go far. I wish to make my arrangements before receiving my payment. Then we can arrange a drop.'

'A drop? Why aren't we going hand-to-hand on this?'

'Let's say that trust is always at issue when breath and bodies are involved.' Bataille with that not-knowing-what-to-do-with-his-hands look again.

'We do the drop at the zoo.'

Bataille smiled. 'A good choice. And in front of which beasts?'

'Giraffe pen, obviously.'

Bataille stepped forward with his hand out. 'That is fair on all counts. I'll meet you in two days with the coins.'

They shook on it. Pillow felt the bones in his hand move in the soft, accommodating way that it is totally fine for bones to move in.

Bataille cast a quick look up at the slaughterhouse.

'I love this place, I actually have a whole theory about –'

Pillow reached over and gently cupped the side of Bataille's neck. 'No more, man. I'm sorry, I can't do it. They're all … Do you know how many times I've heard Breton ramble on about dreams? I just can't listen to these long speeches anymore.' Bataille stepped away from Pillow's hand laughing.

'Oh yes. He was telling me about it once, and I couldn't help thinking, "If you like dreams so much just go to bed." I'd rather talk about someone's big toe than a dream.'

Pillow scratched his chin. 'Well, we agree on that one, Georges. Big toes are super-important: where you put 'em, where everybody else's are. A lot depends on it.'

Bataille smiled. 'You don't want to get me started.'

'True.'

Pillow winked and rubbed Bataille's belly. The old man started to walk away and Pillow caught him by the elbow.

'Sorry about that wink a second ago, I think it kind of came off like an "I'm fucking with you" sort of thing, but that's not what it was. Once you get in that winking zone it's sort of hard to stop. You feel me?'

Bataille had his hands crossed over his crotch, always waiting for that cosmic ball kick. He winked back without moving any other part of his face and disappeared into the trees.

Pillow closed his eyes and took a long, deep breath. Even though he hadn't been famous in a long time, he couldn't shake the feeling you get when someone is watching and liking you.

Pillow spent most of the next morning sitting against the wall of his bedroom massaging his jaw and temples and periodically covering his eyes with flat hands.

He'd been a chump, but somehow he'd backed into the coins. Everyone but him knew Bataille still had the coins. That was why Breton had gone after Prevert, and why Don had let him stash Artaud, because Artaud just didn't matter. But whatever the route, he was there now. Bataille was ready to give up the coins and nobody else knew about it. Pillow didn't like the idea of sitting around for two days, but there wasn't anything he could do. He just had to wait.

After a while Pillow started thinking about cocaine. He didn't want any. Once he'd run out of money, once the parties stopped being parties, Pillow had actually found it very easy to abstain. He was a good abstainer, in general. The only thing Pillow actually missed about it was the part that most people hated: the part where he was just getting rolling, talking, laying it all out there, and he'd get that hard, slow bloom right in the middle of his chest. And in some isolated top shelf of his brain he could tell, objectively, that he was sad, but he was chemically unable to feel it. He just knew it was there.

Eventually, he got up and ate a fruit salad, blended up some food for Artaud and delivered it, and a little taste of morphine, without waking the guy up. After, he went home and did a punishing set of intervals in the courtyard to relax, during which Avida and Simon showed up.

They were still eating a road lunch. Avida was nibbling at a sandwich and Simon was eating a full roasted chicken, holding one leg in each hand and chewing his way across the breast plate, grease shining off and calling attention to each fold in his face. Pillow bit down hard on his own teeth.

Avida took a final rabbit nibble off the side of her sandwich and then threw it in the gutter. 'Hey there, friend, remember us?'

'How could I forget Captain Wordplay and her pet sea monster? It's about time someone threw that thing back in the water.'

Simon tore a long strip of meat off the chicken's breast. His chewing made a sound that was not exactly one a warthog would make getting fed through a grain thresher. He tapped his lips twice with the top of the chicken. 'We want the coins. We know Costes is looking for them, and we want you to tip us off if he finds them.'

Pillow fought through his intense revulsion and reached a strong, instinctive conclusion. 'All right then, let's get our dicks out, I guess.'

Avida reached into her pants, rummaged around forcefully for a bit, and then theatrically presented an empty, vaguely musky palm. Simon sucked an entire leg clean off the bone.

'You two want the coins, Breton wants the coins. Breton pays me, and you guys *think* you can jam me up. And I'm supposed to give up alllll this –' Pillow threw a long arm across the length of the peeling plastic siding of his apartment complex '– to avoid some trouble you can't even make without giving up your shot at the money.'

Avida ran her finger along length of her nose. She was getting more comfortable. 'We're going to get those coins, and you can help us and get protection, or you can fuck with us and be on our bad side. It's all up to you.'

Pillow shrugged.

Simon tossed the chicken blindly over his shoulder, sucked each of his fingers thoroughly in turn and then walked over and looked up at Pillow. 'I've thought about it some, Pillow. I've realized that you're right. What you said to me before, you were right. You are far too stupid to threaten. So I'll try to explain myself. I'll tell you why I want this money. Let me tell you what my dream is, Pillow. My dream is to buy a little house right on the edge of town. Nothing fancy, just a little house away from all the people and all the noise. And I will fill this house to the brim with cats and high-class, vintage pornography. More porn and more cats than anyone could possibly need or hope to use in a lifetime. Then I'll stay inside that house until I die. That's the dream. That's what I'm working toward. And I will not let you get in the way.'

Avida already had her car door open. She called over to Simon. 'Come on, he's useless. We need to talk to Costes.'

Simon waved her off with two fingers no fatter than elephant legs and turned back to Pillow.

Pillow pulled his head back a little bit away from the grease. 'That's good, man. It's good to dream.'

The fat of Simon's cheek split into two discrete segments as he grinned. 'No, it's not, just necessary.'

After the cops left, two very obvious realizations struck Pillow nearly simultaneously: the first was that he didn't have seven thousand for Bataille yet, and the second was that Bataille was planning to fuck him over, take the seven grand and the coins and run. Why else make it a drop? Why else delay two days when he was being actively pursued by two corrupt cops and a well-connected sociopath with a crew?

It only took one phone call to an underground casino and one phone call to the registrar of the university for Pillow to get the address of Bataille's safe house. Pillow wondered how Breton had missed it, and then he remembered that Bobby Desnos had been one of the main searchers, and that Desnos had spent a lot of the time he was supposed to be searching listening to old radio plays.

There were a lot of little steps involved in the seemingly simple act of going straight to Bataille's safe house. He had to decide to go, then he had to stand, then he had to get his gun from the closet, then he had to open the door and leave his apartment and avoid looking up at Emily's door as he left. Then he had to do all the things you have to do to make cars start and move and stay moving in the right direction. And he did each of these steps knowing that it, and the one before it and the one to follow, were huge mistakes, or at least tiny parts of one huge mistake. But he did them all.

Pillow stood on the porch of Bataille's safe house for a few seconds to get his bearings. The porch itself was a tragedy, as porches go. It looked like someone had tried to shake it to pieces from the middle out. The front door had a thin, plastic frame, but otherwise it was all glass. Pillow looked in, and the corridors seemed empty, as if cigar smoke was around but hiding. The windows to the outside were all painted over a half-opaque white and Pillow could sense the presence of a dog lying down, but couldn't see where it would be. His hand knocked aggressively on the door and Bataille seemed to float into view, swinging smoothly around the corner, like he was skating.

Bataille looked somehow calmer than he had at the slaughterhouse, like he'd given up a few minutes prior. He motioned Pillow in and stood by the door, waiting to close it. Pillow reached up, did two quick pull-ups on the top of the door and loped elaborately into the house, peeking his head around the corner into the living room.

'Could you have picked a creepier place to crash?'

'I was not spoiled for choice.'

Bataille wasn't wearing shoes. Pillow got distracted for a second wondering if he'd ever seen a man that old in sock feet before.

'Are we alone?'

'Yes. In fact, I had planned to be completely alone.'

Pillow dipped to the side of the doorway, next to kind of a nice vase, and came up behind Bataille, rubbing at the combination-lock-sized knots in the old man's shoulders. Pillow guided him to and pushed him down on the sofa. He kept standing behind him, stopped massaging and just kept a grip on the old man's shoulder. 'Tell the cushion where the coins are.'

Pillow felt Bataille take a deep, dipping breath.

'I wanted to talk about that big toe first. You seemed interested.'

Pillow tightened his grip. He had a feeling where it was going. From the old man's voice, Pillow could tell Bataille was smiling.

'The big toe is a genuinely *human* part of the body. It's the part of our bodies least similar to any portion of an ape. This is due to the fact that apes live in trees, and human beings are trees.'

Pillow switched his grip and took hold of the back of Bataille's neck. 'Where are the coins, Georges? I never repeat myself.'

'I don't have them.'

Pillow's stomach finally fell from the sky. The part of the sky so high up there isn't much air left. The part where balloons die. He swung around the side of the couch, pulled Bataille on the floor and dropped a knee onto the middle of his back. 'You weren't looking to sell the coins to Gwynn, you were looking to knock off her stash and leave town. Because Artaud has the coins. It was true. Then you saw me and thought you could get the best of me. Tell me some story, get a few grand and hit the road.'

Pillow eased off and Bataille groped for breath; the carpet was old and thick enough that it belched a puff of dust at him in response. He caught his breath and moved up to his knees.

'You know, you're a little bit smarter than they said you are.'

Pillow felt one bead of cold sweat roll out from every pore in his body. He dropped into a beat-up old recliner, the footrest popping out like a cuckoo from a clock. 'I haven't been this mad in a little while, Georges. And I have a feeling I'm going to get a little bit angrier before you're done talking.'

Bataille was in full-on snitch mode now, tripping over himself to get the story out. 'Yes, but there's more. This was all a couple days before the meeting, and I knew I couldn't tell Breton I'd lost the coins, so I went to Lieutenant Avida. I know her from some of the orgies, and I thought that she was smart and crooked and that she'd help me find Artaud before the meeting. I said I'd give her half the money.'

Pillow gripped the arm of the recliner hard enough that stuffing popped out. Bataille was the leak, he'd fed them the whole deal. 'Why would she take half, Georges? You gave her the whole thing, why would she let you have half when she could just take it all?'

Bataille looked back at the ground, hyperventilating but seeming somehow relieved at the same time.

What Pillow knew, and Georges didn't, was that Avida hadn't just gone for the whole payment. She was trying to double her money. That was why she and Simon had shot first that night at the deal, so they'd catch their own case in homicide. Rip off the deal, find the coins and get paid twice.

Pillow stood up and started pacing. He started thinking about everything he still had to do, everything that needed to be done, and he felt tired. His head was spinning, the way an empty bottle spins in outer space.

Bataille was getting himself together; he settled an arm over his knee and took a couple breaths. He started a laugh that became a cough instantly. Bataille got himself into a runner's stance. 'We enter traps of our own free will. Everyone does.' He made a thin whisking sound with his teeth. 'Breton. He's a real piece of beef, isn't he?'

Pillow saw it coming. He saw what he had to do, but all he wanted was sleep.

Bataille made a try for the front door, getting less than halfway out of the living room before Pillow caught him with a clean left hook.

Pillow had thrown enough punches in his life that there was no longer a conscious thought to doing it. So he didn't totally feel himself swing, and he didn't totally feel the thick, wrong crunch when he caught Bataille on the chin. He was fairly sure he saw the old man drop face-first and land on his neck at a bad angle that Pillow knew wasn't so much a bad angle as it was the worst angle possible, his legs twitching once and then settling at another angle that was even worse. Pillow was fairly sure that he watched Georges Bataille die right then in that shag-carpet hell of a living room. He was still pretty sure about it even after it happened, even after it was just another one of the things he had to try to remember.

Pillow left the body in the living room and went to the kitchen. He used the heavy rotary phone on the wall to call Don Costes, who showed up in what seemed like two minutes but could have been any amount of time. Pillow felt like he'd just taken a long drink of alone water.

Alone water is similar to lemon water, but with a sharp, clawing bleakness squeezed into the water instead of half a lemon.

Don asked what had happened, and Pillow told him that he'd seen Bataille at the grocery store and followed him home. Pillow stared at a fridge magnet stylized to look like a really surprised panda as he talked, so he wasn't sure if Don believed him at all. He didn't really care, but some part of his brain knew he should.

Don started rubbing Pillow's back like he was burping a baby. 'Easy, easy, easy, buddy. It's easy, okay? Breton and I will take care of this, and you go home now and see Emily. All right? See her and don't talk about this. I'll smooth it over with Breton, and we'll get rid of the body. You tried your best. It's easy now.'

Pillow thought, but wasn't entirely sure, that the panda on the fridge smiled at that. 'Yippee.'

The kitchen glowed in the sick, buzzing yellow light of a fixture that needed to be replaced.

Don waved a hand in front of Pillow's face. 'Do you have the coins? Did he tell you where they were?'

Pillow figured he was committed by now. 'No.'

'Did he tell you anything about where he kept them?'

'No, he just ran for it, and I ... I don't know, man, it was just an instinct. I didn't ...'

Don shushed Pillow, pulled him standing, walked him to the front door and, pretending Pillow was wearing a collared shirt, fixed the shirt and straightened Pillow's imaginary tie.

Pillow felt that, since he'd strongly considered crashing his car into a bridge pylon on the way home, he was doing a pretty great job of seeming emotionally present as he and Emily spooned and chatted on the couch. Her couch was a cheap and very hard one, so she took the keys out of her jean pocket and threw them in the loud, shiny prayer bowl where she'd started keeping her change. She wiggled around a little bit until the two of them were settled.

'Have you met Matt? From my work.'

Pillow briefly paused in molesting her shoulder blades and thought. 'Oh yeah, he was nice.' He figured that was probably true.

'Did Matt tell you about his puberty thing?'

'What? No.'

'He didn't start hitting puberty until he was eighteen.'

'That's fucked up.'

'That's what I said, except I'm less coarse than you so I just made a sympathetic sound. But yeah, I made my sympathetic sound and he said: "It's cool. It just means I'll live longer."'

'Does it?'

'That's what I said! Yeah, so I go, "Really?" and he shrugs and goes, "I dunno, but that would seem fair."'

Pillow considered this. 'A guy whose balls didn't drop until he was eighteen who still believes in fairness. That's special. That's fuckin' … that's Komodo dragon rare.'

She nodded in a way that made him imagine her drawing a checkmark. 'Wooooo. Okay.' She touched her eyebrows. 'We have one last issue to deal with. Then that's it. The rest of life. Whoosh.'

'Whoosh?'

'That's the sound the rest of life makes. Whoosh. Yes. The issue: I know you think you're sort of hot shit at intimacy, but you're a very humpy cuddler.'

'I was hoping you'd think that was more of a gentle rocking.'

'You can't pull the wool over these eyes. I know a thorough humping when I feel it against my bum.'

'Understood. No more cuddle-humping.'

She rolled back onto the couch and pulled his hands around her.

'That's not what I said. It's like anything, just cut back by about a third and it'll be copacetic.'

Pillow closed his eyes tight and tried to level out his breathing. Life was starting to feel like a pair of pants four sizes too big, sliding further down his hips with every step.

Pillow ran over to the Bureau at a good enough clip that it pushed most thoughts past breathing out of his mind. He hit the front door hard with his shoulder, grinning into the pain and pirouetting into the main room.

As he righted himself he saw Don and Bobby Desnos. Bobby was clapping with his hands raised above his head. Don threw his cigarette into a corner of the room blind, giving him a disgusted once-over.

Pillow sidled up to Don, pulled his bow tie askew. Don didn't even look at him. 'Why thanks, fellas, that was encouraging. You ever thought about personal training?'

Bobby stopped clapping and hooked his thumbs through his belt loops. 'Training isn't training unless it's personal. And learning isn't learning unless you're already mostly dead.' Desnos seemed to get distracted by something above him. 'Good day, Sadness, you are inscribed on the ceiling.'

Pillow was still trying to figure out a whole lot of things more important than whatever Desnos was saying. 'So what's shaking?'

Bobby Desnos cast a sweeping, druggy stare around the room. 'Everything.'

Don jumped in. 'Breton needs to see you.'

'Okay.' Pillow pinched Desnos's cheek. 'I'll catch you later, Bobby.'

Bobby looked six feet past Pillow's eyes.

'Yeah, good to see you too, Robert.'

Pillow and Don walked down the hallway in silence. They entered the room as Breton was polishing a large stick-man candelabrum.

Don peeled off and stood beside the door. Pillow wouldn't have said Don was careful about hiding the gun bulge in his waistband, but he wouldn't have said Don was showing it off on purpose.

Breton stuck his finger up in the air and lowered it. 'Sit.'

Pillow moved to the chair on the left and Breton tsked through his teeth.

'No. Your chair is over there. Sit down.'

Pillow couldn't help laughing at that one. He sat down. 'Subtle. So, I found Bataille. I was buying food and I saw him in the parking lot, and I followed him back there. I figured if I brought him to you,

I could make things right after everything with Louise and all. It was an accident. But I was going to bring him to you.'

Breton allowed a pause so long some species would have called it a hibernation; some others would have called it their whole lives. Don's dry swallow was audible from a couple oceans away. Finally Breton uncrossed his legs and he moved his head, sunset slow, down to meet Pillow's eye line.

'The important thing to know is that we are lost in time, in the second before us – in all senses of *before*, a word that may be cast forward or back with equal ease. You underestimate me to think I am so invested in either planning or perfection. Truth is only and always found in the unrehearsed moment. Accidents are the engine that help this world spin. What I object to is your planning. You have three things to answer for. The first is that you did not call for the help of a person more blessed with good judgment. The second is that you have cost us our best avenue to find the coins, reducing an artful, lived detective novel to another spoiled child's birthday-party treasure hunt. The third is that you wasted my and Don's fucking time. Time is beyond price.'

'Okay, you're right. I thought he had the coins and I wanted to get them, but I was going to bring them in. I don't know shit about coins. I just ... Fuck, man, you know how much money I make. I'm almost forty, I'm a brain-damaged high school dropout, and I need to make it happen. That's why. I knew you'd make me pass it off and I wanted a real share of that money. What else could I do?'

Breton leaned back smiling. 'I know I might seem, at times, severe. I know that I have often been curt with you, and I will continue to be, because I am curt with idiots, even useful ones. All my life I have tried not to allow utility to limit my behaviour. I am a callous man, but not without some understanding. One chance. I am giving you one chance to, if there is anything else going on, unburden yourself. All will be forgiven, and our arrangement can continue. If there is nothing to reveal, reveal nothing. If there is something and you keep it from me ... then you will have ceased to be a part of my community. One's community is the group of people one wishes to keep alive.'

Pillow didn't really have time to wonder if Breton was telling him the truth, and he didn't have time to wonder if Breton already knew about Apollinaire. Fortunately, none of that mattered: his answer was going to be the same either way. He looked Breton in the eyes. 'I'm telling the truth.'

Don piped in from the corner. 'And you really killed Artaud? He's dead?'

Pillow turned to look at him. He nodded.

Breton looked at Pillow with his head tilted to one side. 'You were correct, Mr. Costes. Pillow, you will now follow instructions, and should you have another brainstorm, you will talk to Don about it. I sincerely hope this is the last time we speak of anything so tediously unpleasant.'

Breton stood and Pillow stood with him. Breton didn't bother raising his head to look at Pillow's face as he continued.

'You are in debt, again. And your debt this time may be paid by someone else ending this matter completely. You are to do nothing. If Don somehow finds the coins, your slate shall be cleaner than, and just as empty as, your mind.'

Pillow nodded. 'Okay.'

Breton paused a minute, and finally looked up at Pillow's face. 'Tell me, Pillow, are you able to visualize a horse galloping on top of a tomato?'

Pillow closed his eyes. 'Yup.'

'How?'

'Really big tomato or really small horse.'

Breton laughed and clapped him on the shoulder. 'Then I owe you an apology. You are not an idiot, you are something else. What is admirable about the fantastic is that it is so similar to the basest aspects of reality, too true to do anything but exist. You would do well to remember that.'

'I'd do well to remember to lock my fucking front door, but we all know how that turns out every day.'

Breton was still laughing as Pillow left the office. Don followed Pillow to the door. He pointed to his own eye, then his heart, and then at Pillow, then he stopped, straightened his bow tie and closed the door behind him.

Pillow could hear Breton laughing the whole way down the hall.

After a lot of very long hours trying to sleep, Pillow finally accepted that he needed help. The only person he really had left to trust about the coins was Gwynn. Crossing the street to her apartment, Pillow's attention was arrested by a long, thick stream of steam coming out of a vent. He stopped in the middle of the road and watched it rise and dissipate. Placing his hand over it, feeling the heat and the moisture gather, he felt no curiosity about where it came from or why nobody else was watching. Pillow felt that a car should have come by now, and he wondered why he never seemed to be in anyone's way. Nobody ever asked him to move, or bumped him, or pushed him. He thought about all the people he'd grabbed around the waist and moved, and only just then did it occur to him that most people asked first. They didn't just put hands on someone. Steam was pushing out of the ground so hard in such a tight bundle, disappearing a few feet off the ground. People say that steam doesn't disappear, it just dissolves into the air, becomes a part of it. Pillow knew it couldn't be true. Things are usually just gone, and people will do anything to deny that fact.

Gwynn looked sort of like a ghost moving into the street from the alleyway. Her skin seemed looser, giving off a strong unused vibe. She stood up straight, her long, thin nightgown blowing in the breeze. 'How slow a life is, how stunningly violent a little fiction called hope would be.'

Pillow moved his hand out of the steam but stayed standing where he was. At night, Gwynn seemed smaller, quieter. He looked down at the seeping soak of steam creeping up the fibres of his sleeve.

'Did you want to talk to me about something?'

Pillow looked back at Gwynn. He remembered crowds, and cut men, and referees. He remembered having his face touched, his legs rubbed, he remembered ice on his spine. These were all things he had to remember, because he didn't know them by heart. He knew his heartbeat and the way pavement looks when you're running. He knew sunrises and canvas and the length of his own arm.

'On second –' Pillow closed his eyes and smiled. 'On first thought, I don't need to bother you. I'll … Things you just have to get done you should probably do alone.' He moved his hand back over the steam.

A while later he opened his eyes, saw an empty street, and black where he knew an alley was.

By the time he got home, Pillow felt strangely confident. He had the best line on the coins, and nobody knew it. His plan just might work. He felt so good that he forgot about the time and accidentally woke Emily up by knocking on her door at three a.m.

She opened the door, turned around and set to pulling the large chunks of crust out of her eyes. 'Are you okay?'

Pillow was now feeling a little embarrassed but still quite good. 'Yes! I'm perfect. I'm perfect.'

Emily squinted over at him. 'Well, then you're a jerk. I was soooo asleep. I was literally bathing in a thick soup of melted chocolate. That's what I was doing when you knocked on my door. Drinking it up.' She closed her eyes and made an abstract sucking shape with her mouth, rolling her head around sleepily. 'Do you have any chocolate? I ate mine. I ate all of it.'

Pillow moved over to her and dropped to his knees. He looked up at her.

'What's the deal, baby?'

'I had a thought, and it was one that I would keep to myself. That I've been keeping to myself, and this time I wanted to tell you. I used to have this idea that there are two types of people in the world: people who do great things, and people who *are* great things. And always, as long as I can remember, I thought if I worked hard enough, if I cheated enough, if I loved it enough, I could do great things. And then all of a sudden I couldn't. Maybe I could have, but I didn't. But it's been, it's been so fucking long since I lost it, and in that whole time I never once thought I could be a great thing. A person you like as a person, instead of a person who does things you like. You make me feel like a great thing. I don't, I'm not all the way there yet, and I'm probably not done fucking up yet, but I can kinda see the shape of that now. And I might be stupid. I am stupid. But nobody is dumb enough to fuck something like this up.'

Emily put her hands on his jaw, leaned down as if to kiss him and blew a full hard breath into his mouth.

When Pillow entered the room, Artaud stood on the bed and started swinging the stick in a wide, uneven pattern. Pillow ducked down, waited out a circuit and then snatched the stick. Artaud feebly moved after him and Pillow set him back down with a shove. He was going to take the stick away. Not everyone can be trusted with sticks.

'Hey, you get this back after you talk to me. Do you remember what I told you? About our deal? Okay. New deal, you don't get your stick back until you talk to me.'

Artaud had obviously snorted all the pills Pillow'd left for him; he held the pen rock-steady in one hand.

I remember, Pillow.

I remember well. And I appreciate everything you are doing for me. Seeing your blood at stake was all the guarantee I needed to share the tender of my soul with you, the coins of my being.

It is of the utmost urgency that I leave this corner of the life. Just yesterday, looking out my window I saw a bird emerge, as if birthed from the trunk of a tree. It took off gloriously, and then fluttered clumsily. As if a large circle of its wing had been punched out, chewed on and then reconstituted into the overall structure of the wing.

I am eager to go to Mexico, and to explore South and Central America in general!

Ayahuasca is a most illuminating and therapeutic experience. Perhaps another such treatment is enough to cure my current psychic ailments, which I put down entirely to a case of bad nerves.

I am eager! My soul feels already refreshed!
I embrace you affectionately,
Antonin Artaud.

P.S. I must have my stick back. Her importance is vast enough to be obscure, even to herself. Love, ultimately, slobbers and weeps its hot, invigorating tears into the assholes of even the mightiest.

Pillow put the letter aside. He grabbed Artaud behind the neck and pulled Artaud's forehead to his. Artaud probably wouldn't need the coke to get talking.

'We're going to figure the whole thing out.'

Artaud jerked abortively toward the walking stick. Pillow held him rooted to the bed with one arm.

'You tell me what I want, and I think about giving you the stick back, okay? *After* I have what I want.

Pillow felt Artaud's head nod against his and he slipped back over to his bag. He pulled the food out and started breaking it down as Artaud kept writing. When he was done he dropped the straw in from a height and it bobbed a little before it settled. Artaud couldn't move his head too much, so he rolled onto his front to drink breakfast. Pillow read.

The time has come to sober up, to drink some food and to sit in front of a window closed against the morning's spinning rays, and to make myself fleetingly and imperfectly clear.

All I ask is that you remember how deeply I sighed before doing so.

There were no windows in the room. Artaud took the paper back and kept writing, but didn't quite manage a sigh. Pillow waited for him to finish and slipped into half a sleep. He dreamed about caves. He dreamed about water running through the pitch black, about sounds echoing off walls he couldn't see a foot in front of him.

The address Artaud gave him was for a church. It was a really old one, and was now just used as a soup kitchen. There were tunnels running all underneath it, and apparently Artaud had found himself a little nook and taken to living there. There was a manhole in the church parking lot, and after a quick look around, Pillow climbed in. He had to crouch down to get through the drainpipe, but when the tunnel opened up the ceilings got very high and the passage was wide. Pillow shone his flashlight down the hallway and made out a room. Artaud had a whole set-up ready, oil lamps all the way around the room, and Pillow went around lighting them one by one.

The room glowed dimly in all its creepiness. There were random beakers half-full of liquids Pillow knew better than to guess at. A rope hammock was tied up across the room, and the whole place was lined with trunks. The coins were apparently stashed on a shelf, hidden in the bottom of a broken snow globe. Because it was broken, the thing now just looked like a tiny castle on a wooden stand. Pillow turned it over and found the box. He took the case in his hands and pressed it hard into his forehead. Finally. He had the coins. And nobody knew, not even Gwynn.

Pillow walked over to the hammock, sat down and opened the thing. He could smell stale sweat mixed with the smell of rope, and something somewhere rotting. The coins; the whole thing. They just looked like quarters. Really, really old quarters.

Pillow shrugged, not knowing what he'd been expecting these coins to look like. He took them each out of the box and flipped them, all four heads. Looking at them now, printed in metal, Pillow didn't feel bad for the backward centaurs. Their arms weren't great considering they were legs, but they looked great as arms. Well and evenly defined, like a discus thrower's arms. And they all had great posture. The kind of posture that bought you a little respect when you entered a room. Pillow put them back and closed the box again, tucked it into his pocket. After all that, even with the coins right there, it was still all imaginary. Nobody else even knew he'd won.

Pillow sat on the hammock, rocking gently back and forth, trying to feel like he'd accomplished something. He looked around the room, wondering how the trunks got so filthy. He did not consider himself to be a particularly accomplished interior designer, but at least he'd done better than this place. Pillow then considered how sad it was to congratulate himself on keeping his apartment tidier than a paranoid-schizophrenic priest's underground hideout.

With all the excitement, Pillow had totally forgotten to give Artaud his stick back. Usually, forgetting things upset Pillow, but he was in a good mood. The whole afternoon evaporated when he entered the empty room. He more saw himself go through the motions of checking under the bed, kicking a hole in a wall and pretending that Artaud would ever have been there when he got back than he felt them. His smile set a personal record for insincerity as he realized that this was the first time he'd left Artaud unchained. The lunatic had plastered a note to the door with bloody snot and some pus.

Dear Pillow,

Although I suspect you empathize with me on some level, I also suspect that your kind looks are contingent on your ascribing a 'gentleness' to my soul that does not, in fact, exist. You, sir, have one foot sunk in the grave of kindness and the other nestled in the wondrous incubation chamber of cruelty. I know for a fact that you do not have as clear an understanding of cruelty as a person so violent should. So I am leaving your care.

I once thought you my friend, but the fact that you pried the only object of any meaning from my arms shows you to be a monster of custom and shallowness who thirsts for the sweet, heated milk of my pain.

You know as well as I do that the walking stick belongs, coincidentally, to St. Patrick, and was once the property of Satan himself.

You must be aware of how true and trenchant my love for that walking stick is.

I am obliged to return my beloved to its homeland, Ireland. I have singlehandedly cured all my many ailments, and I have done it with the power of my conviction, and with the ferocity of my energy. I need your feeble caretaking as much as I shall need a stiff breeze across my back when I emerge from the water, having swum across the entire Atlantic Ocean.

I have a mission on this earth, a mission simply to love as only milky blood can love corruption.
A.A.

Pillow folded the note and put it in his pocket. He counted the ways he hadn't fucked up on one hand.

Getting back in the car, Pillow paused to look at the walking stick. He reached over and pulled it into his lap. It had a nice texture to it, you had to say that, but it really wasn't much to look at. The stick was carved out of deeply knotted wood, it had all sorts of weird knobs and bumps along the side, and it was stained a putrid yellowish brown. The handle was weirdly big, a bit larger than could comfortably fit in Pillow's palm. It had grotesque mini-knots curving all the way back into it and was sort of fractured, the splits in the wood palpable as he held it, that chunk of Artaud's lip still stuck fast.

Pillow sighed. He spoke to the cane.

'Well, sweetheart, seems like you made an impression.'

The walking stick stayed silent.

Pillow didn't call ahead before he went to Gwynn's. She tsked three times over the intercom and buzzed him up. As Gwynn opened her door she reached up and pulled Pillow's lips forcefully together. 'Shut your mouth before you open it. It's always an important thing to do.'

'I'll give you the good news first.'

Gwynn waited. 'Before somebody starts to smell my dead body, Pillow.'

Pillow dropped to one knee and whipped out the coins. 'I found them.'

Gwynn clapped once and opened the box. She looked at it for a few seconds, then handed the box back and tented her hands. 'Well, you certainly do know how to make even the most jaded old lady's heart skip the odd beat, don't you, Pillow? But I've been around long enough to know that good news first means bad news to come.'

'I'm in big fucking trouble with Breton and Don. I was supposed to kill Artaud, but he knew where the coins were, so ...'

'So you stashed him and he got away.'

'So I stashed him and he ran away because he fell in love with that fucking walking stick.'

'Story checks out. I maybe should have seen that coming.'

'*Should* you?'

'What's your plan?'

'Find him.'

'That's not a plan, my friend, that's a goal.'

Pillow bounced the coin box between his hands. The reality of the coins hadn't really hit him until he saw Gwynn react to them. It was a trick Pillow had been relying on for most of his life: pick a person you trust and watch them take it in. He'd watch their body react to it, see their eyes twitch this way or that, and that would tell him most of what he should think of the situation. Gwynn pinched a strand of his hair and pulled it straight.

'If you want my advice, just remember what I've always said: one can't just keep carrying one's father's corpse around *everywhere*.'

Pillow stood up and walked over to the window. Gwynn's condo was at that height where people look the size of really big dogs. 'How long until you can get your buyer in line?'

'A few days. Should you get out of town?'

Pillow reached up and ran his fingers down the glass, leaving distinct smudges trailing down the freshly clean glass. 'I can look after myself. Just talk to your buyer. I want this all to be over.'

Pillow heard Gwynn stand and shuffle over, stop a couple feet behind him.

'I thought that too. That I wanted the action to stop, that if I could only rest I would be happy. I thought I would be kind, calm. And then I rested for a few years. I entertained myself with a whole wild life full of memories. But no matter how much you *did*, if you sit around long enough anyone will realize that memories are just hunting horns whose sound dies in the wind.'

'Who hunts with horns? That shit's crazy wrong anyway. Say, Gwynn, just say, you were looking for a crazed priest on a love-quest for a cane, where would you start?'

She tapped him on the back, took his arm and led him to the door. They hugged. Pillow closed his eyes and craned his head down to rest on her shoulder.

'When people wanted to make a machine that could walk they used hard circles as the legs.'

Pillow snorted and grabbed Gwynn in a gentle headlock, tousled her hair, sending it out in wide, spraying wisps. 'Thanks for the help there, Advice Column McRiddlebook.'

She pushed her way out of Pillow's arm and kicked him hard in the shin. 'How did you know my maiden name?'

Pillow didn't put the coins away when he first got home. The only sure way he knew not to lose things was to keep them in his pocket forever. He went to wash his hands and he ended up, basically, playing in the sink for a long time. Pillow was watching the water run pleasantly over his hands and down the drain, feeling the cold slide across his skin, when he remembered Emily's storage key. He hid the coins in the red-model-train box at the bottom of the giant model pile. He looked at the box for a long time, repeated the words 'bottom box' three times, then he left.

Pillow knew for a moral certainty that each minute passing without telling Emily about what he was doing was another minute of fucking up so badly he might not be able to fix it. But he kept not telling her, for hours and days on end. It was a sensation Pillow was familiar with, knowing that he'd made a horrible initial mistake and then just letting it keep going. In fact, Pillow had been sporadically feeling that way since that day when he was sixteen and his coach had frankly and clearly explained the long-term consequences of a career in boxing. It had faded in and out for years, and had disappeared pretty much completely when he'd been making a lot of money and Mike Tyson had been telling him how fun it was to watch him, and the girls he'd been staring at all his life had started propositioning him in hotel lobbies and at signing events. After Solis, that feeling had been so present that Pillow would not have called it a discrete feeling so much as he would have called it the way living his whole life seemed.

Mistakes. It all came down to mistakes, and he'd made so many that he could never fix. Artaud was loose and dangerous, Pillow had no idea how long moving the coins would take, the cops were on him and he was sure he'd been playing that wrong. Somehow he knew he needed to think really hard now. To make a game plan, but he was thinking too slowly, and the faster he tried to think, the more confused he got, and the more confused he got, the more he went back to thinking about Bataille. It took him a really long time to adjust to the light when he re-opened his eyes, and his vision stayed blurry even after he'd gotten used to it.

Pillow still had some of the coke from Gwynn, and an emergency OxyContin he'd been keeping for Artaud. He crushed up the pill and mixed the powder up with the coke. He leaned right into it and came up smiling, one hand plastered over his eye. His dreary, off-white apartment took on a vague bioluminescence. He stood up and moved around to do some thinking.

After a couple minutes he grabbed a pencil and started a chart on his wall. The coins were in the middle, the people were on the outside. All the people had shaky lines pointing to the coins, and haphazardly to each other. Pillow was trying to keep track of who knew what and when, who did what to whom and when. He got all the information down, but he didn't have the order, and soon the wall became a confused mess of lines and scratches.

When he stepped back from the flow chart, he still had his sense of humour, so he laughed awhile, rubbed his eye and wiped the wetness off on his pants. Then he started shadow boxing.

Even shadow boxing, Pillow threw more feints than he did punches, and he spent about twice as much time flashing tricky footwork as he did settling down and throwing. So he moved around his living room, eyes on his shadow, ignoring the tentative knocking on the front door until it went away as he kept faking out the wall. He did that until he'd soaked his clothes with sweat, and then he took the clothes off and went into his bedroom. He got under the covers and twitched slowly toward sleep.

Pillow thought about the time when things had been simple, when the whole world had just been waking, working and sleeping. Pillow thought about whales and thumbs and oil lamps. Pillow thought about balloons leaking air. Pillow thought about running in sand. Pillow thought about rental properties and tiny trust funds and owning a corner store. Pillow thought about a lot of things he should have done when he'd had a million dollars lying around. Pillow thought about baskets and benches and getting away clean. Pillow thought about claws and coffee cups and monkeys holding hands.

Pillow thought about choking on water.

Pillow didn't so much wake up very late the next day as he woke up at a normal hour and stared at one spot on the floor for a very long time. By the time he got over to Emily's she had already eaten breakfast (and a small second breakfast).

Before he managed to say anything she put one flat hand on his chest and said, 'First off, fuck you. Secondly, I work, and this is my day off. And if I start with you I'm going to be mad and stressed out all day. I want to have fun, and I don't want to fight with you, I don't want to nag you, and I don't want to pressure you. I want to chill out. But you listen to me, son, and I will give you this space. Way more than is, honestly, reasonable. So you handle your stuff, and you get no excuses. Just deal with it. I'm going to get a lot more pregnant, and then you're going to be around a normal amount and you're not going to randomly disappear, or you're not going to be around at all. I'm fine on my own, and I don't need anything, I just want you to care and show it. That's it.' She took a long, uneven breath and reset her face into a smile. 'Now, you need to hit this instep. You take that thumb and you dig it the fuck in. I'm no bed of roses, you're not going to crush my petals, just hit it hard.'

She moved backward into the bedroom and flopped on the bed with her foot straight up in the air. Pillow grabbed the foot.

'Ooooohhk. Oooooohhhk. Yeah, you can stay.'

After what was, objectively, a pretty great foot massage, Pillow put his hand up to give her a high five, and Emily just rested her head softly in his palm.

Pillow attempted to shape Emily's pubic hair into a primitive faux-hawk (the attempt actually made the hair look less like a faux-hawk than it had in the first place).

'You should be a pubic-hair model.'

Emily was scanning the ceiling with her eyes, for nothing in particular. 'You should be a pubic-hair stylist.'

Pillow moved his head back and examined his work with a stylist's discerning eye. 'Uhh, maybe not.'

Pillow smeared his eyes across her belly. 'What a nice stomach you have.'

'Yeah, well enjoy it now, 'cause I'm going to get soooooo fat, and it's all your dick's fault! I already have you sucked in, you can't get out now, so I'm going to get extra fat, unreasonably fat, to punish you. I don't know if you're aware of this, but you have some pretty serious body-image issues.'

'You're not going to follow through on this.'

'What? You think it's hard to do? Look outside, buddy. In some cultures it's a sign of prestige. I'm going to get wealthy fat. Corpulent.' She stuck her belly out as far as she could.

'I love you. And I would love you if you were a cow.'

'A cow like how my grandma calls other mean old ladies a cow, or a cow with spots and like twelve teets?'

'The one with all the tits.'

'Mooooooooooooooooooooooooooooooooooooooooooooo.'

'I love you.'

She looked him in the eyes and nodded soulfully. 'Mooooooooo ooooooooooooooooooooooooooooooooooooooo.'

Artaud was a man with very serious needs, so Pillow figured the way to find him was to put the word out to heroin dealers and hospitals. He spent the last of the afternoon dropping in on dealers and some receptionists at the sketchier hospitals, carefully avoiding mentioning Artaud's name.

A person less reliant on physical intimacy than Pillow probably would have spent the whole day looking for Artaud instead of starting the search in the late afternoon with his muscles pleasantly tired and relaxed and his outlook on life warmed and softened with affection.

Pillow was aware of that, but he figured that the only way he would win was to do his unique best. There were always stronger, faster and smarter people, but none of them did things exactly the way he did. When he'd been doing camps that was what he'd always told the kids: the only thing you're guaranteed to be better at than everyone else is being your own stupid, strange, probably inadequate little self. Somebody else is probably a little bit better at everything else. Even at the peak of his fame, Pillow had not been a particularly popular guest coach at youth camps.

Pillow was confident he could find Artaud. After all, it was fairly easy to spot and remember a half-dead lunatic in a priest's outfit with his jaw dangling off his face. The problem for Pillow was that he didn't just need to find Artaud, he needed to find Artaud without word getting back to Breton that he was looking.

After he'd finished his rounds, Pillow bought and threw out a large salad, sat in his car for a few minutes and decided to call it a day.

By the time Pillow saw Don it was too late to turn around. Costes was leaning heavily against the gate of the apartment complex, lazily bouncing his left foot against the joint of the hinge. Pillow pulled up short, letting his hand float a bit above his head to block the sun.

'Is that an autograph seeker?'

Don shifted the large vaguely gun-shaped bulge in his coat pocket to point at Pillow. He used his other hand to play along the length of his scar. 'Have I ever told you why I don't like making out with guys?'

Don kept his hand firmly in his bulging coat pocket. He stood up straight and continued. 'The problem with making out with guys isn't that I'm massively heterosexual or anything. As an idea, I like it. But once you get past the idea, and you're actually doing the thing … it's sort of nice. I mean, it's kissing. But it's a very alienating geography, a man's body. With women, there's a general terrain you're navigating. Places to go, things to do. With a man it's just torso, and these, like, these chest muscles. It feels really empty and barren, but there's also this heft to a man's torso. And then there's a dick, and it just sticks right out at you. It points at you. Like it's asking you a question that needs to be answered right now. Right whenever.'

The setting sun slipped through Pillow's fingers and caught him in the eyes. He looked back to Don with black spots dancing around the edges of his vision. He knew it still wasn't his turn to talk.

'So that's what I was thinking about today, Pillow. I was sitting at the Bureau, taking calls from every heroin dealer in town, and I was cursing my past self. I was thinking that if I hadn't been an open-minded and generally game twenty-one-year-old boy I wouldn't know for sure that I don't enjoy foreplay with other men. And if I didn't know that, maybe you and I could have made an honest go of it. A nice, smooth, erectionless kiss and grope before you fucked me.' Don took his hand out of the scar and snapped his fingers crisply, the bulge bobbing as he adjusted to lean on the gate again. 'But early discoveries are the black cloud floating over adulthood. Aren't they, Pillow? They follow you around, raining, like in Charlie Brown.'

Pillow dropped his hand, let his vision glow orange under his closed eyelids. 'Does Breton know?'

'If he did we'd both be dead. But the word about Artaud is getting out. You weren't exactly subtle.'

'I'm sorry I lied to you, Don. I was going to get him out of town, got kayo'd there, y'know, got a little scrambled, y'know, and Artaud got away from me, and I need to find him. You realize Breton will kill me, and then he'll go out for lunch.'

Don inched closer. 'He doesn't do that sort of thing on an empty stomach. Lunch first. And it's not you, it's us.'

Pillow heard a slow metallic click in Don's pocket. He raised his hands slowly, laced them behind his head. 'What about transvestites? How's that geography?'

Don smiled and stopped. He finally looked Pillow in the face. 'Well, I'm super picky with transvestites. So they've all been really pretty. But let's see …' Don looked at the ground for a second, gathering his reflections. 'I mean I never really noticed. They tend to keep things sort of tucked and out of the way. They're not huge on their own dicks, generally, in my experience. But yeah, they keep it chill. Not the same vibe.'

'So it's mostly a chest issue. It's an empty-torso thing for you.'

'Yeah, man. Male chest and stomach, where's the juice?'

The two men nodded. Don let out a breath.

'Pillow, I want to help you, but seriously. You have really, really let me down at every point here. Anybody else … I have to ask you. With Bataille, now this … Are you after those coins?'

Pillow closed the gap. Don didn't move. Pillow reached forward and took a hold of Don's face with both hands, pulled Don's eyes close to his. 'No. I'm not. I feel you on this.'

Don pushed himself free. 'You don't feel shit. Do you remember who it was knocked you out? Stuck a gun in my face, you remember?'

'I don't remember any of that.'

'It was the cops, Pillow. Avida, Simon. As if a ski mask … Fucking idiots. Are you getting me? You best not be fucking me here, Pillow. I've known you a long time, but we're playing for the whole thing right now. So tell me now, why all this Artaud trouble, why this cop trouble, if you're not in it for the coins?'

'I just … He has a fouled-up brain. And he can't help it, and I just thought … I thought he needed a break. I wanted to cut someone a break for once.'

'If you have the coins –'

Pillow started to interrupt and Don put a flat finger in his face. 'Listen. Do not talk for a minute, and listen to me. If, *if*, you have these coins I can give you one option. Give them to me and leave town. I'll work it out with Breton, no one will follow you. You'll be safe.'

Pillow gave this some real thought. He worked out exactly how to say it, knowing that giving up on things had never gone that well for him. 'I'm sick, Don. I don't talk about it a lot, but I think about it all the time. My brain is really fucking sick, and chances are it's going to get a lot worse. And I just can't do this stuff anymore. I'm done. I was done years ago. I can't hurt any more people. I'm scrambled. Anytime I try to do something … After Bataille, I just wanted to do something nice. And it bit me. It bit me real hard in the ass. I would give them to you if I could, man. Really, I wish I had them.'

They both laughed in short, awkward bursts.

'But now I just want to go home and be with my girl. I want to quit. And if you help me find Artaud, this last thing, I'll be gone. That's it for me.'

Don looked him over, then he looked at the ground. He popped a thin, empty grin. 'Okay, buddy. But you have to know what I'm risking too. If we find Artaud, he dies. We kill him, and we knock out his teeth, bleach and burn the body, whole nine yards, like we talked about. *Then* you're done. We do not half-ass this thing. You stay home and hug your goddamn pregnant girlfriend and teach some kids to box, and you wait for my call. I will find him. I can't trust you on this anymore.'

Pillow took a long, uneven breath. 'You're right. Just call me when you find him, and I'll come help.'

Don took his hand out of his pocket and stuck it out toward Pillow. 'I'm agreed.'

Pillow smiled wider than owl eyes. 'That's good. The world needs more greeds.'

They shook hands, and everyone's hands kept shaking on their own after they let go.

Since he already had it scheduled, Pillow decided to show up for Kevin's training session. Julio's gym had turned into a decent distraction. Pillow felt all right – he wasn't as nervous or upset as last time, but that was mostly because he didn't get sad when he was pissed off. The kid was late.

The way Pillow thought about it, if you're a fighter, if you're a real prospect, you have the right. You can be late for pretty much anything. Doctors can wait, limos, promoters, reporters, fans. They can all wait for you, and they will. You're the talent. You get there when you feel like it. But you can't be late for training. Because being special isn't free, and if you skip the work, you lose the privileges. The ball and the bounce. And if you're some pissant prospect who hasn't even made it yet, you sure can't be late training with a with a champ, somebody who wasn't nobody in his day.

Kevin ambled out of Julio's office. The pair of them walked up smiling.

'Hey, Pillow, I'm so glad –'

'You're late. Go warm up.'

Kevin smiled up at him, waved it off, like it was his beef to dismiss. 'Sorry.'

'Sorry shit, go warm up.'

Julio patted Kevin on the shoulder and the kid slipped off to get his gear.

'Take it easy, Pillow, it wasn't his fault. I was just talking to him. Catching up, you know?'

Pillow nodded. 'Sure.'

Julio looked at him another few seconds and then walked off. Pillow took a couple breaths, then watched the kid skip for a while. Pretty quickly he couldn't take it anymore. He hopped out of the ring and stood in front of Kevin.

'You're going too high.'

The kid kept skipping. 'I'm sorry, what?'

Pillow caught the rope as it was coming down and snatched it out of the kid's hands.

'You're doing it wrong. You're jumping, not skipping. Look.' Pillow brought the rope over, put it under the kid's nose and pointed to it. 'The rope is this wide, so you don't need to go any higher than a hair over this.'

Kevin fell off a step, this little-boy-wronged smirk on his face. 'What's your problem today? I know how to skip rope.'

'You know how to skip rope pretty good. If pretty good's all there is, then you're perfect.'

The kid dropped the smirk and took the rope back. 'I get it, man, I get your point.'

'I'm not making any fucking point. You're doing it wrong.'

The kid tried to do it the right way after that. Half the time he stepped on the rope.

When it was time for him to watch Kevin spar, Pillow put the kid's headgear on him and told him to go hard but controlled, just show him how he fought normally, nothing fancy. They were supposed to go three rounds, but Pillow could only stomach watching two. He never could stand bad boxing, bum-on-bum violence. For the length of the third round Pillow took to looking out the window with the Filipino flag over it. The light was still shining through, somehow still hot, empty and white through the blue and red. There must have been a leak in the window because in the middle of all the stagnant, sweaty air, beside all the other flat, glowing flags, this one flapped just a bit at the corner, puckering up and down in rhythm with the wind.

Pillow snapped back to attention when Julio shouted over from the other side of the ring. Pillow hopped up the steps and squirted some water in the kid's mouth.

'He's got a decent little punch on him, hey?' Julio nodded at the kid, who was gulping air like he'd just fought a hard eight-rounder. 'I know you like that jab.'

Pillow ignored Julio and talked to the kid as he ducked into the ring. 'Look, you're too slow to be using that shoulder roll.'

Kevin shook his head and spat out his mouthpiece. 'What? I'm fast.'

'You have fast feet and shit footwork. You have the reflexes of a fuckin' blind rhino. You want to see what a real fighter looks like? It'll be the last thing you see, so you best really wanna look.'

Pillow was looking down and sprung his left hand out, slapping the kid flush in the mouth.

'Hey, I wasn't –'

Pillow slapped him with a right. The kid backed off and Pillow followed him.

'You weren't what? Ready? Fuck ready, you should be reacting. This guy here is a tomato can, you should be humiliating guys like him, and he feels fine right now. He thinks he's people.'

Julio shouted up from outside the ring. 'Hey, Pillow, take it easy, man.'

Pillow nodded a few times and started to wave it off, but midway through he stopped the wave and hit the kid in the cheek with a closed fist.

Kevin lunged with a hook; Pillow dipped aside and cuffed him hard behind the ear. As the kid stumbled, Pillow tripped him to the ground.

Julio shouted over from the side, fat little legs struggling over the top rope. 'Enough, Pillow, Jesus, I told you take it easy.'

Kevin was still on the ground and Pillow stepped over his head and out of the ring.

'Kid's too slow.'

Everyone was watching, and Pillow figured he might as well give them a show. He kicked a punching bag and threw a spit bucket against the wall on his way out the side door. He muttered as he walked into fabricless sunshine, shaking out his arms, rotating his neck around.

'Too fucking slow. They always think the tall kids can box, but they're too fucking slow. Like it's all just a long-arm contest.'

His headache was bobbing and tipping around his skull now, like a boat without a pilot. He dug into both temples, waited for it to pass. 'I'll hit him and have my hand back in my pocket before he hits the ground.'

When he got home, Simon was parked out front of Pillow's apartment block, his head lolled over the back of the seat sawing logs. Pillow crept up beside the car, making sure to stay below the windows. He threw the door open and wrapped the seat belt around Simon's neck, choking him as he fished the cop's gun out of his holster and tossed it into the back seat.

Simon let out this long, deep gurgle. He looked a little bit like a strawberry coming into season.

Pillow slacked off on the seat belt, holding Simon's head in place with his other hand. 'Hey, howzit going?'

Simon was too busy unsticking the seat belt from his neck to offer much past a grunt.

'So I've got a plan for us today. For both of us. D'you wanna hear it?'

Simon swallowed hard, nodded.

Pillow dug the seat belt in for a second, then relaxed it again. 'Let's use our words. Tell me you want to hear it.'

Simon rasped it out, blotches of white creeping into his tight, red face. 'I want to hear it.'

Pillow pinched some of Simon's cheek. 'Gold star for you. You're going to promise that you're sorry and you're gonna leave me alone, then I'm going to let you breathe again, then you're going to drive away and go eat a small village for lunch, or whatever the fuck. Then we're both going to appreciate breathing air. Really appreciate it, y'know what I mean? Like our whole lives are yoga classes.'

Simon snorted. He looked a little surprised but not too worried. 'What happens if I don't?'

Pillow pushed in, his nose bumping the round red tip of Simon's. 'I'm an adult and I don't make threats. I'm asking you.'

Simon looked at him another second. The seat belt rustled. 'I'll drive away. But I don't have to promise you shit. You really don't understand, do you? You don't understand any of it.'

'Oh I don't? How's about you explain it to me while I kick you to death in a nearby parking lot.'

'I promise.'

Pillow twisted the belt deep into the cop's neck. Simon started feeding shots into Pillow's abdomen. The guy had hands like plates of meat. Pillow braced his foot against the car and dug in harder. Simon's hand floated up in a vague surrender.

'Like you mean it. Like all the cats and porn in the world depend on meaning it.'

Simon went into long, wracking coughs when Pillow let up. Pillow was waiting for him to finish hacking when he heard the side gate of the apartment creak closed.

Emily was holding her hands a foot away from her eyes, gesturing at covering them. Pillow went to yell, but only ended up sputtering. Emily disappeared behind the bars into the apartment.

A hand not quite the size and weight of a filing cabinet hit him behind the ear, and Pillow's legs went from under him. The car door he'd been leaning against vanished, and Pillow fell, watched the door close a few feet away, and watched the whole car turn the corner looping and slow, the way a car with nothing to worry about turns a corner.

The phone woke Pillow from a deeper sleep than was normal or healthy. Don's voice was bumping through the receiver at him. 'I found Artaud.'

Pillow tried to roll out of bed and only realized how tightly the sheets were wrapped around his ankle as he was already falling.

'Are you okay? Were you still sleeping?'

Pillow pulled himself up to sitting, punched himself lightly in the jaw and picked up the phone again. He looked out the window. It wasn't fully light out, but Pillow wasn't sure if the sun was setting or rising. 'I'm good. I'm good. Where is he?'

'He's holed up on the lakeshore. It's perfect, he's alone. Don't bring anything, I have clean guns. Meet me in that parking garage near yours. We have to get organized.'

'Yeah. I know what you're talking about. How did you –'

'Never mind, we have to roll. See you in twenty.' Don sang the last bit. 'We're almost free, bay-bee!' He held the note until Pillow hung up.

Emily hadn't answered her door the night before and hadn't even pretended to be out. Pillow had leaned into the door listening to her scuff around, cook dinner, wash the dishes. He had a loud knock; she must have heard.

After Don called, Pillow popped back upstairs. He paused over the door, realizing he didn't have time even if she did answer. Pillow kissed the door.

Don had done a few of these. He had a whole checklist. First he'd pack his trunk with ice, because his dumping ground was pretty far out of town and once it gets in there, the smell of human corruption just doesn't wash out. Then he'd line the trunk with plastic bags to catch the blood. Then he'd take three Gravol and drink three cold espressos. Pillow'd already downed his hot and burned his mouth. Don was doing all the preparations himself. He needed them done a particular way.

Don was still telling a very long joke while Pillow paced around behind him, bouncing the heel of one shoe off the toe of the other. He was very sleepy.

'So the nun comes down the staircase, and she turns the corner, and before she even has a chance to scream, her arm is already wrist-deep ...' Don looked up from the trunk. 'Are you still listening, Pillow?'

Pillow waved vaguely in front of his face. 'I lost the thread a while ago, to be honest.'

Don turned the rest of his body and sat on the bumper, the car bobbed a little with his weight. 'Are you okay for this? It's your first.'

Pillow thought it over, then he took to stretching his neck, limbering up his shoulders. 'I did Bataille.'

'You're either playing dumb or taking it really seriously. We both know that a punch gone wrong and a job like this are not even in the same ballpark. You felt it with Artaud, I know you did.'

Pillow started reeling off short uppercuts into the air. He finished and paced a little ways off, then he came back. 'I can do it if this is it. I ain't no punk. I can do whatever I need to, as long as it's the last thing I do, y'know?'

Don walked over and hugged him. His voice caught as he talked. 'You're almost done.'

Don moved back to the car, Pillow bent over and touched his toes. He got a bad head rush as he stood up.

'I can load the guns if you want. You taught me how, remember.'

Don's head was back in the trunk. He spoke without looking back. 'Do you want another joke? It's a short one.'

Pillow shrugged.

'A slice of bread will always land peanut butter side down. Butter both sides and it'll float forever. That's not just a joke either. That's wise.'

It was a smiling rather than a laughing joke, and Pillow didn't fake it. He stood still, getting his equilibrium back. Looking at the plastic-lined trunk, seeing the icepacks and watching Don whistling and carefully checking for holes in the plastic, all at once the whole thing seemed obvious to Pillow. He felt about as stupid as he usually did.

'You all right, Pillow?'

'Yeah, yeah. Just a headache. I'm sure you can guess why.'

Don grunted, lifted one leg off the ground to reach the far corner of the trunk. 'Every night at Mad Love was a fucked-up night at Mad Love.'

'Sure was. What were you even doing there? I forget, as usual.'

Don took an extra second with his head in the trunk and then stood straight. He closed the trunk and started cycling through the keys in his hand, rubbing them together and passing them through with his thumb. 'Just going for a drink. Same as you.'

'Right. Yeah. That was it.'

Pillow couldn't remember what Don had actually told him that night. If he'd told him anything. He hardly ever remembered the details at the exact times he needed them, but he could pay attention right now, size Don up in the moment.

The sizing wasn't going well for Don, who looked about as comfortable as a pie at a food fight. His smile dropped an octave. He almost looked sheepish, standing there running through his keys in his hand, but now it was obvious he was never going to pick one. Pillow started measuring the distance. He took a short shuffle closer.

'Do you ever … I've had one idea for six years now. I was counting this money that … that poor Paul Éluard gave me after I snapped his wrist. You remember? You sent me on that job.'

There was just the sound of keys not getting chosen.

Pillow grinned. 'You sent me on this job and I broke his shit, and he was … I mean, that guy was busted, just, his ass was *busted*. And I had to count the money. To make sure it was all there. And I started counting the money, and I was running through it, looking at it, looking like I was counting it, but really I was just shuffling the bills from the front of my hand to the back. No way to tell them apart, y'know? No numbers.'

Don held Pillow's gaze, his chest puffing raggedly in and out. Don laughed a little. 'Do you want to go now?'

'I didn't tell you the thought. It occurred to me that if, just one time, I could run into a wall, that real sheetrock shit, if I ran into it as fast as I could, with my eyes open, not hesitating a little, that I'd feel perfect. That it would solve all my problems. It would make me feel so much *better*.'

Don laughed again. He shifted his weight around a little, favouring his right side. 'You know what'd happen if you did that, Pillow?'

'I just told you.'

'Nothing. Nothing would happen.'

Pillow looked over Don's shoulder at a cloud between cement pillars. A sheep with no legs. 'You're wrong. The answer is: just about. It's just about nothing.'

'We really have to go now.'

Pillow grabbed Don's arm, stopped him from turning. 'I've got a joke for you.' He waited in silence until Don looked him in the eyes again. 'You've probably heard it before, but that's okay. So a moth walks into a dermatologist's office, and he says, "Doc, I have seventeen seizures a day. Every day." And Doc says, "That sounds horrible, but I'm a dermatologist, you need a neurologist. Why did you come to me?" Moth says: "I don't remember."'

Pillow winked.

'He's telling the truth. He's a moth. His memory ain't shit.'

Don reached for the back of his waistband but Pillow lunged forward in time and knocked the gun across the concrete. Don tried to dig his key into Pillow's eye, tearing a patchy, serrated run across his forehead. Blood dripping numbly down his face, Pillow slipped under Don's arm, got behind him and grabbed his friend's neck. They fell to the ground as Costes flailed and kicked. Pillow kept the choke and cranked harder; Don had lost the keys in the fall but he kept punching the same spot on Pillow's temple. Black dots started creeping in around the edges of his vision, but Pillow held on and kept squeezing until the punches lost their steam, and eventually Don's arm fell limply to the side, and a few seconds later Pillow felt Don's bowels release. He kept holding on after that, hyperventilating the smell through his flat, twisted nose, until his arms failed from the bicep down. Pillow pushed Costes off, got standing and swayed across the parking lot, trying to fling the blood out of his eyes by shaking his head and scooping at it with his hands. He felt his shoulder hit a pillar and he dropped to his knees and started vomiting; he kept at it until he was stringing small bits of bile toward the ground, and eventually he was just belching out half-swallowed air.

His arms were pretty much dead, so he had to roll Don's body along the ground and hoist it up into the trunk with his shoulder. He closed the trunk and spent a while in the front seat of the car, trying to staunch the bleeding from his head with some of the spare pocket squares Don kept in the glove compartment.

Pillow'd finally figured it out: the trunk wasn't being prepared for Artaud. Don was going to lure him out to a secluded spot, and then the boys were going to jump him. Don had probably known the whole time; he'd just been setting him up. They'd dangled Pillow out there for Bataille, and now that he'd killed Bataille and lost Artaud, he wasn't useful anymore.

Pillow squeezed the blood-soaked pocket square into a ball and wished, once again, that horrible people weren't his favourite people. He thought about it another minute and corrected himself. Not horrible people – they were usually bummers – but pleasant people who did horrible things, that was who he liked. He went to tuck the square into his shirt pocket, and then because he didn't have one he dropped it into his lap.

By the time Pillow hit the street, the ground under his feet felt like a huge unfolded newspaper. A woman bounced off his chest and said 'Excuse me,' like he'd just run over her dog or son. He didn't stop walking, but he did a sad, slow circle as he moved, the hot swell of tears crowding around the edges of his eyes.

Seeing an entirely silver man standing on a silver box in the middle of the sidewalk was not something Pillow had been specifically hoping for, but it was something for which he was truly grateful. He stopped and watched the silver arms move stiffly around, and his jaw didn't drop, but he felt his eyeballs relax around the outside.

'Hey, d'you ever find it kind of weird and cool and sad that people pay to look at you? Like you're the Grand Canyon, or all the paintings in a museum.'

The silver man stayed looking straight ahead; he twisted his torso robotically away from Pillow, canted over at the waist and then pulled himself back up straight, like he was being turned by a crank.

'I don't know how much time I spent being watched for money, like in minutes. But it might be actual years' worth of minutes. In the gym, in the fights, people watched me, and they paid. If you put it all together, which, I'm finding out, always happens. It all gets put together, added up on you. And then you deal with it, and then that's what real life is like. What I'm saying to you, man, is people pay to look at you, and the Grand Canyon's a big hole in the middle of the desert, and there's a river and a shit-ton of flowers at the bottom of it. There's people who posed for paintings, but it's different to be a hole in the desert, or a tower that's keeled over a little, or a real person standing there sucking air. It's just different. Y'know what I'm saying? You feel me? Y'know what I'm saying?'

The silver man stopped robot dancing and stepped off his block like a real person. He bent over like a real person and grabbed a few coins out of his bucket, then he stepped over to talk. He touched Pillow's arm, which Pillow didn't like.

'Hey, dude, I appreciate you taking an interest, but I'm doing a show here? It's a show, and I can't have you talking and distracting people.' The silver man pressed coins into Pillow's hand, which Pillow hated quite a lot. 'Get yourself some food, bud. I think you've had enough tonight.'

Pillow looked at the silver face and when the silver face looked back, he saw that the eyes were deep brown. Not silver. This man wasn't silver. He was pretending. The busker stepped back onto his block and snapped immediately into an extended running-man dance.

Pillow set himself and threw the coins into the air overhand, then shouted over at the busker. 'Hey, I'm not drunk, man. It's just how I talk sometimes. I'm not drunk. You hear me, I'm not drunk, and I ain't no bum either. You need to look at where you're at. Motherfucker begging for coins calling me a bum. I've never been a bum. Not for a second. You hear me? Where you at, motherfucker? Where you at?'

The silver man dropped his arms like the skin-wearing pinkish thing he really was under the paint. 'Listen, dude, I'm sorry. I don't want any trouble, I didn't mean to upset you. I just want to do my show.'

Pillow nodded, waving his hand vaguely in apology, then looking at the ground. He sensed but didn't see the busker breaking back into his silent robot bit. Pillow stayed looking at the ground a second, letting the scene settle down a bit.

He didn't hurry over to the change bucket, and he didn't feel himself kick it, but both he and the robot-imposter watched it move in a tall spinning arc over the street before landing and getting skittered aside by the glancing blows of tires as it spit coins across the pavement.

Pillow's hands were already extended over his head, and his lips were already curled back by the time the busker was off his box and out of character again, his silver neck showing its tendons, his silver face twisted into a shout.

'What are you doing?'

The mime got closer, and Pillow sensed the range and snapped a crisp jab into the busker's face. 'Do you think this is talent? You mother-raping panhandler. You think this is talent?'

The busker was stumbling backward with his hands out behind him, anticipating concrete. The smudge of bare skin on the busker's cheek only made Pillow angrier, and he walked forward with his hands at his sides.

'Makeup cunt. Where you at?' Pillow skipped forward and kicked the busker's foot out from under him. The man fell to the pavement and jumped up three-quarters off balance. Pillow kept moving forward and shoved the mime down again. The mime tried to get up again, and Pillow pushed him down twice more. He couldn't really tell what he was shouting and what was coming from the crowd anymore. He could hear the fake-robot saying *Okay* over and over, but he wasn't sure what was being agreed to. The mime finally stayed down, and as Pillow pulled his foot back to kick him, someone from the crowd tried to grab Pillow around the shoulders. He spun away from the touch without his balance and tripped over the mime's prone body, tumbling toward the street. Pillow was halfway toward righting himself, still pulling himself up to stand straight, when the mirror of a high-riding truck doing sixty hit him in the side of the head, and he slipped back down the long black hallway he was getting so used to.

3

drinking some hot tea

Pillow woke up in a white room he'd never seen before with Avida's face an inch from his. It took him a few seconds to recognize her.

'So, the mime isn't pressing charges.'

Michael Simon was standing in the corner aggressively digging some lint out of his belly button; he was not using a lot of very complicated mining equipment to reach it. 'What are you talking about?'

Avida stood back up and slapped his arm, she gave a few stage laughs. 'Oh you kidder, you. Pretending you don't remember bullying a lowly busker, pretending you don't know where the coins are. Where is they, Pilla? Last call.'

Pillow tried to think. His lips were dry. 'I don't understand what … Just tell me what you're talking about.'

'You're really quite a bummer. You know that, right?'

Pillow went to hit her, but his arm felt like it had been crushed by a cinder block some years ago. She ducked back.

'You've lost a step. Haven't you? Well, keep us in what you've got left of a mind, Pillowslipping.'

'Get out, get out, get out, get out, get out.'

They were already gone. Pillow tried to get his bearings. He closed his eyes and felt the room spin in a tight, diagonal arc, as if his head were a globe in a stand and some asshole kid had slapped it hard into a rotation. He opened his eyes, and then he vomited across his chest and stomach. A couple of nurses came into the room. They spoke at a pace and pitch that Pillow couldn't understand, and he relaxed into the ambient sound as they changed his gown and cleaned him.

He imagined that this was how it felt to be a dog in a new home and that he had the same choice a dog always had: relax into it and appreciate the warm hands and free baths, or bite someone in a desperate shot to take some control over his life. When the nurses were finished, one of them put her hand on his shoulder. He snuggled in toward the hand and licked it with a short, quick stroke. The nurse pulled her hand back, then she rubbed the side of his head without a massive hematoma on it. She said something, and Pillow chose to think it was a nice thing.

Pillow moved listlessly in and out of consciousness for a while. When his legs felt strong and coordinated enough, he slowly removed his IV (Pillow had once learned the hard way that it was the exact opposite of ripping off a Band-Aid) and stuck it into his pillow. Then he stood up and took a test walk around the room. He made it to the wall before he had to pause and steady himself, but then he did the rest of the circuit under his own power.

He'd tried to take stock of the situation. And he felt like he knew some things: he was in the hospital, the coins were hidden, Don Costes was dead, Breton wanted to kill him, his head really hurt, he needed to get to Gwynn, his shirt and pants were folded under the side table, Emily was pregnant and he had to escape the hospital before they ran a brain scan or, if they'd already done that, before they told him the results. That last one felt the most vital and immediate to him.

Pillow felt tired, but also relaxed somehow, ready to accept things gently, and as they came. He lay back down and slept some more. Waking up, he felt glad there was a clock in his room, and he felt confident that it was three in the morning, not the afternoon. Pillow slid out of bed, dressed gingerly, bit off his ID bracelet and walked out of the hospital in careful four-inch steps.

The first thing Pillow did was head straight down to Emily's storage locker to get the coins while he still remembered which model-train box he'd hidden them in. The bottom box. Pillow carefully set aside the rest of the old models, got on his knees and opened the box. It was empty. Totally empty. No model, no coins, no note, nothing. Pillow stood back up and walked around for a minute. He took the two deepest breaths of his life. They didn't help.

He started his search calmly and reasonably, carefully checking each model box before moving on to the bigger boxes. What set him off was sticking himself on a sewing needle. Pillow pulled his hand out and saw the thin metal reflecting the stark lights of the basement sticking straight out of his index finger. He pulled the needle out. Emily had specifically warned him about the box with all the sharp stuff in it, and he'd forgotten. He'd forgotten if the door was even locked when he got there. If he'd even remembered to lock it in the first place. He'd had the coins, and now he had empty boxes and used ski poles.

If his initial goal, on entering the locker, had been to systematically destroy everything inside of it, Pillow would have done a really good job. He started with throwing the dioramas and scale reproductions against the wall, but he really got going when he'd found the cricket bat. Pillow had just put his foot through a decent-looking oil painting of a shoe when the wall and the floor and the ceiling all tilted sharply to the side. Pillow fell down. He stayed on the floor a long time, his foot in a picture frame, draped across a set of skis, waiting for the spell to pass. Then Pillow rehearsed the speech he would make to Emily, trying not to slur his words, and he got up and swayed down the long cement hallway, lights bouncing off the floor, and the sound of his shoes bouncing off the walls, in a small, empty-enough way that he'd have hardly called it an echo.

Emily's door had a small Post-It note in the middle of it. Pillow peeled it off. He read: Don't knock.

It wasn't signed. Pillow was used to getting more formal notes.

Pillow had already gone to the bathroom and swallowed several too many pills and fetched an ice pack from the kitchen by the time he noticed Breton and Bobby Desnos had been waiting in his apartment the whole time.

Breton was standing behind the couch. He walked down a set of imagined stairs, waving. When he came out the end he stood back straight and offered Pillow the couch with his arm.

'Why, hello.'

Pillow laughed and croaked hello, as he sat down, let his head sink back, closed his eyes and set to icing his skull.

Breton's voice filled the bottom corner of Pillow's eyes. A long, rhythmic throb filled the rest.

'I suspect that your considerable mental handicaps will prevent you from fully comprehending my speech in real time, so I have left you detailed written instructions.'

Breton was pretty much on the money. Pillow didn't even really have the energy to worry about the coins, or the fact that someone was very likely to shoot him in the head within five minutes. He tried to relax into it, take it as it came, that real Buddha-type vibe.

'I know everything that has happened and everything that will. I know that you have lost Artaud, and possibly found the coins; I know that my dear friend Don Costes was supposed to help me deal with you and that he has disappeared. I am aware that, in some reality somewhere, he is likely dead. But, knowing the future as I do, imagining as accurately as my genius allows, I have decided to give you a little chance, for the purposes of my amusement in these dark times of lost friendship. After all, humour is that which allows one to brush sadness aside, like so many pencil shavings, when it becomes too distressing. You and your severed-chicken-head mind have forty-eight hours to return both the coins *and* Don Costes's living body or corpse to me. If you fail to deliver either one, then I will verify the balance sheet, and you will see just what kinds of moral virtues I feel comfortable laying claim to. And it will be amusing and educational for me to watch you. My little project.'

Pillow had been trying to imagine the slow, thick waves of pain as colours, but he wasn't succeeding. He opened his eyes and saw Breton walking out of the apartment, sliding as if on ice and moving his arms in a loose Charleston approximation.

Pillow woke up when the cramp in his hip finally got deep enough that his whole leg spasmed back against the bottom of the couch. He hopped up, fell and massaged himself. He stayed on the floor awhile, propped up on his other knee with his face pressed flatly and firmly into the carpet. His hip started to feel better, and Pillow remembered where he was. It was his own apartment. He felt desperately thirsty and for a minute thought he was hungover. Pillow realized that the problem was the head injury when he accidentally bumped his hematoma lightly against the side of the sink and his vision went a sudden, searing red and he sank to the ground and rolled around.

After a while of that he pulled himself up against the kitchen counter and took to repeating the phrase *Easy peasy, lemon squeezy* over and over until he felt confident enough in his balance to stand. After he'd calmed down he managed to string a few, admittedly swirly and jagged at the same time but still probably accurate, memories together.

Emily was done with him, at least for now. Artaud was gone and didn't matter anymore anyway, so that was nice, one less headache and all that.

He had the strong gut feeling that he'd killed Don Costes, but wasn't strictly sure how, or where he'd left the body. All he remembered was throwing up on a cement pillar of some kind, sopping blood from his forehead in the front seat of Don's car. He remembered those things in quite a lot of detail, though.

So, it was time to go. He had to get to Apollinaire, ask her for some walking-around money, and then run as far away as he could as fast as he could, until such time as he had turned himself into the sort of genuinely caring and unselfish and not accidentally incredibly dangerous person that Emily would allow around her and their child.

He knew that he should probably eat something and went to fridge. Most of the vegetables and fruit seemed rotten, so Pillow took out a box of tofu, an eggplant that was only half-bad and a jar of kimchee. He put the food on the counter and looked at it for a while, and then he felt a sudden overwhelming rage. He smashed the food with his hands, got a really bad head rush and then did a breathing exercise sitting on the floor of the kitchen, feeling the bottom of his pants soak with food and wondering vaguely if the red stuff dripping down his hands was blood or just kimchee juice.

Pillow closed his eyes and, because these things aren't quite anchored to skulls, his brain started spinning, but not in straight-line sort of way, more the way something spins as it's falling off a table. He rubbed his hand and slid down flat on the floor. He felt liquid on the back of his neck and heard the sea.

His hands and toes tingled. Pillow didn't really care. He relaxed into the sounds of the sea, watched the moonlight behind his eyelids catch the dips and swirls in the water. For a second he was in charge of the waves. Not the whole sea, just the waves, and not totally in control of them either. He was in charge of them like a trainer is in charge of a fighter, getting them ready, watching them peak and break. Not a lot of control, but knowing every ripple, seeing every fold, seeing them happen from close enough to feel far away.

The thing about waves is there are millions of tiny waves in each one.

Pillow didn't notice Julio waiting by his car. He dropped his keys when he saw him. Julio had come out of nowhere.

'Fuck you, Pillow.'

Pillow was very confused.

'What? We're going to fight, son. You've got time later.' Julio moved in closer, went nose to nose with Pillow, jabbing his chest with his finger. 'I tell you, I tell you specially that I can't have trouble. I'm trying to cut your broken-down ass a break and you do me like this. You bully some fucking kid, you leave the room I loaned you with blood on the floor, piss, shit, used needles … I don't even want to know what you did to this girl. You don't call me again. I cut you a break.'

Pillow ducked his head back and slapped Julio across the face. He smiled wide and waved his finger in front of him. 'Don't touch me, son. You don't get to touch me now, and you won't be able to touch me on Saturday night. Do your level best.'

Julio flinched as if to hit him, then he took a closer look and stepped back. 'Shit, what happened to you? Are you okay?'

'Fuck your mother if you can find her, you'll know how good I am this weekend. I'm going to take you apart, run a paint job on you, kid. This is *the* fight for me, this is it, this is my last march and I'm going to goose-step right on your chubby little face. You're not even on weight, look at you. You've got a nicer rack than the ring girls.'

'Pillow, listen, I think you need to go to the doctor. We already had that fight, man. That was years ago.'

'We already had it? It's not even gonna happen, fatty. You can't make 154. You and your big, silly right hand, like that's talent. Like that's fuckin' art. Give me a break, I've tricked every fighter who ever tried me. I've got as much punch as a hummingbird, and I beat the best. And I'm gonna beat you too. Pure paint job, kid. Easy work.'

Julio was backing away now. 'Listen, I'm done. You need a doctor. You need a doctor and that's … I'm done, brother.'

'Yeah, yeah, yeah you're done. I float like a butterfly and that's it; stinging is for dumbfucks who can't wait to die.'

Julio walked away shaking his head, and Pillow bounced on the balls of his feet and reeled a quick, loose combination into the air. Then he laughed at something that wasn't funny. He got his car open and sat down, coming back to himself a little. It seemed important to leave, so he left.

Pillow was careful to consciously plot a simple and exact route to Gwynn Apollinaire's house. He went through the route several times in the car before he started to drive. As he moved through the city, consistently failing to shoulder-check when changing lanes and ignoring his mirrors because they were disorienting, Pillow reflected on how strange it was to have been praised for his 'survival instincts' since he was thirteen years old. As a boxer he had always been easily stunned (which probably just had to do with the way his skull and jaw were shaped), but he'd reacted very well to getting rocked. He was able to stay calm and collected and usually even managed to stick to his strategy. He thought there should be no difference this time, and he felt pretty sure he could pull the coin thing off.

Then Pillow came within a second of blowing through a cross-walk and running over a woman pushing a twin-stroller, but he managed to stop in time. The woman froze, then touched the cloth flap that covered the place where the babies were. She kept looking at Pillow, as if expecting something from him. He apologized to the woman with his eyes and the angle of his head.

Pillow pulled up to Apollinaire's building feeling pretty decent. It came and went in waves, the brain stuff, and he felt like he was at the very top of one right now, looking arrogantly at the rest of the water from a couple of fluid feet above.

For no particular reason, Pillow looked up at the roof before he entered Apollinaire's building. He saw Gwynn swaying forward and back with her hands holding the fire escape on either side. There was a man in a suit with a giant head standing behind her. Gwynn looked down and opened her hand to wave at Pillow. Pillow waved back and let out a long, low whistle.

'Well, if that doesn't just fuck me right in the ear.'

Gwynn Apollinaire seemed about to turn around and speak to Breton when he tipped her straight backward and she went over the side, glanced off the fire escape and fell to the concrete in a loose forward circle.

Although he would never be sure of when he'd gone to bed, or how he'd gotten there, judging by the date on his watch and where the sun was, Pillow knew he'd slept for at least fifteen hours. He woke up feeling uncommonly refreshed. After looking at his watch and figuring out the sleep thing, he'd laughed once and then set to making a plan. Obviously he'd needed the Zs.

He'd already decided that revenge was the thing to do now. Emily was a lost cause, they'd killed Gwynn, and while those things were both mostly his fault, they were also a lot of Breton's fault. Pillow'd hurt people for a lot less. Plus he didn't have the coins or any of his own money so Breton was going to be after him, and he might as well take the initiative.

Sitting by the window, tapping his chin in a steady rhythm, occasionally wondering what the thin wooden lines in the middle of the window actually did (they couldn't be weight-bearing) Pillow formulated a plan. There'd be at least five people at the Bureau with Breton, and even at the best of times Pillow had trouble keeping track of that many variables. He preferred more of a one-on-one type thing. To make matters worse, Pillow's equilibrium was not in the ballpark of normal yet, plus he'd never actually fired a gun before, so he cut his odds of shooting his way in to slim. Pillow figured his big strategic advantage was that the Bureau boys were not a particularly organized bunch. They would just rush into the action, all clumped together, like six-year-olds crowding a soccer ball. So if he could distract them, get in around the back and find Breton alone, it might work. The wood bits in the window were probably there to keep the glass from thumping around too much in the wind, and to make people think a little bit about carpenters as they looked at trees.

Pillow had come to understand variety pretty late in life. Early on it had been all about repetition. In boxing everything has to be second nature, there's no chance to think things through, so for a long time Pillow considered repeating something to be the key to learning it, and he'd done that happily. Then he took his first loss in the pros. He'd gone through the amateurs and his first twelve pro fights doing it all by the book, executing perfectly drilled techniques, being fast with his hands, putting his feet in the right places and winning. Then he fought an old gamer from Philadelphia who'd whacked him on the hips, head-butted him, hand-trapped him at every opportunity. And Pillow had realized that the book would only get him so far. So he started learning the tricks, still repeating them, but switching up more, throwing the odd curveball. What he realized then was that he loved new things. If something was new, if it had that little bit of humour, a little touch of style, he could pick it faster. He learned all the flashy tricks twice as fast as he'd learned the basics. He kept on breaking his right hand, he kept on not finishing anyone, but he started dazzling them. Not just stuffing a jab in their face and running, but showing some real style. Some class.

When he retired, Pillow had realized that the whole time he'd been loving variety while only ever doing one thing. To have the whole, giant, wild world of things to choose from had initially been overwhelming to him, and he knew he hadn't handled it well. But in the last couple years he'd been coming around, relaxing into the newness of everything else, and, he reminded himself in case he forgot later, that had been a good thing. That was something that had helped.

As Pillow got to his car he stopped, bent over and rested his hands flat against the hood. He stayed like that for a long time.

The only good thing about Julio Solis knocking him out and ruining his life had been that he'd learned a whole lot of things, or had at least clarified them. Pillow had learned exactly how different it was to casually wish you didn't exist (which everyone does once in a while) than it was to really want to be dead right now. He'd learned that when street lights start looking like they're shedding distinct lines of light, like the world is moving and you're staying still, that it's not either beautiful or a sign that you need to go to the neurologist, it's both.

Pillow dropped to his knees and pressed his head deeper into the front grille of his car, feeling the individual slats digging into his scalp. He kept his hands up on the hood, flat against the absorbed heat of the sun. He'd learned all those things once, and it had been hard and it had hurt and it had taken a really long time, but he'd learned them, and now he'd been taught them all again for good measure. Pillow pulled his head up and opened his eyes. He watched the tops of some sad, small trees move in the wind, their half-bare branches trembling like sheets of paper in his hand. Pillow stood up. He brushed the knees of his pants and got in the car.

In a flash that faded almost as quickly, Pillow remembered where he'd left Don's car and corpse. He drove over, fetched Don's car and abandoned his own, and went to the Bureau. Because he hadn't had his nose fixed the last time he'd broken it, he did not notice the full extent of the smell.

Pillow knew that being alone limited his options. There was no way he could cover the angles he needed to by himself, so he'd have to time it properly. He got out of the car about a half block early, popped the trunk and left the car coasting. Then he sprinted ahead, peeled off into the alley and dove into the dumpster. He closed the lid and waited. He heard the Bureau boys come running out, flocking together like he knew they would, he heard someone take the car and drive off, he heard them realize he could have snuck in the back. Then he waited.

Pillow didn't wear a watch and couldn't see the sky, so he couldn't know how long he was in the dumpster. It felt like a long while. In his mind he knew the smell was strong, but he didn't feel it in his face. Pillow wondered what exactly his septum had deviated from. Itself?

Eventually he heard a whole gaggle of them leave out the back door, a few more out the front. He waited for a bit longer, then he pushed the lid open and peeked. He could see two guys standing guard out front, but they seemed alone. They looked like the sort of people who were alone. Carefully and quietly he snuck out of the dumpster and ambled down the alley. Pillow walked through the back door.

Breton was slouching against the front of his desk with his back to the door, a pistol hanging limply from his hand. Pillow sprang forward, pressed his gun to Breton's spine and fired. He didn't watch the body drop. He just felt it slide down airily against his leg. It was only after he looked down at the body that he realized the head wasn't quite big enough, and there was no blood.

It wasn't Breton. They'd just put those stupid cufflinks and glasses on a creepily realistic Japanese sex doll. Her circle mouth gaped at him neutrally. That was something Pillow had never understood about sex dolls: the best part of lips are the corners. Pillow sighed and did a slow spin, dropping the gun and waving to each of the armed, black-suited, black-haired men in turn.

On the walls: seven madrigals breastfeeding from a cow standing on her hind legs; three melting clocks, one hanging from a tree branch, and in the background a yellow mousetrap just to the right of a marble slab and an empty, hopeless desk; a young boy eating a park bench raw and whole; a monk carrying a young girl in a bundle of sticks; a piano pulling a meat truck overflowing with lipstick cases; a burning bundle of sticks; a naked woman being spoon-fed Greek yogourt by a falcon with baby hands at the tips of its wings.

Pillow relaxed into the arms yanking and pushing him toward the door. He let his feet go slack, let his big toes drag against the floor.

On the door: a hot-air balloon made of clouds illuminated by a setting sun, floating to nowhere in particular.

They shoved him into the closet, which was empty except for two chairs facing each other. Breton was holding a ship in a bottle to the light, looking up through the bottom. He saw Pillow and raised his eyebrows, put the bottle carefully back in its stand on the ground next to him.

'Why, hello. I haven't seen you since I killed that ancient cunt you called your friend. Oh, you really put on a show for me that day, didn't you?'

Pillow took a long, elaborate skip forward, hopping into the chair and crossing his legs in the same motion.

'You have done nothing but betray me and betray the whole vision of this fraternity. Explain why I should not just take the coins.'

'Oooh, I know this one. Two reasons: because I don't have 'em, and because you already tried that once, sent your best guy at me too. And that didn't turn out so good. Your boys are enthusiastic, but they've got other shit on their minds. Nobody frisked me on my way in. So you'll kill me, for sure, but you don't know what I'll be able to do first.'

Breton tented his hands in front of his mouth to cover his smile. 'Who said I was taking the coins from *you*? Where you see sloppiness I see artful disorder in support of a clear, transcendental vision. You do not look your best. A bit past one's prime, would not one say? In any event, I was never intending to kill you. That is another thing you are wrong about. It is, perhaps, easier and less of a waste of time to tell you of the things about which you are not mistaken.'

Breton paused and took an insanely long and loud sip of tea. He lifted his pinky as he tipped the cup back. When he was done he tossed it straight backward. The cup shattered against the wall.

'You were correct about one thing. One. You did surprise me. I really did not think you'd get past Costes. But the reason you are a punch-drunk idiot child is that you thought you had any way to win. You thought I would put you in a position where it was remotely possible for you to best me? You pulled some moves, you had a bit of style, but it is just not possible for you to win. How did you think it would work?'

'I didn't really. I met a girl, I went raw. You know the deal, I'm sure.'

'Knowing me as the open sore of a romantic you do, you probably supposed I would understand and appreciate that motive. But that is the exact reason you are a complete dunce. Because if you had what you thought you had, the last thing you needed was money. You could have just left and been poor and happy together, and you could have slept and woken and laughed in each other's arms for the rest of your lives, and it would have been beautiful. The only reason the proletariat does not revolt is that it is absolutely fine to be poor if you are madly in love. You have an interesting mind for violence, a cleverness and some charm to you, but I cannot sympathize with you because that mistake is too huge and sad and obvious for me to have ever made, in all the years, and with any of the brains, and from any of the childhoods. There is no possible variation of me that is so stupid. I have never had a thought so misguided, not even a single, fleeting, unexpressed thought. You ruined a true, catastrophic love, sir, and for that crime the only reasonable punishment is prolonged torture without the sweet release of death. I will not kill you. I will watch you move into early senility and wretchedness. I will watch you hate yourself to bits.'

Pillow rolled his neck around. It felt a lot crunchier than was healthy. 'Man, I know you and I know me. And I never took a dive for anyone. I never stayed down for anyone, and nobody stayed down for me. I'll fight you 'til it's done. You were going to kill me, that's a fight. So I'm here until it's done.'

'Oh, you poor, sweet ape. You never took a dive, but you did go down, did you not? You even stayed down, you simply never got paid for it. I would never have killed you; that would have been so conventional. Ick.' Breton pretended the idea was on his shirt cuff and flicked it off fussily with his thumb. 'No, no, no. That day with Don we were going to give you an ultimatum, similar to the one you recently received, and then we were going to watch you run about, struggle in your uniquely humorous manner against the brutal tide of reality. Why would I kill you? Your whole being, right now, is my project. My masterpiece. I made you, lovingly, why would I just smash you to bits without first displaying you? That would be to betray the whole frame that has held up my genius. Over some nominally valuable trinkets? No, no, no. See, actually, it was Don's idea. He realized that you were going to make your adorable and senseless little play for the coins. And he thought we could watch it. See you in beautiful, deranged action. Put you in some corners and watch you spasm into the walls. I did not believe him at first, but I was wrong. See, my mistake was that I thought you were a beaten man, and you were not by any stretch. You were just a doomed one, so much so that I will let you leave. And I will watch you try to survive, as the whole of society zeros in on you. Who do you think sent Bataille to you? Did you really think he just plucked you from the world? Appeared from the air? As if beauty were a gift with no giver. Do you remember Avida and Simon? Louise Aragon? Jack Prevert? The warrants are out. Mistakes are so easy and wonderful to make. Don't you agree?'

Pillow tried to keep smiling as he gripped the handle of the razor in his sock. He was close enough to get there with one swipe – if he got the neck it would work. 'Motherfucker, say what you want, but I am too old a bird to get fed an egg.'

Breton ran a hand an inch over his slicked-back hair. 'I am in love with a woman right now. A beautiful, insane, disgraced woman. And last night she endeavoured to bake me a pie. It was supposed to be an apple pie, but her crust was made from the fat of some obscure animal, and there were very few apples. It was a lard-crust pie, basically. When I slept last night I dreamt that giant grapes were falling from the sky, and they were bouncing all about, and bouncing against me. They were hurting me.' Breton pursed his lips and twisted the skin of his hand hard, then he let it go and watched the skin regain its shape. 'I used to think I was a masochist. My analyst said so. But now I know I am not. The best discovery of my life was that my face is actually on the other side of that coin. Minted.'

Pillow tensed up, readied himself.

Breton looked at Pillow's ankle, and then right in his eyes.

'One final question, since I don't care whether you kill Artaud or whether Artaud kills you: when was the last time you were at your apartment? Actually, two final questions: do you think your child-laden girlfriend might have decided to return there? Might she still?'

Pillow let go of the razor. He sprinted through the doors, the blood rushing so fast through his ears that he almost couldn't hear the whole building laughing hysterically at him.

Pillow roughly shouldered his door open before remembering that he almost certainly hadn't locked it.

Emily was sitting on his couch for maybe the first time. She drained the rest of what seemed like a once-big whisky. Then they both listened to the sound rooms with bad light bulbs make when nothing is happening.

Emily did one of those smiles that is actually just resisting a smile. 'The first time I fucked you was here, for some reason. And I woke up and looked at your empty room, and your goddamn statue, and I was so hungover. Your place was so weird and sad. But I convinced myself you were sweet. And for breakfast you tried to serve me a piece of spelt toast with margarine on it. Because that was all the food you had. You didn't think to go out, to take me out. You just slapped margarine on a piece of carbon-fibre toast and gave it me. And you ate nothing. When I left I saw this hanging fruit stand with flies all over it, smelling across the room. I still thought you were a sweetie-pie.'

She ran the glass along the length of her thigh, then she dropped it on the ground where a table should have been.

'I don't know what's wrong with me. I really don't. Because I came back, *champ*, just like you always assumed. I'm here. Well, I have things to work on, I guess. Real-person things.'

'Listen, I can explain …'

'No. Dude. No. I don't want to hear you explain anything else, ever in my life. You told me no one would get hurt. Promised it. You haven't even been to the doctor with me, you've barely asked. When my parents ask me what happened between us I'm going to say that I told you I was pregnant and you instantly went completely bug-fuck insane and lost all sight of fairness and responsibility. Have you been beating people up for money? The whole time I knew you?'

Pillow slumped down onto the couch and dug his palm a little bit too deeply into his eye. 'What did you think I was doing?'

'I thought you were bouncing at underground clubs and dealing steroids, because that's what you told me. And now you're acting like I'm stupid for believing you. I didn't think it was right, but I didn't think it was all that wrong and I thought you would figure it out. Because you said you would, you had it handled. You kept saying you were fine, and you're not.'

'I know. I know. I got really confused and I messed up. But I'll … Whatever you want, whatever you want I'll do.'

'Whatever I want is nothing. I want nothing from you. I say no. I choose not to be a part of this anymore. Not even a little. This is wrong, Pete. You're hurting yourself, and you're hurting other people, and I don't want anything to do with it.'

Pillow stood again. He walked into the kitchen and looked at his plant. He came back into the living room desperate. 'I'm really sorry. And I'll go, but I just want you to know that I'm sorry for everything. Everything.'

'Okay. Okay.' She used the back of her hand to wipe her eye. 'When you were here, when we were in the exact same room together, it was great. We had fun. You're fun. But the second I wasn't around, you just instantly turned into a huge bag of shit, apparently. Fuck, man. I thought you were a good break. I've been jerked around so many times, and when I met you I was so *lonely* in a way I don't think you've ever understood, and I thought you'd be nice. Just nice. You specifically promised me that, it was your idea.'

Pillow gestured with his hand, as if he was about to speak. He moved his head forward as if he was speaking. 'I just need you to know that it wasn't … I didn't decide. I was confused and I fucked up really bad. Worse than I ever thought I would. And I won't bother you anymore.'

She waved a hand at him like he was a wasp who'd been buzzing around so long she couldn't be bothered to care if she got stung. 'Yes. Okay.'

'You should also know that I love you, and I totally believe that you made a shooting star appear with your mind.'

Emily laughed at the ceiling and then the floor. 'Actually, I didn't make that star.'

'Right. You just sensed it.'

'That happened. It was magic.'

'I know. I know it did.'

Emily stood, rifled around in her purse. Pillow stayed still and breathed. The room was canting hard to one side, but in the calm, temporary way he was used to. She flipped the coin box out of her purse, letting it fall to the ground. 'Your coins. I stole them and felt like I'd done a terrible thing. You might want to look in your bathroom.' She shook him off before he could talk. 'Time wounds all heels, Pillow. That's a thing cobblers say.'

Emily walked briskly past Pillow out of the apartment. Nobody turned to look at anybody.

Pillow tried to breathe for a minute, then he moved over to the sink and vomited a small amount of stomach acid. Looking up into the fractured, more-white-than-usual sunlight coming through the glowing leaves of his plant.

Pillow could not strictly account for how correct it felt to push the door to his bathroom open with his toe instead of turning the knob. All he really needed to see was the leg. Not many men's ankles were as skinny and riddled with track marks as Artaud's. Pillow went the rest of the way into the room anyway.

Artaud was lying across the tiles, the needle still in his arm. There was a little bit of white froth foaming out the slack, double-hinged corner of his mouth. His skinny wrist was bent back, wedged under the toilet. He'd popped his abscess with a hatpin. There was a thin puddle of dark brown urine underneath him. Artaud had left a note propped up against the faucet. Pillow picked it up.

Dear Pillow,

First I think it important to tell you that I still wish nothing but despair, loneliness and deep pain upon you. That walking stick was my final chance, my first and final chance at happiness; you knew it and you stole it from me anyway. Even if I were the sort of person to ever forgive another, this sin would be beyond my imagined and hypothetical benevolence.

I have not been one to think much about tragedy. But I have in the last few quiet minutes of my horrific shouted lifetime, this

hoarse, exhausted denouement, come to realize that my whole
world of thought has been dominated by one central tragedy.
That I wish for the only impossible thing: to be understood in
thought. Unmediated, unheard, unseen. Merely understood,
nothing else.

   Insomuch as life is   , cruelty and error have taken
its place.

   &c,
   Antonin Artaud

Pillow didn't spend as long as he usually did reading Artaud's notes. He got the gist. Pillow looked in the mirror and recognized himself. The cut on his forehead sectioned off into descending drops of dark red scab, his hand scraped and puffy, a swelling as big as a baby's head on the side of his. This was a version of himself he knew well. He pinched his nose, tried to remember a time before it was flat.

Pillow stopped out on the hallway balcony, leaning heavily into the railing. He looked out at the dingy apartment courtyard. It was that time just before morning when the yellows that used to be bright, and the greens that used to be neon, took on a muted pre-emptive glow. He rubbed his eyes and let them come back into focus slowly, allowing water to collect. Pillow took the coins out of his pocket. He opened the case and shook them one by one into his hand. He bounced them around in his palm, letting them touch each other for a while, and then he put the coins back in the case and the case back in his pocket.

Pillow took off running in what he guessed was the vague direction of the water. He kept his head up, distantly observing the line of the horizon bumping up and down with his steps. His legs were sluggish, and he had to stop several times because he felt dizzy. He arrived at the far edge of the waterfront and stopped to look out over the water. Pillow looked at the water for a long time, then got down on his knees and plunged his head straight under, keeping his eyes open.

Keeping his eyes open had always been one of Pillow's more natural skills. Even when he'd first started, all the other kids would close their eyes and flail, and Pillow flailed with them, but he always paid attention, kept his eyes open and looked for spots. He didn't remember Solis, but he must have closed his eyes; the only way to get knocked out that badly is to have no idea it's coming. He casually recognized that his air was running out, pulled up, curled into the fetal position and gasped for a long time. He rocked back and forth, listening to the sound of the water kissing the shore, and he hoped that they loved each other. That the shore knew how badly the water wanted to stay in one place, that the water knew how badly rocks wanted ripples. He stayed like that a long time, a good rest period. Then he stood up. He was still good at catching his breath.

Pillow spat and took another look at the thin films of water pushed off the tops of the waves by wind, and then he started up running again, firing telephone-pole jabs into his flickering shadow.

As he ran, Pillow took stock and started to make a plan. What he needed to do felt clear. He had to kill Breton. Pillow thought that once it's decided that you'll never see your child because you're a murderer, all bets are off. He thought that was a decent general rule. He spent the rest of the day poking around houses near the Bureau, circling the surrounding blocks on foot, trying to pick a good angle of attack. Nobody really seemed to notice him.

Pillow kept almost fainting and falling down, and his legs felt a little bit foreign and too long to control properly. He'd gone through a whole series of plans to kill Breton that kept getting derailed by losing his bearings, or forgetting the second phase of his plan once he'd done the first. So he thought he should hole up somewhere and try to sleep again. See if he could string together four good thoughts in a row. He made few vague guesses about where he'd left his car, got disoriented, then remembered that he'd come on foot, so he decided to just steal a new one.

Pillow waited through several stop lights, supporting himself against the street-light pole, dozing off and rousing every few minutes. Finally a huge, old, maroon car pulled up, driven by the exact median of twenty-five-year-old men at the wheel. Pillow looked both ways, and the street was clear and dark now, full of calm quiet air, the car just sitting there waiting at the empty red light. He staggered across the street. The average face was sitting in his car like a racehorse, staring straight out in front at the stop light, waiting to get the signal and trusting the straight line as if it were the only direction.

The guy didn't seem to notice Pillow until he'd already gripped the door handle. He threw it open, and the man shouted something. Pillow grabbed him by the average-length off-brown hair and threw him to the ground. Pillow dropped heavily into the seat with his legs still out in the street. He rested his elbows on his knees and rubbed his eyes, trying to focus them up for driving. The car hummed hollow under him.

Pillow looked down at the young man again. The guy was sitting up a bit, bracing himself on one arm, the other plastered to his forehead, blood leaking thickly through his fingers. Pillow raised one hand, acknowledging a foul. 'I'm so sorry. Had to do it. I'm not here to make excuses.'

The man started inching himself backwards toward open road using his three-sets-of-twelve-reps forearms.

Pillow continued: 'I don't feel bad anymore, I just feel things. Call 'em what you want. And sorry, I've always thought that, y'know, sorry's not a thing you feel. It's a thing you are. And I am sorry. You take enough shots and you lose the thread a bit. Like, there's people who have been punched in the head once, and it's the biggest deal of their lives. Y'know? This is … Shit, I probably did the worst thing that ever happened to you just now. I'm getting that idea. Hair pulled, head bonked on the sidewalk, that's, like, a Wednesday for me these days. But everyone's take is important, y'know? I know how bad that was for you, and I'm sorry. I can't make it right, but I am sorry. I'm a sorry thing.' Pillow tapped his head. 'It's a couple stitches, max. They freeze it up. Like they glued a tiny piece of somebody else to you. It's cool. You'll like it.' Pillow sighed and looked up at the sky for a second. 'I liked it, you might not. I've been having trouble keeping track of that lately.'

The guy wasn't going to talk or look up or stop leaking anytime soon, so Pillow turned around in the seat and pulled his knees into his chest. He kissed both of his kneecaps, then he cranked the seat back, adjusted the mirrors and took off.

Pillow sat still as the car floated absently and the city became small in the mirrors. He pulled over into a small clearing and parked and looked out the windshield at the grass swaying in the wind. The whole scene looked as if it was being crowded in along the edges, that little bit of forgetting creeping in even as he looked.

Pillow hyperventilated. He started to cry a bit, but his eyes gave up on that pretty fast. His mouth was dry. His hands were tingling in long waves through his fingers.

He took to slamming his head against the steering wheel and he didn't stop until he passed out.

Pillow woke up too out of it to notice the headache. He hadn't even forgotten anything. He briefly entertained the notion that he'd just concussed his way through to the other side, that maybe he'd dug himself such a deep brain-damage hole he might pop out in China and be super-good at math. He laughed.

Pillow got out of the car. He looked at the field again, and it wasn't how he remembered it from a few minutes before. There was one tree in it, mostly bare but with three bushy little circles of leaves at the tips of its tallest branches. Underneath there was the frame of a bench, but there weren't any slats to sit on. A hill sloped up gently on the other side of the tree and someone had carved a set of stairs into the hill, stairs that were just holes. Pillow walked over and climbed the stairs, hopped over the bush and kept walking.

After a couple minutes he emerged on the edge of a farm. In the distance there was a farmhouse and a tractor shed, and Pillow followed the incredibly long driveway toward the house. It was a log-cabin-style place. Out front there was an old rotted-out sign that had some vague faded colours on it, but no clear writing. Behind the sign there was a huge, half-rusted metal mailbox that said *Leg Farm* on it. There was no address. As Pillow got up to the door he saw that the knocker was shaped like a woman's leg, rounded and smooth with detailed toes. He pulled back the leg and let it kick the door. After a few seconds a man came to the door. He was wearing a flannel shirt with no pattern on it and jeans. The farmer had a deep tan; he was very thin and a lot shorter than Pillow.

'Shit. Are you all right?'

Pillow reached up and touched his head, and then he looked down at his blood-soaked shirt and smiled. 'Oh yeah, I'm fine. I had a run-in with a … with a steer.'

The farmer angled his head to the side and smiled up at Pillow. 'Steer, huh? Well, who in this wide world hasn't run afoul of the oh-casional steer. You ain't here to hurt me or rob me in some way, are you, fella?'

'No sir.'

The farmer nodded agreeably, considering all his words carefully. 'Looks like you had your bell rung pretty good.'

'You could say that.'

'Did you come to see the legs? You must have heard of the legs.'

Pillow decided to roll with it. 'Yeah, uh, yes I have. Is that okay?'

'Oh yes you may, not too many folks come to see those legs anymore.' He made a sweeping gesture with his hand and then he put the hand in a pocket. 'In the realm of agritourism, I am a bit of a one-hit wonder.'

The house had high ceilings, an open kitchen and a huge window facing the driveway. The farmer walked toward the kitchen and asked Pillow if he wanted some coffee. Pillow said no. The farmer went to the coffee pot anyway.

'This is a really nice house.'

The farmer looked at the ceiling, then he poured some coffee into a mug that didn't have a picture on it and didn't say anything at all. 'Well, we should get to the legs, that *is* the serious business.'

They walked out the back of the house. He had a white plastic table on his porch and dirty white plastic chairs all around it. All Pillow had to do was lift his eyes a little bit and he could see the field. It was littered with hay bales. The rounded hay-bale parts were smaller because the farmer had used the rest of the hay to make legs coming out the top. They weren't at all what Pillow had expected a leg coming out of a hay bale to look like. They looked smooth, more like rock than anything. The only inaccurate part about them was that the toes were further apart than a person's toes. The feet were maybe a bit wider and longer than usual, but still feminine, volleyball-centre feet. Pillow could tell they were supposed to be a tall woman's feet, and through their strange and painstaking details, he could tell that they were all supposed to be one specific tall woman's left leg.

All the way to the back of the field these bales with legs coming out of the top. Pillow couldn't count how many there were and didn't really want to. All of a sudden it felt like something was crowding into his eyeball again and it was hard to see. He kept trying to look at the field but all he kept catching were fractured, blackening pictures, disappearing. His own legs were weak, and there wasn't a cloud anywhere, and sometimes unadulterated sky crept into his vision. The leg farmer eased Pillow into one of the chairs and asked if he could bring a water. The farmer came back with two mugs, his full of coffee, Pillow's water. He put the cup down next to Pillow. Pillow said thanks.

The farmer leaned forward in a way that let Pillow know his back had been hurting for a decade or two. 'Now, son, I hope you don't mind me calling you that. I don't mean much by the word; it's just an advice-giving sort of thing to call another man. But, son, you look to be mixed up in the sort of fun I resolved to give up after meeting a lovely red-headed woman with legs taller than your ...well, my head. So I can't say I'm going to help you out much. But I'll let you stay out here, hell, I'll even leave you alone a minute with your thoughts, let you get sorted. Does that sound about okay to you?'

Pillow didn't say anything. He tried to look at the legs, losing them even as he did it.

And Pillow sat there quietly with him, as the farmer chewed on what was either his lip or just air for a while. Then the farmer rocked forward in his chair and said one perfect piece of nothing.

The zoo. The zoo. The zoo. He said it to himself as he left the farm. *The zoo. The zoo. The zoo. The zoo. The zoo.*

Pillow figured, finally, that there was no point dying if you were going to do it without at least seeing a giraffe in person one last time.

Life had, for many years, been a wonderful and familiar routine for Pillow. Every day he would wake up and run, and every day he would run enough that he felt a little bit joyful and loose and prone to laughing by the time he stopped. Then he'd eat and drink a pre-measured meal, and then he'd go to the boxing gym. And the gym never changed, sometimes he'd go to other gyms, to spar new guys, to see new trainers, but the activities would all be the same. Chin down, hands up, quick feet, moving that head. And in the evening he would go out and have a bit of light fun and socializing that took place in one of a few familiar places and always ended in time for him to get his rest. So, if it could be said that Pillow enjoyed anything in his post-fighting years, what he enjoyed was just the whole world. How big it was, how little of it smelled like sweat and leather, how grey and loose the air was sometimes. All the weird things he'd never seen before in addition to all the weird things he'd only seen a couple of times.

Once, on the way out to the zoo, he'd seen a tiny old man dragging two full-grown, bleeding elk carcasses into the woods, one on each shoulder. The little guy was just zipping along, no problem. Pillow had pulled over to talk to him, and the man, who must have been eighty, had a hunch the size and shape of a basketball on his back. He was wearing a polyester shirt with a repeating print of someone carrying a yoke on it and no pants. Pillow ran up alongside him and didn't say anything. He waved at the man, and the man saw him, looked him up and down (his eyes sunk halfway back into his skull), nodded once and kept walking, carrying the massive elk like they were nothing, and leaving thick, twin lines of half-congealed blood in the grass behind him.

So it wasn't just the zoo that was so amazing it seemed like no one would believe him if he told them about it (he had told a few people about the zoo, and they didn't 100 percent believe or disbelieve him), it was the whole way to the zoo, the whole way home, the whole space in between. The world seemed so random and interesting that nothing felt impossible to him. It could all float away attached by giant strings to a huge balloon with tall, knotty trees growing out of it, and he'd be surprised, sure, but it wouldn't exactly blow his mind. He wouldn't say it was impossible.

He pulled the car he'd jacked to the gates of the zoo. Then he got out, jumped the fence and remembered that he still had the coins when he saw the box fall out of his pocket as he dropped to the ground inside the zoo. He picked up the box, tossed it in a short tight spin in the air and put it back in his pocket. When he tried to whistle, it came out as a flat, tuneless flop of lips.

The parking lot was like any large parking lot at night: a bit creepy, like an open field but where the animals who might sneak up on you are people with knives and things like knives. Pillow made sure not to step on the white lines of paint marking the parking spaces. He wasn't really sure why, but it seemed important.

Climbing the fence into the zoo itself was a bit harder. Eventually Pillow found a way to scale the oversized wooden board with a map of the zoo on it, jump from that to the roof of the hut where they take your money and walk past the fence. As he climbed off the roof, Pillow took care to focus extra-hard on making his feet go to the exact places he wanted them to, knowing that he would have plenty of time to think about what to look at in the zoo, and what animals with which to hunker down and sleep, after he had not hurt himself on the large and surprisingly sharp-edged donations bin just below him.

The zoo closed at five p.m every day, so Pillow was very excited to see it at night. He hoped that more of the animals would be awake, but he knew that they were probably all just sad enough to sleep for eighteen hours a day. Which was fair enough. A lot of animals and people felt that way.

The big downside to entering the park through the front gate was that they displayed the saddest animal at the zoo first, right after you'd paid. It was the caged eagle. Pillow walked to the cage and peered in. He had to go pretty slowly because the zoo was very dark. The eagle was sitting quietly and coldly and sadly on its perch, its neck hunched straight down, wings tucked tight in to his sides. The bars were also cold, and touching them reminded Pillow once again of how insistently the two middle fingers on his right hand had been tingling for the last little while. Pillow had a sudden and complete change of heart.

'Fuck this eagle. Fuck you, Eagle. Flap your wings a bit, make a thing of it if you hate it so much. We all know you do. You've made that clear, you killjoy. Don't just sit there pouting. Fuck you, fuck your family. If I was an eagle, I'd just glide until … until there was no more … up-gusts?'

Pillow laughed and dropped his head down to gently touch the bars, enjoying the feel of the cold metal rolling against the top of his head.

'Sorry, Eagle. You're not who I should be saying that stuff to. Pals?'

Pillow held up his hand for a fist-bump (fewer germs). The eagle kept sleeping. Pillow shrugged and moved on.

As he walked down a footpath lined with trees so tall he could easily have forgotten they had tops, Pillow wondered idly why no one had stopped him to talk, or kick him out of the zoo, or arrest him, or shoot him in the chest a few times. More actively, he hoped that he was heading for the giraffes.

On the way, Pillow got distracted by the Southeast Asia pavilion and pushed the amazingly unlocked front door open and walked in. The humid air felt nice and close, intimate in relief from the dark, hollow early-morning air from outside. The moonlight filtered weakly through the window and the ceilings that were all glass like a greenhouse. Pillow quietly shuffled across the room, feeling his way along the wall.

He came across a locked door with a yellow sign that was way too blurry and indistinct to bother reading. He leaned back and kicked the door, denting it beside the handle, then he waited out a head rush and kicked it seven more times until it opened.

Orangutans are apparently very heavy sleepers, because six of the seven stayed slumped in their cages, their arms hanging through the bars, swaying and twitching with sleep. Pillow wondered if it was still making sounds when he hit things. It didn't really seem like it. There was one small orangutan who was awake; he had pulled himself up on the bars, gripping them with his leathery hands. Pillow walked up to the cage and kneeled in front of it.

'Hey, pal.' The little guy tilted his long, oval head to the side and flipped his lip inside out. 'I know what you're about. I'm about that too. You know what I'm saying. For people the time is four-thirty in the morning, maybe five o'clock. Nobody's there, nobody wants anything. You can stay in your own apartment and feel how empty the street it is, or you can go running and feel how empty the rooms are. You can hear street lamps. They make this thunk. You beat the sun up. Sleep's just something you need.' The orangutan scratched his belly, then he brought the hand back up to pull on the bars some more. The metal made a barely audible groan from the pressure. 'Why fuck around dreaming when you can just wake the fuck up and hear some street lights?' Pillow reached forward and wrapped his hand around three of the scratchy black knuckles. They felt like a leather bag that had been buried for years and grown hair. The orangutan snapped his head forward and tried to bite off Pillow's finger. He got the hand back fast enough and the orangutan drove his teeth straight into the bars, then he lurched back and curled against the back of his cage, sucking on his fingers.

Pillow put three fingers in his own mouth. The orangutan had a blanket in the cage with him, which seemed wrong to Pillow, what with the hair and thick skin and stuff. He thought about it a second and realized it wasn't a sleeping blanket, it was a playing blanket. The orangutan was having fun with how the world looks different when you put something over your head. He could see how that would seem pretty cool to a monkey. Pillow pulled the fingers out of his mouth.

'I was super into doing that too, when I was five. Hey, are you like a five-year-old? No, fuck it, don't answer that. It was wrong to ask you to compare yourself to stuff. I don't actually know how old I was. I don't know how old I was for anything. I just said five.'

The kid wasn't getting it. Pillow stood to leave, listening to the snorting rhythms of sleep for a bit. He turned around at the door and squinted for one last look. The orangutan was still pulling the blanket on and off his head, enjoying the sliding movement of darkness and air and cloth.

In the bright light-blue glow of the fish tanks, Pillow watched a turtle have sex with another turtle twice its size. Mostly the couple just looked around blankly and spasmed in short, awkward jerks. Once in a while the big turtle would take a couple half-hearted steps forward and the tiny turtle would move with her, thrusting as he followed. He dropped to his knees and tried to catch the male turtle's eye. The turtle seemed like somebody who got it, the kind of creature that inspired a little respect.

'I'm glad I got to watch you in the saddle, my friend.' He reached out and touched the glass in front of the turtle's fully extended neck. 'You're a stamina machine. I know you're not having sex for fun, just babies, which is a sad thing about your life. But you picked a hardy gal.' His finger slid across the glass toward the female turtle's shell. 'Child-bearing hips, am I right?' He cocked his head to the side, looking with deep and sudden sympathy at the larger turtle. 'Hang in there, sweetheart. Kids can make your whole life feel right.'

It didn't seem like the turtles would be done anytime soon, so Pillow cracked his knees straight and walked over to peek at the Komodo dragon, which wasn't having sex but was still interesting because it was a dinosaur. The dragon was awake and Pillow watched it move around, walking toward him in a weird zigzagging way, scattering wood chips aside with its long, dexterous-looking claws. Pillow watched the creature in satisfied silence until he heard some jaunty humming and footsteps not quite heavy enough to wake the dead.

As had become common to him, Pillow felt smart and stupid at the same time. He laughed and spoke in a sidelong, jocular sort of way to the dragon.

'Riiiiight. I totally forgot about them. Well, okey-dokey, Smoky, time to rumble, I guess.'

The dragon didn't move or blink. Its tongue went out and back in again quickly. Pillow reached into the back waistband of his pants and then remembered that he'd left his gun in his car and his car somewhere really far away a really long time ago. He took the razor blade out of his sock, moved slowly over to a dark spot by a tall metal pillar. He angled his body behind it, saw a flashlight beam moving and bouncing at the rhythm of walking down the other end of the pavilion. Pillow quietly cleared his throat.

'How does anyone still *care*?'

The beam stopped moving.

Lieutenant Avida's voice was surprisingly chipper, given the hour. 'Why, hi there, Pillow. How are you this fine evening?'

The Komodo dragon was stuck in a corner now. Pillow wondered where its asshole was in relation to the tail.

'Oh, you know, pretty decent considering you stitched me up for a bunch of murders. That aside, I'm feeling daaannndy.'

'You're not sounding too good there, Pillow. Sounds like you could use a rest. You gave it a run, Pillow, you did. But it's time for you to recognize that some of us are meant to be covered in linen, and some of us are real people who sleep on it.'

Simon wasn't talking. Pillow figured he'd probably snuck out to block the other exit while Avida covered the front and kept him talking.

She continued. Pillow could easily imagine how big her hand gestures had gotten.

'We fucked your life pretty darn hard, Pillow. I'm not going to sugarcoat it. But you have to admit your life was just begging for that dick. Your life was giving it away, like candy. Loose as all hell and dripping, was your life. We had to do it. We were so dirty on this coin thing, we couldn't leave you out there with a credible story. But hey, we are not crusaders, we can do business. So how's about you give us the coins, and you skate on the murders.'

'How?'

'We're in charge of the thing, we fuck up on your rights, you get away clean on appeal. Never hear from us again.'

Pillow chuckled and ran his hand along the smooth metal of the pillar, then he hustled quietly through the arch into the river-fish area and settled into another corner. He admired this new pillar for another second, then got back to the conversation.

'Clean, huh? I dunno, that's a too much delayed –' Pillow fully intended to say *gratification*, but his brain and mouth caught just as the *T* met the *I*, and when he still couldn't get over it after three restarts he quit. 'The answer is no. I don't want that. I'll get away and fuck off and a while later I'll die.' Pillow was finding it easier to talk now that he was really leaning into the slur. Not trying to fight it, but using it to round off the edges of speech, give it some shape. 'No, wait, I forgot. Actually I have to kill quite a few people first.'

Avida paused a second. The flashlight beam wavered into his old corner. She continued.

'You want to go right now? Give us the coins and we let you walk out of the park. We've been following you for two days. How hasn't anyone recognized you yet, by the way?'

Pillow switched razor hands, shook out his right fingers and then replaced the razor. 'For once, I'm lucky nobody watches boxing anymore.'

The footsteps of the beam stopped again. The turtles were still jerking half-willingly back and forth. Avida's voice came out shaky with anticipation this time.

'What was that, Punchy? You're slurring like a motherfucker. I imagine motherfuckers to be a heavy-slurring demographic.'

Pillow knew she'd figured out where he was by sound. He crouched low and moved around the corner. He took a pen out of his pocket and tossed it lightly toward the other side of the archway. Pillow heard Avida moving closer, shuffling and trying to keep her feet quiet. He heard the hum of the fish tanks. He imagined the little turtle coming. He imagined the dragon laying its giant, poisonous head down to sleep.

Avida made the final lurch through the arch and she pivoted toward the wrong corner. Pillow jumped out and she turned and got off a shot blind. Pillow parried her arm and took her eye with the razor blade. Blood and clear viscous fluid flopped out, mixing dark, dark red and clear. Avida dropped her flashlight, screaming, and the room went black. Water and beautiful idiot fish flowed invisibly past her writhing body. Pillow turned and ran straight into the pillar. He reset and ignored the blood falling down his face and made it out the front door just as he heard Simon rumbling in.

Pillow finished running when he got to the picnic area behind the giraffe enclosure. At the back edge there was a vending machine that Pillow had never seen before. He supposed it could have been there for years, and he could have missed it, once a month, for years. He hadn't given vending machines a whole lot of thought before, so it seemed worth it to pause, and give it some attention.

Pillow figured that there probably weren't very many happy vending machines in the world. It was sort of a pathetic station in life to be a vending machine, but this was the worst he'd seen. The front of it was dirty and scratched up, and the candy inside looked dry somehow, dusty even. Pillow cupped the vending machine's cheek.

'What about you, buddy? What animal would you be if you had to be an animal who wasn't human?'

Pillow put his fingers against the glass. He thought about rain and dead eyeballs and trees. He thought about big toes and killed chickens and blood. The vending machine just sat there, picking up dust by the second.

'Are you very old and sad?'

Nobody had even told the vending machine that candy cost more than a dollar now. Pillow shrugged and pulled the case out of his pocket. He shook out the coins and put them, one by one, into the machine. He watched the springs uncoil and drop the chocolate bar heavily into the tray.

Pillow had bought his first adult chocolate bar. He pushed back the sleeve and grabbed the candy bar. His hand felt almost numb now, so he more heard the wrapper crinkle than felt the thing in his right hand. Unwrapping it, he smelled the chocolate.

It was fucking gross.

Pillow shrugged and threw the bar in the garbage can, heard the hollow sound it made when it hit the bottom.

Pillow walked all the way around the empty giraffe enclosure, looking up at the trees, accidentally soaking his pants by falling in the fake river and throwing one of the giant red balls around for a while before he noticed the after-hours pen. Of course they wouldn't keep them outside. Pillow moved over to the pen at a leisurely pace, enjoying the night air and the sound of exotic animals sleeping far away. He casually smashed a window with his elbow and stepped through, trailing blood.

There were four of them sleeping in a loose circle. They slept lying down, with their necks coiled all the away around resting on their hinds. Pillow had never seen a giraffe sleep before. For a second he thought maybe this would be the last new thing he saw. But he realized quickly that the least likely thing in the world was not seeing something new. Because each second was actually a new thing, if you thought about it. No matter how hard you pulled at its saddest threads, life could never unravel into something worthless. Pillow remembered how tired he was. He climbed the stairs down to the giraffe pen, opened the door and walked in.

He approached the largest sleeping giraffe and rubbed the giraffe's flank, which felt firm, almost leathery. The giraffe kept sleeping, looking peaceful. There was a little opening below where the giraffe's neck was looped around, just by the torso. Pillow lay down and curled into it. Even though it's not really a spoon unless the person holds you with their arms and hands, Pillow thought it was close enough. The giraffe was the big spoon. They slept.

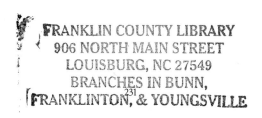

231

Sources

This book owes a large debt to the work and thinking of Surrealist writers of the 1920s to '50s. Particular thanks are owed to: Elsa Triolet, Phillipe Soupault (in particular 'The Silent House'), Paul Éluard, Man Ray, Vladimir Kush (who is actually much younger/ still alive), Georges Bataille (in particular 'The Big Toe'), Georges Franju (in particular *Les Sangs des Bêtes*), Guillaume Apollinaire (in particular *Alcools*), Salvador Dalí and Luis Buñuel (in particular *Un Chien Andalou*), Dieudonné Costes, Arthur Cravan, Louis Aragon and, of course, Antonin Artaud and André Breton. Two later works concerned with Surrealist literature and culture were also very helpful to the completion of this work: *Life Among the Surrealists: A Memoir* by Matthew Josephson, and 'Come to the Edge' by Christopher Logue, a poem commonly misattributed to Guillaume Apollinaire.

Also, thanks to Dr. James Cahill for telling me who any of those people were/are and what on earth they were even talking about (and from whom I also stole a story about getting a pimple on an eyelid for use in this book).

Also, I would like to acknowledge the influence that the craft, style and careers of Pernell Whitaker, Willie Pep and Paulie Malignaggi, and the shit-talking of James Toney and Ingemar Johansson, all had on this book and my outlook on art in general.

Acknowledgments

Thanks to Pasha Malla, who facilitated pretty much every aspect of this book, from listening to the germ of an idea that began it and saying 'It sounds like you have energy with that, why don't you do that?' to reading several plotless half-drafts to putting me in touch with Alana and Coach House.

Thanks to Coach House Books as a whole beautiful thing and to Alana, Heidi, Taylor, Stan, Evan, Shannon, Ingrid and Veronica for putting their work into this book and thus making it into a thing I can like and be happy with.

Thanks to the Ontario Arts Council's Writers' Reserve Program for its generous support of this project.

Thanks to Rick, Rosemary, Jess, Cheryl, Nadia and Sofs for the learning and fun times.

Thanks to Jeremy and Andrew (Sullivan) for the reading and advice and chuckles.

Thanks to all my *Dragnet* friends, mostly for the dancing.

Thanks to Terence for showing me all the tricks.

Thanks to Peter (Dad), Kelly (Mum) and Claire (big sis!) for the support and love and genuine, in all senses of the word, family.

And, of course, thanks to Zani for the happiness.

Andrew Battershill is a writer and teacher currently living in Columbus, Ohio. A graduate of the University of Toronto's MA in English in the Field of Creative Writing, he was the fiction editor and co-founder of *Dragnet* magazine.

Typeset in Aragon and Emily Lime Pro

Printed at the old Coach House on bpNichol Lane in Toronto, Ontario, on Zephyr Antique Laid paper, which was manufactured, acid-free, in Saint-Jérôme, Quebec, from second-growth forests. This book was printed with vegetable-based ink on a 1965 Heidelberg KORD offset litho press. Its pages were folded on a Baumfolder, gathered by hand, bound on a Sulby Auto-Minabinda and trimmed on a Polar single-knife cutter.

Edited and designed by Alana Wilcox
Cover design by Ingrid Paulson
Author photo by Suzannah Showler

Coach House Books
80 bpNichol Lane
Toronto ON M5S 3J4
Canada

416 979 2217
800 367 6360

mail@chbooks.com
www.chbooks.com